About the

Carol Westron is a successful short story writer who now writes crime fiction, children's fiction, articles and reviews. She is an expert on the Golden Age of Detective Fiction and has published four contemporary police procedurals, set in the south of England. Strangers and Angels is her first Victorian Murder Mystery.

Copyright © 2017 Carol Westron

Carol Westron has asserted her right under the Copyright, Designs and Patents Act, 1988 to be identified as the author of this work.

This book is sold subject to the condition that it shall not, by way of trade or otherwise, be lent, resold, hired out, or otherwise circulated without the publisher's prior consent in any form of binding, cover other than that in which it is published and without similar condition including this condition being imposed on the subject purchaser.

All characters and events in this publication, other than those clearly in the public domain, are fictitious and any resemblance to actual persons, living or dead, is purely coincidental.

ISBN 978-1979733953

First published in the UK 2017 by Pentangle Press
www.pentanglepress.com

pentangle
press

Dedication

To Elizabeth Sirett

Dear Lizzie, you believed in me at a time when I had lost belief in myself and inspired me to go on and achieve. Thank you for being my friend.

And to Jane Finnis

My good drinking buddy through many crime conferences who encouraged me to write a historical crime novel and assured me that, one day, I'd grow to love research.
In the words of the immortal Oliver Hardy, 'Here's another nice mess you've gotten me into!'

Acknowledgements

Beta readers are the wonderful people who read your book in its infancy, spot all the mistakes and offer you the chance to put them right, and I've got some of the best. Thank you Jennifer Palmer and Jane Finnis, for your early readings, advice and encouragement, and enormous thanks (and a well-earned bottle of wine) to Lesley Talbot a true super-star amongst Beta readers.

Thanks also to Jane Finnis for her advice and encouragement with the historical research.

Thanks to Christine Hammacott and The Art of Communication for another great cover design and for your support and friendship.

Thanks and love to Jack Halsall for producing the original photograph that said everything I wanted to convey about my book, and for an author photograph that I am pleased to allow the world to see. You are always there, camera in hand, to capture the images I need, often before I realise that I need them, and the search to find the perfect picture is so much fun with you.

Gratitude to the Portsmouth Central Library and Gosport Discovery Centre for the help and support they gave with my research.

As always, my love to my family, Peter, Jo, Jack & Adam, Paul, Claire, Oliver & Henry, Alan, Lyndsey, Thomas, Tabitha & Pippa. Thank you for being there for me.

Glossary of Victorian terms

lummox	stupid or foolish person
to peach	to tell tales
vapours	tearful hysterics
nubbing cheat	gallows
top lofty	arrogant
To offer slum	To try to deceive or cheat.
watering pot	constantly tearful
toadeater	a servile flatterer
to maudle	to upset, throw into confusion
to cast up accounts	to vomit
gut foundered	extremely hungry
lawks	Lord have mercy! an exclamation used by those of the lower class
heavy wet	mixture of beer and porter
cap over the windmill	defying social convention; giving up all for love
bosom bows	close friends/confidantes
purse proud	contemptuous of those poorer than oneself
cove	man
to grease a palm	to give a bribe
haut ton	high society
queer in the upper storey	mad/crazy
dicked in the nob	mad/crazy

to clap up	to imprison
to cut up rough	to make a fuss
to croak	to die
dibs not in tune	to run out of money
to nick	to steal
to open one's budget	to admit or tell everything
under the cat's foot	under the control of a woman, usually a wife
trull	prostitute
barker	gun
to leg it	to run
high in the instep	proud; aware of one's superior position
flash (language)	to use slang
flash (person)	ostentatious, showy
nob	aristocratic or high-born person
reticule	a small bag
vinaigrette	A container for smelling salts made of aromatic vinegar
cooper	barrel maker
hansom cab	two-wheeled cab with driver's seat behind
hack/hackney carriage	a carriage for hire
nag	a horse, usually not of the highest standard
to prig	to steal

Strangers and Angels

Carol Westron

*'Be not forgetful to entertain strangers; for
thereby some have entertained angels
unawares.' (Hebrews 13, 1-2.)*

Chapter 1

Gosport, Hampshire. December 1850

"Kemal, wait!"

Molly knew it was improper to shout in the street, especially to shout a man's given name, but, for the life of her, she couldn't remember his full name, or pronounce it if she did.

"Kemal!" she called again. She had to stop him before he reached The Crescent and knocked on the mistress' front door. She'd left her summons too late. He passed St Mark's Church, moved on past the imposing bulk of the Anglesey Hotel and turned the corner, disappearing from her sight.

"Stupid lummox! What's he playing at?" Molly gathered up her skirts and bolted after him, as fast as she dared on the icy pavements. At least here, in the most affluent part of Gosport, the ground was well kept, not rutted like the ale-brewing district near the docks where she'd been born and raised.

The hood of her cloak slid off but, carrying a lantern and holding up her dress and numerous petticoats, she had no hand free to hold it in place. Smart clothes were essential for a lady's maid but she hated the way they slowed her down.

What was Kemal doing here before first light? She'd spotted him soon after she'd left her father's house but, in the grey mist that crept inland from the harbour, he hadn't noticed her. She hadn't called out to attract his attention, fearing he'd think her bold. Nevertheless she'd felt safer knowing he'd hear if she screamed. She'd never before walked through the streets before dawn alone and she'd soon regretted her folly.

She rounded the corner at full speed, stumbled and almost fell over Kemal's sprawled body. "Kemal?"

He lay face downwards on the road, close to the railings that enclosed the communal garden that served the houses opposite. She glanced around. The street was deserted. There was no one to ask for aid. Kemal's lantern lay broken on the ground but she had hers and there were street lamps to light the scene. Heart thumping, she knelt beside him and struggled to turn him over. There was an ugly gash on his forehead and she could see a dark stain on the nearby kerb.

He moaned and opened his eyes. At first he looked at her blankly, but then his gaze sharpened and he muttered, "Mistress Molly?"

She helped him to sit up. "What happened? Did you trip?" He looked puzzled then shook his head. "No. I was hit... from behind." His fingers explored the back of his head and he winced.

Startled Molly stood up and looked around more thoroughly. The gaslights that lit the street failed to penetrate the darkest corners. To her left the communal garden was still and shaded, while on her right the tall half-crescent of terraced houses towered white and ghostlike. Their small gardens offered sparse concealment but the steps to the basement door were in darkness and the front doors and the steps leading up to them were in the shadow of the porch that ran the length of the terrace. Kemal's attacker could be lurking there, hiding behind the elegant pillars. She shivered, fearful that they were being watched by an unseen enemy.

"Kemal, are you able to move? I don't like it here." As she bent over him she swung her lantern and saw the gate that led to the central garden was wide open.

"That's odd!"

"What is wrong?" Kemal staggered to his feet.

"The garden's unlocked. Only people who pay for keys can get in there."

"I will look." He pulled open his coat and reached down to his side. "My jambiya... my dagger... it has gone."

"You must have dropped it when you fell." But there was no sign of any weapon on the ground.

"It has a sheath. It would not easily fall out." Kemal spoke with quiet certainty. It reminded Molly that, although he was not yet twenty, he'd been a fighting man since he was twelve. He felt through his pockets and produced a money pouch. It was far from plump but the coins inside it chinked as he weighed it in his hand. "Apart from my dagger, I have not been robbed."

"He must have heard me coming and fled," suggested Molly, although she didn't really believe that. Surely such a desperate felon wouldn't be scared away by the approach of a girl? The whole business was strange. Such assaults happened every night down by the sailors' taverns but this was Angleseyville, the most respectable and wealthy part of town.

"There's a gardener and his wife who live in the basement beneath the Reading Room." She pointed to the darkened building, near to the open gate. "He can't have heard anything going on or he'd have come out to investigate."

"Perhaps he would prefer his bed on such a cold night," suggested Kemal.

"I think he'd have looked. He's very proud of his garden. But there are Bath Houses on either side of the Reading Room and they'd muffle any noise. Do you think we ought to rouse him?" She spoke reluctantly.

"You do not wish to do that?"

"I'll get into trouble with my lady if she knows I've been here with you." Lady Adelaide was an indulgent mistress but she would not accept loose behaviour, moreover she was a guest in her aunt's house and would obey her rules. If Molly disgraced her she'd have to turn her away.

"In that case do not disturb the gardener. I will search the garden. It will be better that you return to your lady's house."

Through the iron railings the garden looked dark and menacing. Molly longed to flee into the safety of the house but it would be wrong to leave Kemal here, injured and alone. "I'd rather stay. I might be able to help."

He considered her, then said, "As you wish." He walked towards the garden, stepped inside, halted and said something sharp and foreign. He turned swiftly to bar her way. His face was taut with shock.

"What is it?" Molly pushed past him. "Oh dear Lord!" She was looking at her second body of the morning, but this one was definitely dead.

Chapter 2

The woman was lying on her back upon a neatly arranged dark cloak. Molly thought it strange that everything was formal and decorous about her, becoming to a respectable lady of middle years. Apart from the terrible wound in her throat. Shuddering, she dragged her gaze away from that horror and looked at the grey silk gown, trimmed with fine lace. Molly had been with Lady Adelaide for eight months and she recognised quality when she saw it. The woman's hands were folded at her waist. In their white lace gloves they looked like a fallen dove.

Kemal asked, "I should search the garden?"

"No!" Molly grasped his arm. "Please, don't leave me."

"As you wish." His tone was curt and she wondered if he was angry. Perhaps he'd planned to slip away and abandon her.

"I'm sorry." All the same she kept hold of his arm.

"No, it is I who am sorry. A lady must not be forsaken in such a place. I will not let harm come to you." Despite his brave words, she felt him trembling. She saw his free hand stray to his side and knew he was instinctively seeking for his dagger.

She wished she could get clear of the whole business and tell Kemal to slope off to his ship. She could slip into the house by the kitchen door and hope no-one peached about her being late. But, in the nearby houses, lights glimmered in the attic windows as servants prepared to start their day's work. What if someone had seen them entering the garden? Or saw them leaving?

How, in sweet Heaven, had she got into this fix? It wasn't as if she really knew Kemal. She'd only met him once before today, when they'd talked outside St Mark's Church last Sunday. She'd felt sorry for him, the only Christian amongst a Muslim crew, and not made very welcome in England either. She'd heard the mutterings about the arrival of the Turkish ships and how Gosport always got the dross that Portsmouth, on the other side of the harbour, turned away. But it was too late to worry how it had come about. They were both in danger. Justice was for the rich and powerful, and this was a hanging matter.

"Would it be dishonourable of us to leave? To pretend we were not here?" Kemal's voice broke in on her jumbled thoughts.

"It could be dangerous. We may have been seen."

"Yes, you are right. I spoke like a fool. I wonder, who is she, this poor lady and how did she come here?"

Reluctantly Molly turned again towards the corpse. The scene looked unreal, like in the Crown Inn Assembly Room, when she'd cajoled Pa to take her and Grandmama there to see a play. For that matter she felt unreal herself, as if she was standing outside her body looking on. She forced herself to look at the dead face, thankful that the eyes were closed. The woman had a fine web of lines and wrinkles on her skin, but her fashionably arranged hair was dark and glossy. That thought lit up a memory in Molly's mind and she clasped her hands over her mouth to suppress a cry.

She remembered Lady Adelaide's aunt saying crossly, 'I wonder her mistress allows it. I would never let any servant of mine dye her hair. But, having so little sight, Lady Dewsbury may not know. I will mention it to her when we next take tea.'

Lady Adelaide had answered with gentle firmness, 'I think it would be better not to meddle, ma'am. After all she has been with Lady Dewsbury for many years and a companion is not the same as an ordinary servant.'

Kemal spoke quietly, "She is not young and her gown is fine, surely she is not a..." he hesitated, clearly searching for an acceptable phrase, then finished apologetically, "a woman of the streets?"

"No." Molly's eyes filled with tears. She wiped them away and sniffed defiantly. "I recognise her. She lives here in The Crescent. Her name's Miss Berry. She works for old Lady Dewsbury. She's her companion." She felt the words pop out in uncontrollable bursts and couldn't blame Kemal for looking puzzled.

She was about to explain more simply when Kemal said, "I comprehend."

"Did you see anything of the man who hit you?"

He gave a hopeless shrug. "I saw nothing. I heard a footstep but before I could turn something struck me. I remember nothing more until you were there with me."

"Why did you come here this morning?" When she'd first seen him, she'd assumed he was heading for the church, that's why she'd panicked when he walked on past.

He looked bewildered. "But you asked me to... you wished to speak with me."

"I asked you? Kemal, I didn't!"

He stared at her. "But a boy came. Yesterday, in the evening. He said to meet you in the garden of The Crescent at six in the morning... I am late, I know. I am sorry but it was not easy to obtain permission to leave my ship."

"Who was this boy? What did he look like?"

Kemal shrugged. "He was a tall, thin boy, not richly dressed but clean. It was hard to comprehend all he said. I think he was weak in his wits. He kept saying, 'Molly Bowman wants you to meet her tomorrow at

The Crescent garden at six in the morning.' He spoke like a parrot... a bird that repeats without understanding."

"I don't know anyone like that, Kemal."

"But he gave me this as a token. I knew it belonged to you. I saw it on Sunday, when you dropped your Book of Prayer, although then it was not soiled."

He rummaged in his pocket and produced a silk bookmark. It was stained and crumpled. Molly gave a cry of protest and disbelief. She took it from Kemal and tried to smooth out the embroidered angel. Her mother had made the bookmark as a Christening gift and she used it to keep her place in her prayer book. Her mother had died when she was six years old and Molly treasured her memory.

"Some person wished me to come here." Kemal's voice was sharp with fear. "Why should they do that? I know no-one in this town."

"I don't know." Nevertheless Molly was sure he was right. Someone had lured him here. The body was positioned so that no casual passer-by would see it from the street. If they hadn't stepped inside the garden they wouldn't have noticed her.

This was not the first time Molly had seen death. Her grandmother was a good neighbour, aiding childbirth, tending in sickness, and laying out those who died. For the last four years, from the age of fourteen, Molly had helped her. She knew it was no good shrinking from what she had to do. She had to find out if the body was still warm.

Reluctantly, she crept forward and laid her fingers on Miss Berry's right arm in the gap between her glove and sleeve. It felt icy and looked strangely discoloured, like a mottled bruise. Surprised, she pushed the lace cuff up a little. The dark colouring continued for as far as she could see.

"There is too little blood," said Kemal.

"What do you mean?" There was quite enough for Molly.

"In battle I have seen death from wounds like this. It is only when life has left there is so little blood. If she died in this place, there should be a pool of it on the ground."

"You mean she wasn't killed here? That's what I thought. My grandmother told me that if a dead person's left too long in one position the blood gathers there and discolours that part of the body. I think the poor lady died lying on her side. I wonder..." She broke off as the glint of metal caught her eye. It was lying on the path, almost hidden by Miss Berry's skirt.

Molly put out a cautious hand and picked it up. It was a dagger, about eight inches long, and the slender, curved blade was blotched with blood.

Kemal stared at the weapon. "That is mine."

"I know." Molly had recognised it immediately. Kemal had worn it last Sunday when he'd attended the morning service at St Mark's Church. The churchwarden had scolded him and locked it away until it was time to leave. The bone handle was intricately carved and when Molly had seen it after Church she'd thought it a pretty frippery, but then it was safely contained in its velvet-covered wooden sheath. Now, unsheathed, held in her trembling hand, it looked the deadly weapon it was.

She stared helplessly at the dagger and then at Kemal. She saw his fingers twitch. Was he about to lunge forward and wrest it from her grasp? She began to shake more violently than before.

Chapter 3

Instead of coming nearer, Kemal stepped back. "I did not harm that lady."

"I know," she said again. She was sure Miss Berry had been dead for some hours. Kemal's attacker must have stolen the dagger whilst he was unconscious, smeared the blade with blood and left it there to incriminate him. Stubbornness and anger surged through her. She wouldn't let the killer make Kemal his scapegoat.

The first thing was to get the blade clean. She bent down and rubbed it against the ice-rimed grass. Her fingers tingled with the cold but she kept at it until she was sure no trace of blood remained. Kemal watched silently, neither protesting nor questioning her actions.

At last she straightened and handed the dagger to Kemal. "You never lost it. Your dagger had nothing to do with this."

He nodded, his face still taut, as if he was holding all his emotions in. "Thank you." He slid the dagger back into its sheath.

She knew she should feel guilty, but she didn't. There wasn't a court in England that would give Kemal a fair hearing.

"What's going on here?"

The gruff voice startled Molly. She squeaked and clutched at Kemal's arm.

"Be quiet, girl. No need to be alarmed." The tone was testy.

"Dr Russell!" She bobbed a curtsey. "Oh sir, something terrible has happened!" She thought it was typical of her luck that Dr Russell should turn up in the garden at this hour. He was an elderly, heavy-set man, old-fashioned in his dress and in his ways. Of all the residents of Angleseyville he and his wife were the most censorious. Molly wondered what he was doing here. He didn't live in The Crescent but in a substantial house in an adjoining road, not far from St Mark's Church.

He pushed past them to stare down at Miss Berry.

"Who has done this?" There was accusation in his tone. His fierce blue eyes glared at them from the shade of his bushy eyebrows. Molly couldn't see his mouth, which was concealed by his formidable moustache, but she was sure it was set in rigid disapproval.

Behind the doctor's back Molly gestured to Kemal to keep silent. "Oh sir, isn't it dreadful? We found her like this, just a minute or two ago, and we didn't know what to do. It's Miss Berry sir. I don't know what Lady Dewsbury will do without her. Oh who could have done such a terrible, terrible thing?"

She started the rambling speech deliberately, knowing the doctor was the sort of man who despised women, but she found it frighteningly easy to slip into the role of tearful, hysterical female. She reminded herself to keep a firm hold on her emotions and on her tongue.

"Be quiet, girl. No need to have the vapours. Leave that to your betters." He moved to Miss Berry's body and, grunting with the effort, bent down and laid his gnarled fingers on her wrist. "Have you touched her?"

"Her wrist, sir. Just to check she was gone. She felt so cold I knew she was."

"At which university did you study medicine, girl?"

She was tempted to retort that it did not need a doctor to be sure that anyone with such a terrible wound was dead but she kept a still tongue. She knew from bitter experience that it was no good arguing with the gentry. "She is dead, isn't she sir?"

"Of course she is. You're William Bowman's daughter aren't you?"

"Yes sir, I'm Molly Bowman." She wasn't particularly surprised at the doctor's recognition. Her father's family had been barrel-makers in Gosport for generations and Pa and Grandmama were well known and well respected in the town.

"What were you and this young man doing here? The Crescent is no place for such as you."

"I'm Lady Adelaide's maid, sir." She tried to banish all trace of insolence from her voice, although she was sure he already knew that she lived here and was snubbing her. As a doctor, he attended Lady Adelaide's aunt and many other wealthy ladies of the town. Also he and his wife were frequent visitors to the mistress' house. If he recognised her as Pa's daughter, surely he'd have noticed her in attendance on Lady Adelaide?

"That does not explain why you're in company with this Turk."

She sought for a plausible explanation for being here with Kemal. Dr Russell was known as a stickler for the maintenance of working class morality. "Kemal's with one of the Turkish training ships that arrived last month.

They're here to learn about navigation from our sailors. It must be terribly hard to learn difficult things like that in a foreign language. They must be ever so clever to do that." Molly played the ninny for all she was worth. If he thought she was a foolish, tattling maid he wouldn't believe she was capable of spinning a false tale. If only she could think of a good false tale to spin.

A surge of angry colour rose in Dr Russell's face. "That doesn't explain what you are doing here with this poor lady's corpse. I mean to have an answer from you. Do you hear me, girl?"

"They can probably hear you across the harbour in Portsmouth."

The sound of a fresh voice startled them yet again. In unison they spun round to face the newcomer. Molly stared at the tall, dandified, young man. Frustration welled up within her. It occurred to her that gentlemen were like hansom cabs, never around when she was sent to summon one but turning up by the dozen when they'd be a hindrance.

"Good morning, Mr Corfield." She bobbed a respectful curtsey.

"Molly, are you all right?" She wondered how he knew her given name when ladies' maids were known by their surnames. Lady Adelaide must have mentioned it to him. Mr Corfield was a visitor to Gosport and staying at the hotel at the end of The Crescent. He was one of Lady Adelaide's most persistent admirers but Molly wasn't sure how her mistress felt about him.

"Molly, are you all right?" he said again.

"Yes. Thank you, sir."

His gaze went past them to poor Miss Berry. "Oh dear!" he said.

The inadequacy of his words caught Molly in the throat and she gave something between a gulp and a giggle. Horrified she clapped her hand over her mouth to stifle further sound. She felt Kemal's arm around her shoulders and turned to bury her face against his chest.

"Bowman, behave yourself with propriety." Dr Russell's voice thundered in her ear. His hand clasped her upper arm with harsh fingers, forcing her to turn.

"The child's terrified," said Mr Corfield. "This is no sight for a young girl. And the boy looks as if he's about to swoon."

Molly twisted round to look at Kemal. He was ashen and his dark eyes were hazy and unfocused. "Someone hit him on the head."

She wrenched free of Dr Russell's grip and moved to support Kemal, although she knew if he did collapse there was little hope of her holding up his weight.

In three strides Mr Corfield was beside them, hoisting Kemal's other arm over his shoulder. He did it in a matter-of-fact way, with none of the reluctance most gentlemen would show. Molly liked him for that. They made a strange contrast. Kemal was dark-haired and olive skinned, with high cheekbones and strongly defined features. Mr Corfield had pale blue eyes and his hair and neat moustache were so fair they were almost white. Molly preferred Kemal's more striking looks but she had to admit Mr Corfield was handsome in a skim-milk sort of way.

"Have you raised the alarm yet?" His tone was curt.

"No sir. I'm sorry. Kemal and I were about to when..." she broke off as she realised he was not speaking to her.

"Not yet." Dr Russell sounded huffy. "You go and do so, Corfield. I'll stay here to ensure these young people don't make off and to stand watch over this unfortunate lady's corpse."

Indignation overwhelmed the caution Molly usually kept for dealing with the gentry. She opened her mouth to protest that she had no intention of making off anywhere.

Mr Corfield said, "It would be wiser for you to take them into the house, Doctor. I'll stay here and search the garden. I am a younger and fitter man than you."

Dr Russell harrumphed and grumbled but it was obvious that Mr Corfield's plan made sense. The doctor's grip on Kemal's arm was more like holding a felon than supporting an injured man but he agreed to Molly's plea that they should go down the steps that led to the half-basement rather than demanding admittance by the front door.

It was evident the hall boy had not yet ventured out to clear the steps of frost and their stone surface glistened treacherously. Dr Russell released his grip on Kemal to make his way down. Although he took care, he slithered and almost fell. Molly felt a bleak satisfaction at his discomfiture.

Kemal said softly in her ear, "Pray mind your step, Mistress Molly. Let me help you."

"I'm supposed to be helping you."

By the light of her lantern she saw him smile at her. "My head is painful but the dizziness has passed. I am used to such things. I have climbed rigging in conditions worse than these."

True to his word, he went down the steps with sure-footed certainty and his hand on Molly's arm gave her confidence.

Chapter 4

Dr Russell reached the door and rapped a loud demand for entry with the head of his stick. Molly winced. At the moment there was no butler, but the housekeeper would be outraged by this disruption to the household routine and she would blame Molly. She saw the hall boy's wary face as he opened the door. The tall footman lurked behind him, struggling to put on his coat and not yet wearing the powdered wig that was part of his uniform.

Once admitted to the house, they made their way to the kitchen. For Molly, the next few minutes passed in a blur of shrill voices and startled questions. She heard Dr Russell bellowing instructions and the footman was sent to seek an officer of the law.

She steered Kemal to a seat by the large, wooden table in the centre of the kitchen and sat down beside him, hoping, when the chaos died down, someone would help her tend his head wound. She soon realised she could hope for little aid from the servants, who would follow the example of their seniors. Mrs Bradbury, the housekeeper, was a Tartar, and very jealous of her dignity. Cook, who was usually a kind-hearted, jolly woman, was angry at the invasion of her kitchen when she was making her preparations for the day.

Molly looked around for Dr Russell but he had disappeared. She thought he must have returned to the garden. Of course he'd not wish to treat a common sailor. It was well known that Dr Russell's wife was wealthy and he could afford to be fussy about the status of his patients.

The range had been banked down overnight but now it was burning well and the kitchen felt warm.

Molly slipped off her cloak and helped Kemal remove his coat. Pulling back her hood had disarranged her hair. It broke free from its coil and tumbled down her back, but there was little she could do to remedy that without leaving the room and she had no intention of abandoning Kemal. She folded the garments and put them on a chair. This was a breach of domestic discipline but a small matter compared to the trouble she was in.

Kemal's quiet words echoed her thought, "I am sorry to have caused you so much trouble, Mistress Molly."

She smiled at him, liking the way he addressed her as Mistress Molly. In his perfect but heavily accented English it sounded respectful and old-fashioned. The removal of the dark, naval coat revealed that he'd dressed in his best to come and meet her. His white shirt and the bright red waistcoat might have passed without comment in the seaport, but his gaudy sash and the full trousers, gathered just under the knee, emphasised his foreign air. But it was more than his clothes. He was different in every gesture he made and every word he spoke. She thought he looked like one of the exotic birds she'd seen pictured in illustrated books of foreign lands. One of Grandmama's friends had owned a small bird, brought home for her by a sailor son. The tiny thing had been so beautiful and sung so sweetly. It had escaped its cage and been pecked to death by the drab native birds.

She looked swiftly around the kitchen to make sure no-one could overhear. "Kemal, when you first saw Miss Berry's body, what was it you said?" That foreign exclamation had been worrying her.

He frowned, clearly thinking back. "Kyrie eleison. Lord have mercy. It is the language of the Church to which I belong, and my patron also, although once he was part of your English Church."

That reassured her. It confirmed that Kemal was a good Christian, as she'd thought. Why else would he have visited St Mark's Church? That brought to her mind the sermon the vicar had preached last Sunday about being kind to strangers because they could be angels in disguise. Molly thought he'd chosen that message because he'd invited Kemal to attend St Mark's and he'd seen the hostile looks that had been directed against the foreign visitor.

Her father had told her there were mutterings in the town about how Portsmouth should have kept the Turks and not shipped them over to Gosport, the way they did with anything they didn't want. When it came to Portsmouth, Molly shared the local resentment. Portsmouth and Gosport lay on either side of the harbour but Portsmouth claimed the whole water as its own. Both had strong links to the Queen's Navy but, according to Pa, Gosport always got things like the Powder Magazine transferred to their side when the rich folk in Portsmouth wanted the stored gunpowder moved from their Square Tower. What Molly didn't understand was why people hated the Turkish sailors. The Ottoman Empire had been Britain's enemy but the two great empires weren't quarrelling any more. It seemed to her that most countries were at odds with each other at some point in history and if everyone kept up their bad feelings they'd be at war with all the world.

Last Sunday, as she'd sat in Church, she'd wondered what the stranger's own country was like. It must be very different from Hampshire. She'd thought it would be interesting to talk to him, if Lady Adelaide permitted and she could make herself understood.

After Church Lady Adelaide had been trapped in conversation with Dr and Mrs Russell and other friends of her aunt, but she'd given permission for Molly to speak to Kemal. To Molly's delight, Kemal spoke good English and she'd discovered that he was an orphan, brought up in the household of an English soldier of fortune. His patron had fought for the Ottoman Empire and made enough money to retire there. He'd used his influence to get Kemal a place on the training expedition, and Kemal was the only Christian in the Muslim crew.

"Mistress Molly?" Kemal recalled her attention.

"I was thinking of when I met you last week." Embarrassed, she refused to look at him, focusing instead on her fingers, tracing a pattern on the table top. The soft wood had been scoured so many times with sand, soda and water that the surface had worn away, leaving the hard knots of wood to stand proud against the rest. It reminded her of Grandmama's table, where, from early childhood, she had learned to cook and clean. That memory gave her courage. "Kemal, I wouldn't have sent for you to meet me in the garden at such an hour. I wouldn't be so bold." She feared he considered her a creature of easy virtue.

"I thought you wished to talk to me about the celebrations of the Holy Birth."

"Oh, I see." She'd said that Pa might invite him to celebrate Christmas in their home but it was three weeks until the feast and she'd only touched on the matter last night. Pa had been grumpy because Grandmama was away from home and he didn't like fending for himself. "I haven't arranged anything yet."

Kemal looked apologetic. "Mistress Molly, I know little of the customs of England, but is it proper for a young lady to walk the streets alone at such an hour?"

She felt her colour rise. Perhaps he did think her a loose woman after all. "No. The lad who was meant to accompany me was unwell and I didn't want Pa... my father... to be angry with him."

"Lad?"

"One of my father's apprentices."

"It was not wise to come alone."

"I know."

She was not sure which part of the two mile walk had frightened her more: the restless streets of the garrison town or the silent emptiness of the country roads that led to Alverstoke. Perhaps the worst moment of the solitary walk had been passing through the High Street Gate, one of three arched gates in the fortifications that ringed the land part of town. The lewd looks she'd received from the guards as they allowed her through made her fully aware of how unwise she'd been.

She pushed the thought away and changed the subject. "Kemal, before you came to meet me, were there people who could vouch for you? Your shipmates, did they see you at the Mirat-y Zafer?" She stumbled a little over the ship's foreign name.

"But yes. My lieutenant. He is senior to me but I think he means me well. It was he who wrote my permit. Without it I could not have left my ship, nor could have I passed through your town gates at such an hour. He yielded to my request unwillingly. He warned me it would be better not to come. He said it would cause me trouble if I paid attentions to an English girl."

Molly hadn't sent for Kemal and she hadn't encouraged him to pay her attentions, so it was ridiculous to resent this Turkish officer and his advice, but she did.

She saw the housekeeper approaching them and lowered her voice to a whisper. "Kemal, if anyone comes to see you again and says they have a message from me, it will only be truly from me if it contains the words 'stranger' and 'angel.' And you do the same if you want to contact me. Do you understand?"

"I comprehend."

The housekeeper's considerable bulk loomed over them. "I've informed her ladyship of your conduct, Bowman. At last she'll realise what a troublemaker you are. You can pack your trunk, you'll be leaving today."

*

Chapter 5

"If you please, m'lady."

Adelaide jerked from restless, haunted dreams to find the upstairs maid standing at the foot of her bed. The room was dark, lit only by the candle the girl was clutching.

"What is it?" she asked, pushing herself upright. "Put that candle down, before you set my bed alight." Her aunt's reception rooms were fashionably furnished but she had not replaced the bedroom furniture since her marriage and the curtains on the old-fashioned four-poster were dangerously near the flame.

"Yes, m'lady. I'm so sorry. I didn't mean... I'm all of a flutter."

"What has happened?" Adelaide put a sharp edge to her voice.

"Oh m'lady, it's so dreadful. There's been a death."

Adelaide felt a cold shiver run through her. Last night she'd dreamed of her late husband for the first time in months. Perhaps it had been a premonition of another death. "Is it Mrs Tate?" Her widowed aunt had been in her usual health last night but she could think of no other reason the maid should come to her.

"Oh no, m'lady! It's not the mistress. Your maid..."

"Molly! Are you saying Molly Bowman's dead?" Adelaide was shocked at how desolate she felt. Surely it was wrong that her maid meant more to her than her aunt?

"No m'lady. Bowman's not dead. She's sat down in the kitchen. She's brought in a Turkish sailor. Staggering drunk and covered with blood. Mrs Bradbury sent me to tell you."

Only the last statement made sense to Adelaide. If Molly were responsible for disruption to the household, the housekeeper would prefer to inform Adelaide than disturb Mrs Tate. Bradbury was strict with her underlings but she'd grown old in the family's service and had known Adelaide since she was a baby.

She swung her feet out of bed and stood up. "Who has died?"

The maid quailed at her tone. "It's Miss Berry, m'lady. Lady Dewsbury's Companion. Found in the garden she was. Dr Russell told Mrs Bradbury."

"Dr Russell?" Adelaide wondered how many more inappropriate people were assembled in her aunt's kitchen. "But what has Molly Bowman to do with this?"

"She was found standing over the body, m'lady. Along with this Turkish sailor. That's what the doctor said. They shouldn't let them murdering savages loose in a respectable town."

Adelaide didn't reprimand her. It was not her household and she knew the servants' prejudices were shared by her aunt. She recalled that Molly had spoken with a Turkish sailor after Church last week. Surely this must be the same man?

"Tell Bradbury I'll come as soon as I'm ready," she said curtly.

"Yes, m'lady. Do you want me to help you dress?"

"No. You can light my candles and get on with your work." That meant she could not be laced into her stays, but she was naturally slender and most of her morning dresses did not require a corset to make them presentable.

The maid departed and Adelaide made a hurried toilette. She pulled off the pretty, lace-trimmed nightgown and cap that her aunt frowned upon as frivolous and put on her drawers and camisole, stockings and four petticoats. Without assistance it took longer than she'd foreseen.

She was winding her long, fair hair into a coil when she heard footsteps in the corridor. They paused outside her door. Instinctively she grabbed up her modest grey dress, desperate to fully cover herself. The footsteps passed by. Just one of the maids going about their work. She was trembling. It was absurd to still feel so afraid but the memory of her late husband could not be banished. She still remembered his heavy footsteps in the corridor and those fear-filled moments when he stood outside her door. Sometimes he'd move on, but often she had watched the door handle turn and then he'd enter. Looking back, she knew he had never loved her but her reluctance had kindled his lust and his determination to possess.

Bernard had died over a year ago but when her memories were rekindled she could still feel his hot breath on her naked shoulders and smell the intrusive odour of brandy and cigars. She shuddered. She had been betrothed at sixteen and the wedding took place on her seventeenth birthday. Marriage had been five years of misery. She knew it was wicked but she was glad he was dead.

One thing Bernard had taught her was that meek, dutiful women were trampled underfoot. That which she valued, she'd have to fight to keep. She grabbed a black lace shawl and hurried to the door.

As she hastened downstairs Adelaide arranged the shawl around her shoulders to conceal any errors in the fastening of her dress. This reminded her of the shame-filled days when she'd first arrived in Gosport. All her servants had been paid off and she'd been dependant on her aunt's elderly maid for help. That was before she'd met Molly.

At the foot of the basement steps she hesitated. As a guest in her aunt's house, this was a region she had not ventured into before. The corridor was deserted. She knew the closed doors towards the front of the house would open onto the rooms inhabited by the senior female servants, the housekeeper, cook and her aunt's personal maid. Nearer the kitchen were the rooms belonging to the butler, footman and the hall boy. Her aunt ordered her male servants to sleep near the butler's pantry, to safeguard the household silver from housebreakers, and to keep the men at a distance from the young maids who slept in the attics.

As Adelaide ventured down the corridor, she saw the kitchen door was ajar and she heard angry voices. She pushed the door open. The servants were too flustered to notice her. Molly was seated at the table, beside the Turkish sailor. He looked bloodstained and battered. Molly's brown hair was wild and her green eyes were bright as she glared defiantly at the housekeeper.

"How dare you bring that Turk into the house?" said Bradbury wrathfully. "I don't know what the mistress will say when she finds out."

Adelaide pushed the door fully open and entered the fray. "My aunt would say this is a Christian household and gives succour to those who are injured and in distress." She moved across the kitchen to stand near Molly and the sailor, who both stood up respectfully.

"Pray be seated," she said gently.

"Thank you, madam." The young man's voice was slurred but Adelaide had seen enough of drunkenness in her married life to be sure alcohol was not the cause.

Mr Corfield entered through the outside door, followed by Dr Russell.

"Lady Adelaide, you shouldn't be here! It isn't proper. I beg that you withdraw." That was Dr Russell, pompous as usual.

"Thank you for your concern, Doctor, but I have a duty to remain." Mr Corfield wasted no time on protestations. He bowed and said, "Good morning, Lady Adelaide."

"Good morning, sir." Whatever was Edwin Corfield doing here at this hour?

Before she could ask, he turned from her to Molly and her companion. "I know you must both feel shocked and distressed but it would be helpful if you answered some questions. An officer of the law will soon be here, but I would like you to tell me what occurred."

Molly looked doubtful. "Please m'lady, do you think we ought?"

Adelaide was not sure what advice to give. Although the new police service had been in action for some years in London, they had only recently been set up in Hampshire and she wasn't convinced they were an efficient body of men. At some point, Molly and the Turkish boy would have to tell their story to the representatives of the Law and it might be wise to gain Mr Corfield as their advocate.

"It would be best to tell Mr Corfield what you know."

Molly still looked reluctant but she turned to face Mr Corfield, "Very well, sir."

Adelaide surveyed the other servants, who were all listening avidly. "Leave us. Bowman will summon you when we wish you to return."

There was some sulky muttering but they all shuffled out of the kitchen and Mr Corfield shut the door behind them.

Dr Russell said, "Lady Adelaide, such matters are not fitting for a lady. You need a man to lean upon and advise you in such matters."

Adelaide struggled to control her temper. How dare he suggest she should depend upon the judgement of a man? Her father had ordered her to marry when she had barely left the schoolroom. Her husband had squandered his fortune on loose living and women of ill repute. Bankrupt, he had shot himself, leaving Adelaide dishonoured and penniless, dependant on her family's charity.

Mr Corfield said quietly, "Lady Adelaide, please stay. Your maid will be more comfortable with you here."

He smiled at Adelaide and, to her surprise, she found she was smiling back at him. She sat down in the chair he'd set for her beside Molly and said encouragingly, "Answer Mr Corfield's questions."

Mr Corfield intervened, "Thank you, Lady Adelaide, but it is not your maid that I must question first." He turned to the young sailor, "First of all, we need to know your full name."

To Adelaide the young man's response was incomprehensible but Mr Corfield was not disconcerted. "Kemal, son of Halil? Of course, in your country, family names are derived in a way different to ours. Perhaps, with your permission, it would simplify matters if we continued to call you Kemal?"

The sailor nodded. "That would be best."

"And your rank?"

"Deniz Astegmeni. In your navy it is nearest to the rank of midshipman. What is it you wish to ask of me?"

"I wish you to tell the truth." Mr Corfield's manner hardened as he rounded on Kemal. "It's time to end your lies."

Kemal stared at him. "I do not lie! I have done nothing wrong!"

"Then why were you here at such an early hour? Why did you go into the garden?" Mr Corfield's incisive voice sliced through the room. "What is your connection with the lady who was killed?"

*

Chapter 6

"Stop it!" Shaking with anger, Molly leapt to her feet. "Stop bullying him! He's not lying. He didn't harm Miss Berry." She turned to face Lady Adelaide, "I don't wish to disobey you, m'lady, but I'd rather wait for a police officer to arrive."

"You may be right, Molly. That is not the behaviour I expected of a gentleman."

Mr Corfield met Lady Adelaide's cool gaze and gave a rueful smile. "My apologies, ma'am. Sometimes a situation is too urgent to maintain the proprieties. I wished to see if I could startle him into telling the truth."

"He is telling the truth. Neither of us know how Miss Berry died," said Molly.

"Very well, Molly." Mr Corfield's voice was gentle but compelling. "Please sit down again and tell us what you do know."

Reluctantly Molly resumed her seat.

"What were you and your sailor friend doing in the garden at that hour?"

Molly took a deep breath, forcing herself back to composure. "Yesterday was my day out and Lady Adelaide said I could spend the night at my father's house. When I left this morning, Kemal met me by chance outside my father's yard and we walked along together."

"You saw nothing out of the ordinary?" said Mr Corfield.

"No sir. Not until Kemal was attacked."

He pounced upon the weak spot in her story. "If you were with Kemal you must have seen who attacked him?"

"No sir." She'd got this ready but she didn't rush into it. She spoke slowly and clearly in the hope that Kemal would follow what she said. "When we got to the house I was going to go round the back to the servants' door but Kemal wanted to take a look at the fine garden I'd told him about. I said I couldn't go with him, it would be an impertinence. So I waited at the end of the road while he went to peer through the railings." She saw Mr Corfield raise his eyebrows and knew she'd made a mistake. The garden was indeed very fine, with a terrace that looked out over the bay, but none of its glories would be visible on a dark December morn. She hurried on, "Then I heard a noise and I was worried so I peeped round the corner and Kemal was lying on the ground with that dint upon his head."

"And you didn't see who struck him?"

"No sir. But when Kemal regained his senses, he said he thought the person had come out of the garden. So we went to look and that's when we found her, poor Miss Berry." As she reached the end of her story she felt it was safe, even wise, to show distress.

"I see. Molly, how long have you been acquainted with Kemal?"

"We met last week, sir, after Church."

"And you arranged an assignation with him?" spluttered Dr Russell. "Lady Adelaide, I fear you allow your servant too much liberty."

This made Molly angry for Lady Adelaide as well as for herself but there was nothing she could say that wouldn't make matters worse.

"What do you mean 'assignation'?" Kemal entered the fray.

Dr Russell looked at him coldly. "An improper meeting between a man and woman."

Kemal scowled. "Mistress Molly has done nothing improper. She did not know I was coming to see her."

"Why did you, if you received no encouragement?"

Molly's heart ached for Kemal; she was sure his head hurt too much for him to think straight. It also ached for herself because, by admitting that he'd planned to come and see her, he'd made things worse.

"On Sunday Mistress Molly lost the angel she used to mark her place in her book of prayer."

"And you wished to return it to her?" prompted Lady Adelaide.

Kemal smiled at her gratefully. "I did."

Relief washed over Molly. Kemal had offered the only explanation that might pass muster and not get her dismissed. "Yes, that's right." She took the bookmark out of her reticule and laid it on the table.

"Not much of a thing to make a fuss over," said Dr Russell disparagingly.

"My mother made it for me. She died when I was a child."

"I'm sure you can get it clean again," said Lady Adelaide gently.

"Yes m'lady." Molly scrubbed her tears away. They had more to worry about than a bookmark, however precious.

"How did you know Molly would be leaving her father's house at that hour?" demanded Mr Corfield.

"I told him," Molly cut in, seeing Kemal was at a loss. "I mentioned I was allowed every Wednesday off and how Lady Adelaide was kind enough to let me spend the night. I said maybe my pa would let him take pot-luck with us sometimes. It's lonely for him in a strange place and Pa's a good Christian."

She said the last words with an edge of insolence and looked defiantly at Mr Corfield. To her surprise he grinned and said, "As are you, my girl."

She didn't answer. She was more afraid of Mr Corfield's sharp wit than of Dr Russell's bossy blustering.

The silence was broken by a crash, as if someone had fallen down the back steps, followed by knocking on the scullery door.

"You'd better answer it, Molly," said Mr Corfield. "You're the only one of us a tradesman might expect to find here and there's no advantage in spreading the news around the neighbourhood before the police officer arrives."

Obediently she went to open the door. A tall, thin figure stood there. He was wearing a dark blue swallow-tailed coat and tall hat. Her heart sank. The police constable had arrived but she couldn't believe he would improve the situation. "Good morning, Jeremy. You'd better come inside."

"Good morning, Molly. Good morning, ma'am."

He tripped on the threshold and only saved himself from falling by an undignified flailing of his arms. Molly sighed. She'd known Jeremy Bray all her life. They'd lived in the same road and, as children, they'd played together. It was Molly who'd taken the lead, even though Jeremy was three years her senior. Not that Jeremy ever realised that. He was opinionated and stubborn but easily led. When Molly reached fifteen she'd realised he had a liking for her that she could not return and, for the last five years, she'd kept her distance. He resented this and made his displeasure clear.

"Good morning, Constable," said Lady Adelaide. "Thank you for coming so quickly. Mr Corfield, perhaps you could tell the officer what has occurred."

"I think it would be better if Molly told the story in her own words." Mr Corfield pulled Molly's chair out for her and indicated that she should sit down.

Molly hated the thought of going through it all again but she knew there was no avoiding it. This time she added in the reason that Kemal had invented for meeting her at her father's house. Most of the story got easier to tell as she went through it, but describing Miss Berry's dead body was even harder than before.

While she was speaking she kept her eyes on her fingers, which were twisting together nervously in her lap. When she finished she looked up and saw Jeremy glaring suspiciously at Kemal. "So this here foreigner wasn't actually in your sight all the time. There was a minute or so when he could have been getting up to anything."

"He was knocked senseless," said Molly sharply. "He didn't have time to get up to anything." Even as she spoke she knew it was a lost cause. Once Jeremy got an idea in his head, he wouldn't have room for reasonable arguments.

Dr Russell chuckled. "I have often observed, officer, that females have little sense of time."

"Yes, sir." Jeremy gave Molly a resentful look. "So, Molly, does your pa allow you to keep company with a Turk?"

"Officer, you are unmannerly," protested Lady Adelaide.

"It's not important, m'lady." Molly wouldn't let Jeremy goad her. "Kemal couldn't have done anything to Miss Berry. She'd been dead a while. She was stone cold."

Jeremy looked towards Dr Russell. "Can you confirm that, sir?"

"When you have as much experience of death and disease as I have, you realise that it is not wise to claim with assurance matters which could, on further investigation, prove incorrect. I cannot state with absolute certainty the time of death on such a bitterly cold morning."

Molly stared at him in disbelief. He really was a malevolent old man.

"I see. Thank you, sir." Jeremy grabbed hold of Kemal's arm and hauled him to his feet. "You'll come with me, m'lad. My superiors will want to talk to you. You Turks are murdering savages, everyone knows that. It's the nubbing cheat for you."

Molly saw the flicker of fear and anger on Kemal's face. "Kemal! No!"

She was too late. He wrenched free of Jeremy and drew his dagger.

Chapter 7

There was a moment of total stillness and a silence broken only by the sound of Kemal's panting breath. He slanted the dagger, holding them all at bay.

Molly stood up. "Kemal, this isn't wise. You're going to make things worse."

"Molly, tell me, what is it that I should do?"

Molly didn't know what to say. If Kemal harmed any of them there'd be no escaping the gallows. But if he gave himself up he'd be hauled off to gaol, the stranger from a savage land who was easy to blame for any crime. And, knowing Jeremy Bray, Kemal would get a beating as soon as he was shackled and unable to defend himself.

"Very well, boy, leave." Dr Russell stepped in front of Molly as if to shield her. He was a large man and she could no longer see Kemal. "There's a clear path to the door. You're frightening her ladyship."

Instinctively Molly glanced towards Lady Adelaide. She looked pale but more troubled than afraid.

"Kemal, it would be better not to run," Lady Adelaide spoke gently.

"Molly?" Kemal looked towards her.

Molly saw Dr Russell's hand slide into his greatcoat pocket, gripping something large and heavy. Her stomach lurched. It couldn't be a gun? All her instincts told her that it was.

"Get out of here, boy." Dr Russell's sharp words sounded more like a command than acceptance of defeat. Molly was sure he planned to shoot Kemal. There'd be no penalty for killing an armed and dangerous man.

"No! Kemal, don't go!" she shrieked. Shaking with terror, she pushed clear of Dr Russell and stood in front of him. She didn't think he'd dare to shoot Kemal with her in the way. Not with Lady Adelaide as a witness.

"You ungrateful girl! Have you no care for your mistress?" bellowed Dr Russell. "Lady Adelaide, I beg you to leave the room."

"Certainly not," said Lady Adelaide. "Molly, you must do as you think best." Molly loved her for that but it wasn't easy to think straight. She knew that Kemal was desperate and soon someone would make a foolish move. She wondered, if by some miracle he made it back to his ship, whether the English authorities could force his captain to hand him over.

Mr Corfield said quietly, "If you give yourself up, Kemal, I will make sure you are treated fairly."

Dr Russell snorted. "You can't bargain with an animal like that. Those creatures have no sense of honour. It's obvious he's as guilty as hell and deserves to go to the gallows." He glanced towards Lady Adelaide. "I beg your pardon, madam, for my intemperate language."

Lady Adelaide did not acknowledge his apology but she looked at him coldly, her lips tightly compressed.

Molly took advantage of the doctor's preoccupation to edge forward until she was standing in front of Kemal, shielding much of him, although he was taller than she was. She turned so that she could see everyone's expression apart from his. She felt safer that way, even though he was holding a dagger. How could it be, after such a short acquaintanceship, that she trusted Kemal more than these English gentlemen?

She spoke to Mr Corfield. "Don't give me any slum. Do you mean the same as the doctor? Even though Kemal's innocent, he'll be hanged?"

Mr Corfield did not react to her insolence, nor to her flash language, although Lady Adelaide looked startled and Dr Russell frowned.

"No Molly, I didn't mean that. I'm not giving you slum. I too examined the unfortunate lady's body and I agree she had been dead for many hours."

"But what about this business?" She nodded towards Kemal and the dagger.

"I'm sure the police officer won't wish to take the matter any further. He was over-zealous and he didn't realise Kemal is still dazed from that head wound. Don't you agree, constable?" Despite his courteous manner, Mr Corfield spoke with authority.

"You mean let him off?"

"I mean we should forget this incident, which does no credit to anyone. I am acquainted with Captain Harris, your Chief Constable, and I would not hesitate to inform him of this matter."

"There's no need to do that, sir." Jeremy spoke quickly. Molly understood his worry. A complaint about his conduct from an eminent man would lead to his dismissal. He had to placate both Mr Corfield and Dr Russell or he could lose his job.

"You cannot be serious!" exclaimed Dr Russell. "To be intimidated by this ruffian."

"I'm very serious. The political situation with the Ottoman Empire is extremely sensitive at the present time."

"Rubbish! The Ottoman Empire's the sick old man of Europe. Anyway, what would their rulers care for the fate of one common sailor?"

"Sick old men can prove dangerous enemies," said Mr Corfield, "and when people are looking for trouble the slightest spark can cause a dangerous flare."

Molly wasn't sure what they were talking about but Mr Corfield's grave words alarmed her. It was as if

Kemal had drifted into deep and dangerous waters and taken her with him and neither of them had a chart to navigate their way.

"Molly, if you have any influence with Kemal, I beg you to exert it now and persuade him to end this situation," said Mr Corfield earnestly.

It seemed that Mr Corfield was their only hope. "Please, have I got your word of honour that Kemal won't be punished for this? And he won't be mistreated? You'll go with him to make sure he's not ill-used?"

"You have my word." Rather than sounding offended, Mr Corfield smiled as if approving of her caution.

"And I want your promise too, Jeremy. Swear to me he won't be beaten as soon as you've got him away from witnesses." Jeremy Bray had always been a bully.

He scowled at her. "I got my duty to do."

"That duty is clearly defined," said Mr Corfield, "and you are not permitted to offer violence to witnesses."

Jeremy coloured and shifted uncomfortably. "If you say so, sir. All right, I agree," he muttered sullenly.

Molly turned towards Kemal and held out her hand. "Kemal, please give me the dagger. I know you didn't kill Miss Berry and if you run away we won't be able to find out the truth."

She prayed she'd made the right choice about this. If she was wrong to trust them, Kemal would die.

Chapter 8

Kemal lowered the dagger and stepped towards her, holding it out, hilt forward. She took it and passed it to Mr Corfield. Jeremy Bray grabbed hold of Kemal who stiffened but did not struggle.

At this inopportune moment the housekeeper peered round the door. "If you please, m'lady, the mistress is awake and wanting her morning tray."

Lady Adelaide spoke with her usual composure, "Thank you, Bradbury. We're almost finished in here. I'm sorry we've put you behind with your work."

She smiled so sweetly that even the disapproving housekeeper could not resist. "Thank you, m'lady. It's no trouble at all for you."

Molly kept her gaze lowered. She was uncomfortably aware that Mrs Bradbury might be happy to oblige Lady Adelaide but Lady Adelaide's trouble-making maid would have a hard time from the upper servants.

The door closed behind the housekeeper and Mr Corfield said, "Indeed it is time we removed ourselves. I think the best plan would be for this police officer and myself to escort Kemal back to his ship. There we can discover whether his shipmates can speak for his presence on board earlier last night, at the time when we must presume the poor lady was killed."

"Begging your pardon, sir, but that won't prove a lot," protested Jeremy Bray. "These foreigners 'ud say anything. They lie as fast as they can open their mouths. You can't rely on a word of what they say."

"We will go to the ship," insisted Mr Corfield. "And we will listen with civility to what the officers have to tell us. Kemal, which of the two ships is yours?"

"The Mirat-y Zafer." When pronouncing the Turkish name Kemal's accent sounded far more deeply foreign. "Hasan will be able to speak for me. He is my lieutenant." With a contemptuous gesture he indicated Jeremy Bray. "But if this one says that Hasan is not speaking the truth, he will be angry. Hasan does not lie."

Mr Corfield nodded gravely. He was still holding Kemal's dagger and he looked down at his hands as if uncertain what to do with it. It was the first time Molly had seen Mr Corfield at a loss. After a moment's thought he removed the silk scarf he was wearing around his neck and used it to wrap the dagger, then he placed it carefully into the capacious pocket of his greatcoat.

"Your servant, Lady Adelaide." He turned towards the door.

Kemal pulled his arm free of Jeremy Bray's grip and bowed first to Lady Adelaide and then to Molly. "I thank you, Madam, and you, Mistress Molly." He made a dignified exit.

"I too must leave you, m'lady," said Dr Russell. "I must go to Lady Dewsbury and break this sad news to her."

"But it is early and Lady Dewsbury is elderly and frail," protested Lady Adelaide. "I am sure she will still be in bed and if any members of her household have noted Miss Berry's absence I doubt if they will alarm her. I will go and break the sad news to her. I believe she would prefer to hear such tidings from one of her own sex."

Molly expected the doctor to protest but he said, "Yes, maybe that would be better, if your ladyship does not mind engaging on such a sad task. I must go home to my dear wife. She has been unwell and I have been out all night attending a patient who is not long for this world."

"I'm sorry to hear Mrs Russell is indisposed." Lady Adelaide ushered him towards the door.

"My wife is always so busy with her good works. She never spares herself and then her nerves fail her. I've ordered her to bed to regain her strength. We must have her fit for when Henry comes down from London to spend Christmas with us. He gets little time away from his political duties." His voice softened as he spoke of his only son. "We miss him but his duty to his country must come first."

Molly struggled not to smile. The way the doctor and Mrs Russell carried on anyone would think their son was Prime Minister instead of a junior civil servant.

"I'm sure Mrs Russell will feel much recovered when Mr Henry Russell comes home," said Lady Adelaide. "Is this your stick, Doctor?"

"Ah yes. Thank you. I almost forgot it. It's not the one I usually carry. I could not find my favourite stick when I left my house last night. Servants, you know. They never put things in the right place."

"Indeed, servants can often be a problem. The door, Bowman." Molly kept her gaze lowered as she hurried to obey.

The housekeeper must have been listening at the other door because, as soon as the doctor left, she came bustling in and the other servants streamed after her.

Lady Adelaide said, "Bowman, change your dress, then wait for me in my bedchamber."

Molly hurried up the narrow backstairs, jerking impatiently as her skirts brushed against the wall. Unlike housemaids, it was permissible for a lady's maid to wear full skirts and many fashionable ladies preferred their attendants to do so when accompanying them into Society. Molly had been wearing three stiff petticoats for over half a year but still the weight and bulk of them irked her.

Her small, top floor bedroom was sparsely furnished, not appropriate to her rank as lady's maid. That was because Mrs Tate disapproved of her.

She'd failed to empty her wash basin yesterday and a thin layer of ice had formed. Her teeth were chattering as she broke it and washed her hands and face. The chill water stung her skin. Hastily she towelled her face and hands.

She opened her chest of drawers and got out her mother-of-pearl hairbrush, part of a set Pa had bought for her from a sailor who was in need of drinking money. A maid was not allowed personal property on show, especially fripperies as fine as this, so she kept it concealed beneath her undergarments. She brushed her hair, twisted it into a knot at the nape of her neck and pinned it so ruthlessly it made her eyes water.

She changed her dress. The one she put on was dark blue and modestly cut, as became her station in life and her mistress' mourning state, but it was made of soft wool and trimmed with fine lace and she knew it was very becoming. If Lady Adelaide dismissed her there'd be no reason for her to wear any of her pretty furbelows.

But until that happened she had work to do. She hastened downstairs to Lady Adelaide's bedchamber. The disorder in the room showed that her mistress had risen in haste and dressed without help. Molly set the room to rights. As she drew back the curtains, she paused for a moment, looking out.

Lady Adelaide's bedroom was situated on the second floor and at the front of the house. Her window commanded views not only of The Crescent and the garden but of the fields beyond and the sand and water of Stokes Bay. The sea was grey and stormy but Molly saw a ship forcing its way through the rough waves. At this distance it looked like a toy but Molly had lived all her life in a naval port and she recognised the shape of a Royal Naval steam ship striking out in the channel between the mainland and the Isle of Wight. She wondered if it was heading for foreign shores. The thought filled her with envy. It was strange to think that the supplies it held were in all probability contained in barrels made by her father and his men.

In this bleak December the view looked grey and dismal but last summer it had been a delight. Molly sighed. It seemed unlikely she would be in Lady Adelaide's service to enjoy it next year. If she returned home in disgrace, Pa would push her towards a respectable marriage, the way he'd been doing for the past two years. She'd never escape Gosport and never visit all the wonderful places she'd read about. And Pa would never allow her to see Kemal again.

*

Chapter 9

Adelaide stood outside her aunt's bedchamber, hand raised to tap upon the door, then she saw how much it was shaking and lowered it again. She was afraid. Aunt Susan had taken her in when nobody else would and, if her aunt turned her away, she'd have nowhere to go.

Of course, she knew her aunt had her own reasons for her charity. It had been a triumph for Aunt Susan to offer gracious help to her sister, the Countess, who had married so far above her, and to the Earl, who was so top lofty in his ways.

What if her aunt ordered her to dismiss Molly? Adelaide imagined loneliness engulfing her again and shivered. When she'd first met Molly she had been her aunt's guest for three weeks and each day had seemed more bleak than the one before. Then, by fortunate chance, her carriage had lost a wheel outside Mr Bowman's house, and Molly's Grandmama had invited her in while it was being repaired.

Molly had been in the parlour, reading Mr Dickens' *Pictures From Italy*, which had surprised Adelaide, although she'd realised that Molly's Grandmama was a well-bred woman. She and Molly had started chatting. Molly had never thought of going into service until then, but she and Adelaide had taken a liking to each other straight away.

Adelaide thought about the tale Molly had told Mr Corfield and frowned. She did not know why, but she felt sure Molly hadn't told him the whole truth.

The approach of her aunt's maid startled Adelaide. She must not be found here, standing like a statue outside her aunt's door. She abandoned her intention and hurried along the corridor to her own room.

*

As soon as Lady Adelaide entered her bedchamber, Molly curtsied and spoke hastily before her courage failed. "I'm sorry, m'lady. I didn't mean to draw you into any of this."

"I'm sure you didn't." She spoke quietly and Molly found it impossible to read her feelings in her manner or her face.

"I'm sorry," she said again.

Lady Adelaide sat down, her long slender hands clasped together lightly in her lap. "Tell me what happened," she said. "All the truth this time."

"Yes, m'lady." How did Lady Adelaide know she hadn't told Mr Corfield everything? And how many more times would she be forced to repeat this ugly story?

She told Lady Adelaide all that had really happened. All but one thing. She didn't confess that Kemal's dagger had been stolen and hidden underneath Miss Berry's skirt. She feared Lady Adelaide might not believe her protestations of his innocence.

At last she stopped speaking and waited to hear her fate. Lady Adelaide frowned. "Did your father not order one of his workmen to escort you? You told me he would do so when I permitted you to spend the night at his house."

"Yes, m'lady. He told Tom to walk with me. But he wasn't well... Tom, I mean... he was suffering from the gripe. I didn't want to tell my father because he'd be angry. Whenever Tom can get any sweetmeats, he eats too much, that's why he gets gut ache. I'm sorry, m'lady, I shouldn't have said that." Molly felt flustered. 'Gut' was a vulgar word.

Lady Adelaide seemed more concerned about her behaviour than her language. "Your father would be rightly angry. It's wrong of you to conceal his apprentice's misdeeds."

"I'm sorry, m'lady, but I won't peach on Tom. He came from the workhouse and he never had enough to eat, so now he can't seem to help himself. There was no real danger in walking by myself, m'lady." She thrust away the memory of how afraid she'd felt, out in the dark alone.

"You know that's not true. You could have been in great danger, especially from the rough sea-faring men who frequent the docks."

"I won't do so again, m'lady."

"When you saw Kemal why did you not call out to him to escort you?" persisted Lady Adelaide.

Molly felt hot colour flood into her face. Whatever course she had chosen, somebody would have condemned her for behaving improperly.

"Well?" Lady Adelaide's tone was sharper now.

"It was because of what happened after church last week, m'lady. When we got back to the house, the mistress sent for me."

"Indeed? What did my aunt want of you?"

Molly kept her eyes lowered, staring at her fingers as they wound themselves into a tight knot. "The mistress had Mrs Russell with her. They scolded me. They said I'd been forward, talking to Kemal the way I did. Mrs Russell said I was on the path to become a Fallen Woman. So when I saw Kemal, I didn't call to him." There was a lump in her throat. She swallowed. "I'll pack my things and leave the house today."

"Don't be absurd, Molly. I don't wish you to leave."

Molly felt tears well up. She rubbed her hand impatiently across her eyes. She was turning into a regular watering pot. "You're not turning me off, m'lady?"

"Of course I'm not." She smiled. "After you left the kitchen I expended some time reconciling my aunt's housekeeper to your continued employment as my maid and I have no intention of wasting my efforts."

"But the mistress, she'll have something to say about that."

"I respect my aunt but it is not for her to dismiss my personal servant."

Molly stared at her in dismay. If Lady Adelaide quarrelled with her aunt she'd be cast off. In most ways, Lady Adelaide was more alone in the world than she was. Unlike Lady Adelaide's parents, Pa and Grandmama would never turn her away.

"I am grateful, m'lady. I won't let you down."

"I know that, Molly. I trust you."

In that moment Molly was tempted to tell her mistress the whole truth about Kemal's dagger but Lady Adelaide had already moved on. "Tell me, does your father wish you to marry that gauche police officer?" Her smile was tinged with mischief.

Molly wasn't sure what gauche meant but it sounded like a suitable word to describe Jeremy Bray. "Oh no, m'lady! My pa's got more sense than that. He's told Jeremy he won't have him hanging around me. The man he's got in his eye for me is a widower, a cooper like himself, and in a good way of business. Pa's not a harsh man. He doesn't want to force me to a marriage that I can't like, but he wants to know there'll be somebody to provide for me once he's gone. But I don't want to settle down in Gosport... not yet." In all her life she'd never visited a larger town than

Portsmouth or travelled more than twelve miles from her home.

"You are fortunate." Lady Adelaide sounded wistful. Molly knew that her mistress hated the thought of the marriage she'd be forced into as soon as her term of mourning was decently past.

"Ring the bell. I require breakfast before I visit Lady Dewsbury."

While waiting for the food, Molly helped Lady Adelaide to don her corsets and dress suitably for her visit.

The maid returned with a tray, laden with bread and butter, cold meat, poached eggs and a jug of coffee. As soon as the maid had left, Lady Adelaide said, "Sit down, Molly, and join me for breakfast."

"M'lady?" Servants didn't share their mistress' food.

"You must be hungry. I do not wish you to faint while we are out."

"Out m'lady?" Molly stared at her.

"You're coming with me to visit Lady Dewsbury."

*

Chapter 10

"Where have they taken her? I wish her to be brought here to her home." Lady Dewsbury's voice was sharp and imperious and Adelaide could not tell whether she was angry or distressed. She was dressed with quiet elegance in purple silk and lace but there was nothing soft about her. Her grey eyes were clouded and close to sightless but, despite her age and infirmities, she was formidable.

"I'm sorry, ma'am. I do not know where they have taken her." Adelaide chose her words with care. "I think there may be formalities that have to be fulfilled concerning the manner of her death. Doctor Russell would know. Forgive me, I should have allowed him to break the sad news to you. He could have told you more."

"No. I don't require the doctor. He's a tedious man. A toadeater, trying to claw his way up in the world. Well I'm not a ladder for any such to climb. That shocks you, doesn't it?"

"It did surprise me a little, ma'am. I'm not used to such... bluntness."

"Of course you aren't. I've been acquainted with your family for many years and there's not one of them who would look facts in the face if they could avoid it."

"My aunt hopes you'll feel well enough to allow her to visit you very soon." Adelaide struggled to keep this strange visit on conventional lines.

"A visit of condolence? Surely not? Susan Tate wouldn't think the death of a companion merited such an attention. I presume she wishes to visit me out of curiosity. Well she won't be the first or the last to do that."

Adelaide could only assume that Lady Dewsbury was referring to her own visit. The knowledge that she had been curious added to her discomfiture and she felt herself blush. She rose to her feet and, with what dignity she could muster, said, "I'm sorry to have troubled you, ma'am. I did not mean to intrude."

"Oh sit down, child! You're not a fool, so don't act like one. I'm willing to believe you came to break the news out of kindness, but if you were curious what's the harm in that? When I was your age I used to know all the warmest stories and I've been the centre of a good few tales as well. In poor Prinny's day that was."

Adelaide was uncertain what to say. She knew her aunt would be shocked. The Prince Regent, later King George IV, had been a man whose improper way of life meant he was an unsuitable subject for discussion in a lady's drawing room.

"I suppose I will have to see Dr Russell," said Lady Dewsbury. "I can't rest without knowing exactly what happened to Ellen, but I can't abide the man." The sparkle of her remembered youth dropped from her and she looked old and frail.

"Perhaps I could see Dr Russell for you, ma'am. If you would not think me presumptuous," said Adelaide, still wary of being snubbed.

"Thank you, I would be grateful. I dislike being so helpless. Sight is a precious gift. I did not value it as I should have done until it failed me."

"I'm so sorry."

"For the past four years I have seen only shadows. Ellen... Miss Berry... has been my eyes. Without her support I don't know what I will do." She raised a lace handkerchief to dab at her trembling lips. After a few moments, she regained her composure, lowered the handkerchief and spoke fiercely, "I want to know what happened to Ellen. I want to know who did this evil deed. I want them punished. But I'm just a blind old woman and the men in charge, those kind, considerate men, will pat my hand and tell me to leave it all to them." Her voice dropped into biting mockery, "Because it is man's work and it is better if I don't distress myself."

Adelaide flinched. She knew how Lady Dewsbury felt. She spoke on impulse, "I have my maid, Molly Bowman, here with me."

"I heard her enter. I did not expect you to come unaccompanied."

"Molly was one of the young people who found Miss Berry lying in the garden. She can tell you more about the matter than I can."

Lady Dewsbury's indifference disappeared. "Come here, girl. Sit down and tell me everything you know."

*

Chapter 11

Molly perched nervously on the edge of a chair and again told the story. Although it was not yet noon, it seemed as though the day had gone on forever. It was hard to remember exactly what she'd told everybody and she wondered how she was going to keep all the versions of the tale straight in her own mind. At some point, she was bound to get confused, or she and Kemal would contradict each other. She tried to gloss over the harsher details but Lady Dewsbury asked such probing questions that she ended up describing more than she'd intended.

When she finished speaking, Lady Dewsbury was silent. Molly sat, waiting anxiously, her eyes on the old lady. Lady Adelaide removed her vinaigrette from her reticule and proffered it.

Lady Adelaide's gentle touch on her hand brought Lady Dewsbury out of her reverie. She became aware of what she was being offered and said sharply, "No, thank you. I've no need of smelling salts. I've never been a swooning fool of a woman and I've no patience with them."

"But what Molly has told us... it was so terrible... it must have distressed you."

"Of course it distressed me, but I've seen worse than that in my day. I was a soldier's wife. I accompanied my husband across most of Spain and Portugal during the Peninsula War. I tended the wounded brought back to Brussels during the Battle of Waterloo. And, afterwards I walked the battlefield searching for my brother's body. Not that I boast of that. Many women performed that sorrowful task. High-born and low-born, grief and desperate times bring us together."

Molly gave an involuntary gasp. It turned the old lady's attention back to her. "That shocks you, does it, girl?"

"Oh no, m'lady." Molly knew it was not her place to enter into conversation with so distinguished a personage but her unruly tongue overcame her discretion once again. "It's what you said... about Spain and Waterloo... it's like my grandmother's story. She followed my grandfather just like you did your husband, and she tended the wounded and searched after the battle like you did and found my grandfather's body." She stopped speaking. "I'm sorry, m'lady. I forgot my place."

"Nonsense girl. You have the right to be proud of such a story. And what was your grandfather's name?"

"Dorrington, m'lady. Major James Dorrington."

Lady Dewsbury leaned forward, suddenly intent. "And his wife was Elizabeth?"

"Yes m'lady."

"I remember Lizzie Dorrington. We shared many a flea-ridden lodging in Portugal. She had a daughter, a pretty little thing. I can't recall her name?"

"Mary, m'lady. She was my mother. I was named after her."

"Ah yes, I remember. What happened to Lizzie and her daughter? My husband was gravely wounded during the battle and I devoted myself to nursing him. I lost contact with many people I would have liked to retain as friends."

Molly found this whole situation awkward. It was clear Lady Dewsbury had forgotten she was reminiscing with a servant but, by her expression, Lady Adelaide had not. "After my grandfather's death my Grandmama and mother had little money. They were forced to seek shelter with Grandmama's sister.

She's married to a tenant farmer a few miles out of Portsmouth."

Lady Dewsbury looked puzzled. "Surely your grandfather's family were wealthy?"

"They were angry when my grandfather married Grandmama and they cut him off. They wanted him to marry a wealthy lady not a vicar's daughter."

"I see." Lady Dewsbury's tone was grim. "And then your mother married?"

"Yes, m'lady. My father's a Master Cooper." That should effectively remind her ladyship of Molly's station in life.

"You said that Mary was your mother. Does that mean she is no longer alive?"

"Yes, m'lady, she died when I was a little girl."

"A pity. I would have liked Mary Dorrington to visit me."

The regret in her voice touched Molly and nudged her into further indiscretion. "My Grandmama is still alive, m'lady. She keeps house for my father. When she returns from visiting her sister, I'm sure she'd be honoured to visit you."

"Lizzie Dorrington has been living in Gosport all these years and has never come to knock upon my door?" Lady Dewsbury sounded genuinely hurt.

"She would have thought it presumptuous, m'lady." Grandmama had never complained or shown any shame at the change in her circumstances but she had a quiet pride and would not risk being turned away from an acquaintance's door.

"That's folly! Tell her I will be in her debt if she will solace my loneliness."

"Yes, m'lady."

Lady Adelaide stood up. "I will leave you now, ma'am. Please accept my condolences. As soon as I have spoken with Dr Russell I will inform you of the official procedure. I hope that soon you will be able to make arrangements for..." Her voice trailed away as she searched for suitably tactful words.

"For the interment of my friend," completed Lady Dewsbury. "That's what she was, for all I paid her wages. Ellen Berry was my companion for close on twenty years and I want to know who killed her. For that reason I'd be grateful if you could spare me a little more of your time."

"Of course, ma'am." Lady Adelaide's polite agreement didn't match the clear reluctance with which she resumed her seat.

Lady Dewsbury turned her misted eyes back towards Molly. "This Turkish boy, Kemal, how old is he?"

"I don't know his birth date, m'lady but he told me he'll be twenty in the next few months, before he returns home."

"Hmm, that's younger than I thought," muttered Lady Dewsbury, clearly talking to herself. Then addressing Molly, "You said he speaks good English?"

"Yes, m'lady. He told me he's an orphan and he was brought up in the household of an English officer who'd served the Ottoman Empire and made his home there."

"I see." She seemed to fix onto this point. "It is possible an orphan's birth date might be confused. Tell me, where in the Ottoman Empire was he brought up?"

Molly racked her brains. "I'm sorry, m'lady, I can't remember. Those foreign names all sounded the same. I can't remember his family name either. But I do know he said he was brought up on an island and it was very beautiful."

"And he was brought up a Christian?"

"Yes, m'lady. He said he was a dhimmi." She stumbled over the unfamiliar word. "That's a..."

"A Christian who is allowed to practise his religion in a Muslim country," said Lady Dewsbury crisply. "Thank you, Molly, that's very interesting." She turned back to Lady Adelaide, "Now I have one last favour to ask of you. Would you permit your maid to go to Miss Berry's room and select suitable garments? I wish those who have care of my friend's body to have clothes of her own to dress her in."

"Of course, ma'am, but surely your own maid...?"

"My maid is elderly. She is devoted to my interests but she and Miss Berry never got on well. I would not trust her to make an appropriate choice."

"I understand," said Lady Adelaide. "Molly, pray do what Lady Dewsbury requires of you. I will enquire of Dr Russell where the garments should be sent."

As Molly followed the footman up the stairs she noticed that Lady Dewsbury favoured less paintings and ornaments than Mrs Tate, who scarcely left six inches of wallpaper visible between the ornately framed pictures on her walls. But, like Mrs Tate's house, everything looked well-polished and in excellent repair.

Miss Berry's room was comfortable and elegantly furnished, more the bedchamber of a friend than a servant. Molly longed to look around for clues. Perhaps, if she knew how Miss Berry lived, it would help her understand why she'd died. But snooping was wrong and the footman was waiting outside the closed door.

She searched through Miss Berry's attire, looking for a suitable gown for laying out. She took a bag from the wardrobe and packed the clothes. In the bottom drawer she discovered a lace shawl, laid up in lavender. It was exquisite, worked in an intricate pattern she had never seen before. It would be an appropriate garment to do honour to the dead. She picked it up and shook it out. A slender packet of letters fell onto the floor. The lavender silk ribbon that confined them came untied and they scattered. She bent to pick them up and stared at them in horror.

There were seven letters in all, written in a foreign language with a strange curved alphabet. Last week Kemal had traced out her name in Turkish on the path outside the Church and, as far as Molly could tell, these letters looked like the same alphabet.

Chapter 12

As Molly stared at the letters her brain went numb. Were they indeed written in Turkish? Could it be a coincidence? Surely these letters must have something to do with Kemal?

A trickle of doubt seeped into her mind. It was possible Kemal had lied to her. Had he known Miss Berry, or known of her? Perhaps they'd been corresponding. If so, could he have harmed her? When she thought of Kemal as a murderer she felt a great weight crushing her.

Of course he couldn't have killed Miss Berry this morning, Molly was still sure of that. But it was possible he'd committed the deed last night. If so, he must have returned this morning because he'd forgotten something or needed to cover his tracks. Surely he would not have forgotten his dagger? But Molly had found it concealed beneath Miss Berry's skirt. It seemed foolhardy to return to the scene of his crime, but perhaps he'd been heading for this house, to retrieve these very letters. And yet, she couldn't believe Kemal had deceived her. 'Would not believe it', a small cautious voice crept into her mind. Pa had warned her that there were men who'd try to take advantage of her innocence, although she knew he'd not been talking about getting her involved in brutal murder.

She felt an impulse to thrust the letters back into the drawer. She was deep enough in trouble as it was. At the same time, everything stubborn and curious in her rebelled against giving up. Providence had offered her a valuable clue about Miss Berry's life and possibly about her death. It was not for her to reject it because she was tired, disillusioned and afraid.

But how could she smuggle the letters out of the house? She'd left her reticule in Lady Dewsbury's drawing room. She considered placing the letters in the carpetbag she'd taken from Miss Berry's cupboard to hold her clothes but she might have no chance to retrieve them. Desperation made her inventive. In one of Miss Berry's drawers she'd seen sewing needles, thread and pins.

She retied the ribbon that bound the letters, then, in trembling haste, she raised her skirts and pinned the ribbon firmly between her petticoats. She'd have liked to sew it, but the footman outside the door might wonder what was taking her so long. As she left the room she prayed that the bundle pressed against her leg would not work loose and tumble down.

*

Adelaide glanced at the elegant clock on Lady Dewsbury's mantelshelf. She was discreet about it, even though she knew her hostess could not see. She wondered how long it would take Molly to find and pack the clothes.

"Would you care for tea, Lady Adelaide? Or coffee or chocolate or perhaps a glass of wine?" The words were those of a civil hostess but Adelaide was sure Lady Dewsbury knew how ill at ease she felt.

"Thank you. I do not require any refreshment." If she accepted she'd be trapped here until she'd drunk it.

"Very sensible. I wasn't brought up to maudle my insides with tea throughout the day."

"You've had a very eventful and exciting life, ma'am."

"Don't sound so wistful. You have your excitements still to come."

Adelaide looked down at her hands. "I've had enough excitement already." She felt embarrassed to hear the telltale tremor in her voice.

"Nonsense, child, what you've had is pain and humiliation, and none of it of your own making, if what I've heard is true. For you the good things are still to come, whereas my day is done." She lapsed into brooding silence.

Adelaide did not argue about this positive view of her future. Sometimes, when she looked back, it seemed like somebody else's story. Perhaps that was the only way she could bear to think of it. She had been Lady Adelaide Lyndhurst, eldest daughter of the Earl of Charlton, and just out of the schoolroom when she became betrothed to Bernard Talridge, the young heir to a mine owner.

Adelaide had not objected. She had been brought up to render strict obedience and her mother had told her it was a woman's duty to endure. Adelaide knew what she meant without unladylike explanations. Her mother had been worn to a wraith by the Earl's constant demands upon her to produce an heir. After four daughters and five babes who only survived a few days, Mama had presented Father with a son, but little Arthur was frail and Father required another boy to be sure. Adelaide wondered whether Father would prefer Mama to die, leaving him free to marry a new wife.

"Is that child, Molly, in love with her Turkish sailor?" Lady Dewsbury's question jerked Adelaide out of her dark thoughts.

"I don't know, ma'am. I think not. She is sorry for him but she hardly knows him. She has only been in company with him once before today."

"One minute is all it takes for a girl to fall in love with a dashing young man, especially when he's unsuitable. Tell me, do you trust Molly?"

"Yes ma'am."

"And I trust you. You may decide whether you share with Molly what I'm about to tell you but I'd prefer it not to go further than you two."

"Do not fear, ma'am. I have learned to be discreet."

"I realise that, but I'm still uncertain how much I have the right to tell you. If Ellen Berry had died a natural death, she could have taken her secret with her to the grave and I would never have said a word. But in the circumstances..." Her voice trailed away, then she rallied and said briskly, "I used to be fond of drawing. If I might trouble you to go to the bureau in the corner, the lower drawers are filled with my sketch books, take out the one marked 1830." Adelaide obeyed and brought the book back to her hostess.

"Place it on that small table and look through. After my husband's death, I was restless and I travelled extensively. It was during my travels that I met Ellen. We both enjoyed drawing and shared sketching expeditions, although she was a finer artist than I. In that book you will find pictures of Ellen as I first knew her."

Adelaide turned the pages carefully. Lady Dewsbury had possessed skill with both paints and pencils, keen powers of observation and a lively sense of humour. There were pictures of dark-haired, savage-looking men, their garb reminded Adelaide of Kemal's clothes. She bit back her questions. Molly could return at any moment and Adelaide wished to hear all that Lady Dewsbury was willing to confide.

At last she found the first picture marked *'Miss Ellen Berry. Constantinople.'* A full-length study, it showed a modestly dressed young woman, tall, slender and dark-haired. Over the page there were two head portraits. One was in profile and showed a most distinctive set of features, a firm mouth and determined chin, an aquiline nose, arched brows and elfin, pointed ears. Adelaide thought the whole did not add up to a conventionally beautiful face but it was a very striking one. The other portrait was full-face. Ellen Berry's eyes dominated this picture, dark and wide-set, they stared out of the page with a heart-rending gaze of desolation and bewilderment.

"Oh!" The soft cry broke from Adelaide before she could control it.

Lady Dewsbury seemed pleased by her reaction. "Yes, I think you'll understand. Come and sit down. I will tell you Ellen Berry's secret."

Adelaide thought she'd already guessed but she did as she was bid.

"As I told you, I encountered Ellen when I was travelling. I met her when she was searching for employment. Before that she had spent a roving life, accompanying her two brothers, her only family. They were botanists who hoped to find new species of plants and bring them back to this country. There is both fame and fortune in such discoveries. Before I knew her, Ellen had encountered a man and formed a liaison. I think it must have been in one of the island provinces of the Ottoman Empire. She refused to speak of him. All I know is his name, Habib."

"She would not tell even you, her benefactress?" exclaimed Adelaide.

Lady Dewsbury gave a small, grim smile. "She was a stubborn woman, self-willed and independent, never more so than when she was in need. I did not wish to force her confidence. As for the rest, I think you have guessed what happened. She had a child, a boy, and for some time... she never told me how long... they lived together as a family. Then her lover died. Of course, Ellen's brothers had cast her off. She found someone to care for her baby and fended off starvation by working as a seamstress for a French family who were stationed there. I heard her story and contrived to meet her. I took a liking to her, in much the same way, I would think, as you did to your Molly, so I offered her a job as my companion."

Adelaide thought that Molly might flout the conventions but she was not a fallen woman. She did not say so. Such opinions would anger Lady Dewsbury and she did not wish to be unkind about a woman who'd suffered so much and been killed so cruelly.

"Of course, when we returned to England, no-one was aware of her past history," continued Lady Dewsbury.

"What happened to her baby?" asked Adelaide.

"She said he had been adopted into a respectable household. It is strange. Recently, she has spoken more about the child. Talking of him as the man he must be now and she said something about seeing a ghost. Ellen was a sensible soul, not given to foolish fancies. I'm not a superstitious woman but it's as if she felt a foreshadowing of her death."

Adelaide hesitated, embarrassed by the strangeness of this confidence. Before she could find a suitable response the drawing room door opened and the butler announced, "Mrs Russell, m'lady."

Chapter 13

Adelaide saw a swift glint of annoyance cross Lady Dewsbury's face. "Very well, you may show her in." Her voice was cold.

There would have been no chance to deny Mrs Russell entry, for she followed close on the butler's heels. As always her thin, stiff figure was stooping slightly forwards, as if following the lead of her sharply pointed nose. Her beady eyes glittered as they flashed around the room, taking in everyone and everything.

"Good morning, Mrs Russell. How kind of you to pay me a visit of condolence."

"Good morning, Lady Dewsbury. Good morning Adelaide. I confess I am surprised to find you here."

"As I am you, ma'am. Only this morning your husband told me that you were indisposed and confined to your room." Adelaide noted Mrs Russell's pallor and the incessant twitching of her hands. "Forgive me, but are you well enough to be out?"

"I was unwell, but I heard of these terrible goings on and felt it my Christian duty to visit dear Lady Dewsbury. In such a situation one must overcome one's own infirmities." She sat down without making any effort to arrange her plain grey skirt and leaned towards her hostess. "Pray tell me everything."

"There is little I can tell you." Lady Dewsbury's voice became even more aloof.

"My husband came across the tragedy when he was returning, after visiting a patient who is not long for this world. He tells me that villainous Turkish sailor was responsible. The one who had the impudence to come to our Church last week. Such appalling effrontery, pretending he was a person like ourselves.

He must have been crazed with opium or some such thing. Tell me, has he been thrown into prison?"

"The matter is in the hands of the authorities," said Lady Dewsbury.

Mrs Russell sniffed. "In the hands of Edwin Corfield, more like. That young man takes too much upon himself."

"I do not wish to discuss this matter..." Lady Dewsbury broke off as the door opened again. This time it was Molly who entered. She looked flustered.

"Have you found everything you need?" asked Lady Dewsbury. Something in her tone sounded conspiratorial. It made Adelaide wonder if Molly had been prying through Miss Berry's room and whether that had been Lady Dewsbury's intention.

"Yes, m'lady. Thank you."

To Adelaide's eyes, Molly's bobbed curtsey was unusually awkward. The poor girl must be exhausted.

Adelaide rose to her feet. "We'll leave you now, ma'am. Please accept my sincere condolences on your loss."

As they were leaving the room she heard Lady Dewsbury say, "I am grateful for your visit, Mrs Russell, but I regret I feel unfit to entertain a visitor."

Adelaide glanced at Molly and they both quickened their steps to escape before Mrs Russell emerged. They were silent. Ladies do not converse with their servants in the street and Adelaide had trained Molly to stay three decorous paces behind her.

It was a short walk along The Crescent. In fact the eighteen tall, white houses and the hotel formed only a half crescent, built in a sweeping curve. Adelaide had always thought this was a pity. There were larger mansions in Gosport but, in her opinion, these were the most elegant. Adelaide wondered if her aunt was correct when she claimed that Mr Cruickshank, the man responsible for The Crescent, had run out of money while his plans were incomplete. She thought it unlikely. In his prime, Mr Cruickshank had been a clever businessman who'd grown wealthy by his innovative schemes and he'd cared for The Crescent so deeply that he and his family still lived in one of its houses.

Twenty years before, he'd transformed the quiet area of Alverstoke, planting in its heart the fashionable resort of Angleseyville, named after a nobleman who was revered as a hero of the Battle of Waterloo. Opposite The Crescent stood a Reading Room, and Baths in which people could take health-giving plunges in water pumped from the nearby bay. The private garden was for the use of those Crescent residents who wished to pay the annual subscription for the privilege.

Today even those who'd paid their thirty shillings could not enter the garden. A glum looking police officer stood beside the gate and blocked the way of anybody who wished to go inside, although, at this moment, the only people standing in the street were Mr Corfield and the gardener who lived beneath the Reading Room. It was his job and to keep the garden in a pristine condition.

Adelaide paused on the pavement, torn between curiosity and the knowledge it was unladylike to show interest in such sordid matters.

"Lady Adelaide!" Mr Corfield hurried across the street and stood in front of her, hat in hand, bowing respectfully. "I have been hoping to speak with you. I am about to travel out of town and I have hired a carriage. Would you do me the honour of sitting in it for a few moments while we talk? The wind is too cruel for you to stand outside."

Adelaide allowed herself to be handed into the carriage although she knew her actions were being observed from drawing rooms all along the road. She wondered where Mr Corfield was bound. There was a note of demure mischief in her voice as she said, "Why did you not await me in the house? My aunt would have been delighted to entertain you." Aunt Susan would declare her nerves were in shreds but she'd be eager to hear the gossip surrounding Miss Berry's death.

Mr Corfield realised he was being teased and his pale face turned pink. He waited for Molly to clamber into the carriage and seat herself next to Adelaide and then he got in and sat down opposite them. "I was uncertain how much Mrs Tate had been told about the tragedy. I did not wish to distress her."

"Very considerate of you, sir." This time Adelaide smiled at Mr Corfield, inviting him to laugh with her. He smiled back, apparently forgetting what he'd wished to say.

"Please sir," said Molly, "Have you escorted Kemal safely back to his ship?"

"Yes indeed. We saw him safely aboard. Several of his shipmates and the officer who is his immediate superior all confirm that he was on board until past five o'clock this morning. The officer also spoke of a note Kemal had received, appointing an assignation."

Mr Corfield turned his pale, sharp gaze on Molly. "I do not think you mentioned that you had sent Kemal a note?"

"Did I not? I must have forgotten."

"I think the term 'assignation' is inappropriate, sir. I hope you do not intend to cast any slur upon my maid's character?" Adelaide moved in to rescue Molly.

"Not at all. I have the greatest respect for her character and her intelligence. Kemal's lieutenant called Kemal a fool for responding to your message." The humour was back in Mr Corfield's voice. "I fear he distrusts English women." He smiled wryly. "The lieutenant has no English but fortunately his French is fluent, a circumstance the police officer found suspicious."

"But surely there's nothing strange in that? The French have had a presence in the Ottoman Empire for much longer than we have," protested Adelaide.

"So I tried to tell him, but, I fear, with limited success. He resented not being able to ask questions without using me as his interpreter. Between our crass young police officer and the arrogant and fiery Turkish lieutenant, I was beginning to dread an international incident."

"I trust you averted it, sir?" said Adelaide.

"Narrowly." Mr Corfield directed his next words to Molly. "On the way back, I spoke with the men in charge of manning the gate in the fortifications. They confirmed that Kemal had passed that way early that morning and you were close behind him. How discreet of you, not to be seen in each other's company."

Molly flushed but she met his eyes squarely and said, "Girls in my position aren't allowed followers, sir. If anybody saw us and told Mrs Tate I'd lose my place."

"I understand your reticence." He turned back to Adelaide. "Apart from Molly, whom I know you trust, does your aunt keep a close watch on her servants?"

Adelaide found this impertinent but she preferred not to challenge him. "My aunt is a strict mistress."

"So none of the servants could get out at night? Even though you have no butler at this time? I presume your footman and hall boy sleep downstairs to guard the plate?"

"Yes, and Bradbury, my aunt's housekeeper, has charge of the keys. She has been in my family's service since she was a girl and would never allow impropriety."

His lips quirked slightly but he spoke gravely enough, "Very proper, ma'am."

Adelaide was weary of always feeling at a disadvantage when conversing with Mr Corfield. She said bluntly, "Forgive me, sir, but it seems you are taking great interest in this unfortunate death. May I enquire why you are so concerned?"

Mr Corfield looked surprised at her directness. "I have a certain diplomatic interest but I regret I cannot elaborate. You will have to take my word for it."

Adelaide thought bitterly that no lady could tell an English gentleman they wanted more proof than his word. Mr Corfield's involvement was no clearer than before, but now it was covered by a cloak of diplomatic secrecy.

She changed the subject. "Did the gardener have anything to tell you? Surely he should have heard the... trouble in the garden last night?"

"He says that he and his wife slept the whole night through and I'm inclined to believe him. He is angry at the desecration of his garden and even more outraged that the police officer will not let him inside the gate."

"I am sure that's true. My aunt has told me he is a most conscientious man." Adelaide hesitated, uncertain whether to broach the matter but then said, "Mr Corfield, I've just been with Lady Dewsbury and broken the sad news. She requested us to bring away suitable garments to clothe Miss Berry's body, but I don't know where she has been taken."

"There is a mortuary where a surgeon connected with the police will examine the body. If you wish I will take the garments there. As soon as possible I will visit Lady Dewsbury and offer her assistance in arranging the funeral and interment."

There was a gentleness and respect in his tone that pleased her. "Thank you, sir."

Mr Corfield opened the carriage door, climbed out and handed Adelaide down. When she reached the pavement he retained her hand in a gentle but firm clasp. "Lady Adelaide, please believe I am your servant to command."

Adelaide stood and watched Mr Corfield's carriage drive away. She felt shaken and slightly breathless, as if she'd missed a step and almost fallen.

"We'd better go inside, m'lady," said Molly. She cast a nervous glance towards the first floor of the house. "The mistress is at her drawing room window, watching us."

Chapter 14

As soon as she entered the drawing room Adelaide saw that her aunt was angry. She was standing beside the window, her lips clenched into a thin line and her dark eyes snapping with barely suppressed temper. Adelaide shut the door and moved slowly towards the centre of the room, endeavouring to appear unworried.

"You wished to see me, ma'am?" The footman had informed her of this the moment she entered the house.

"Indeed I wished to see you, Adelaide. What have you got to say for yourself?"

An unfair question, inviting confession of unsuspected sins. Adelaide had been interrogated too often by her father to fall into such a trap. "What would you wish me to say, ma'am?"

"I wish you to explain why you were flirting with that young man on my very doorstep! Don't bother to deny it, I saw you with my own eyes."

Adelaide was startled. It hadn't occurred to her that she'd been flirting with Mr Corfield. She had progressed from schoolroom to betrothal within three months, and her late husband had not been the sort of man to waste gentle attentions upon a creature he'd already purchased. But it was true she enjoyed Mr Corfield's company. The deference with which he treated her made her feel safe and restored to her some sense of her own worth.

"You wrong me, ma'am. I was not flirting with Mr Corfield. I have been with Lady Dewsbury, breaking the sad news of Miss Berry's demise. I was distressed. Mr Corfield wished to comfort me."

Aunt Susan sniffed. "Indeed? And why, if his intentions were so proper, did he not enter the house and ask to speak to you? His carriage has been standing outside my door for the last twenty minutes."

Adelaide offered the excuse Mr Corfield himself had used, "He did not wish to distress you, ma'am. He is aware of the delicate state of your nerves. He merely wished to ask if there was any way he could serve Lady Dewsbury in her hour of sorrow."

Aunt Susan sniffed again but took the bait Adelaide had dangled in front of her. "Hardly a great sorrow. It is not as if Lady Dewsbury has lost a member of her family. How did she take the news?"

"With great dignity, ma'am." Looking at her aunt's face, avid for gossip, Adelaide could not bear to tell her more. To speak of Lady Dewsbury's grief at the loss of her friend would seem like a betrayal.

Thwarted, Aunt Susan swung back into anger. "About that girl, Bowman. How dare she sneak away to consort with that young savage, much less bring him into my house? I trust you've dismissed her!"

Adelaide struggled to keep her voice steady, "No, ma'am, I have not."

"Then do so immediately! I won't have her in this house."

"Molly Bowman is my servant, ma'am, not yours." It took all of Adelaide's courage to say this but if she bowed to her aunt's decree she would lose not only Molly but all she'd salvaged of her independence and self-respect.

"Indeed? If you intend to defy me, you may pack your bags and return to your father's house. I trust you know what that will mean, Adelaide?"

Adelaide knew too well the consequences of her rebellion. Her father had said, if she displeased her aunt, he'd place her in seclusion under the supervision of the strictest chaperone he could hire. Even if she defied her aunt, her father would not let her keep Molly.

She suspected Aunt Susan would enjoy discomfiting her parents. She had always been jealous of her sister's great marriage, although Adelaide had often thought her aunt more fortunate than her mother. She remembered her Uncle Tate with affection. He'd been a wealthy widower, years older than her aunt and a kindly, generous man.

Adelaide tried one last, desperate gamble. "As you wish, ma'am. I will tell Molly she must go. If you will excuse me, I will write a note for Lady Dewsbury. I am sure she would be pleased to employ Molly as her companion. She is going to feel the loss of Miss Berry and she knows Molly's grandmother. They were friends years ago, during the war with France." As she spoke she moved towards the door.

"Wait!"

Adelaide turned and looked enquiringly at her aunt. "I won't have that wretched girl telling tales about my household to Lady Dewsbury."

"I understand your feelings, ma'am, but once she has left my service I will have no control over her."

There was a simmering silence. "Very well, she can stay. But she had better behave herself." The unspoken message was clear, 'And so had you.'

"Thank you, ma'am." Adelaide left swiftly, careful to allow no glimmer of triumph to show.

In the hall she encountered Frederick, the footman. He moved hastily back from the door and she wondered if he'd been eavesdropping. Recalling Mr Corfield's questions about her aunt's domestic staff, she looked at him with fresh interest, secure in the knowledge that he was too well-trained to meet her gaze. He was tall, footmen were paid extra for their height, but apart from that he was unimpressive: a gangly lad, with dark eyes and a swarthy complexion that accorded ill with his white curled wig. She noted that one side of the wig was straggly and knew she should warn him to have it dressed. The butler and footman proclaimed the smartness and affluence of a house and her aunt would have no truck with slovenliness.

Before she could speak she saw the drawing room door open. She abandoned reproof and sped upstairs to her room, where Molly was waiting for her anxiously.

"Is the mistress very angry, m'lady?"

"I'm afraid so." She saw that Molly looked stricken and she said reassuringly, "I have convinced my aunt to give you another chance. Sit down. I have something important to tell you. After you left us to go to Miss Berry's room, Lady Dewsbury told me more about her." Quietly she told Molly all that Lady Dewsbury had recounted to her about Miss Berry's Turkish liaison.

Molly centred on the part of this tale that concerned her most, "What about the baby? What happened to him?"

"She told Lady Dewsbury that he had been adopted."

"And you think Kemal's Miss Berry's son?" Molly choked out the words.

"It seems possible."

"But he didn't speak to her last week at Church."

"Perhaps he did not know her identity then. It's possible she sent for him to meet her at some point yesterday. It would be easy enough for her to acquire Lady Dewsbury's key to the garden and there are places they could be unobserved."

"And you think Kemal sneaked away from his ship in order to meet her and kill her?"

Adelaide felt sorry for Molly but she had to be honest. "He may have known nothing about his circumstances. It could have come as a terrible shock to him if she told him she was his mother. It is not inconceivable that he lashed out in rage. But, if Kemal is the culprit, I cannot think of any reason why he should return here today."

To her surprise Molly stood up and said, "Excuse me, m'lady." Without further explanation she lifted her skirt and, after a struggle, removed a small bundle of letters and held them out to Adelaide. "I found these, m'lady, in Miss Berry's room."

Adelaide knew she should feel shocked at her maid's descent into theft but instead she felt eager and curious. She took the bundle and untied the ribbon. "You fear that Kemal knew of the existence of these letters and returned to steal them?"

"I know it's possible, m'lady, but I don't think he did. It's Miss Berry who'd be shamed if these letters became common knowledge. I cannot see that it would make much difference to Kemal's chances in life. He may be Miss Berry's son but if he is, somebody is using their knowledge to make him a scapegoat."

"I think you may be right. Unfortunately we have no proof, just these letters that neither of us can read."

They both stared in silent frustration at the spiky writing.

"Kemal could read them," said Molly, "but we couldn't be certain he was telling us the truth."

"There's that officer Mr Corfield mentioned," said Lady Adelaide. "Surely it must be the same man that Kemal spoke of. He said, 'Hasan does not lie.'"

"But he doesn't speak English," objected Molly.

"He speaks French and so do I." Her eagerness faded. "But it's useless to speculate. We have no discreet way of sending a message to Kemal or his lieutenant."

"I can manage that, m'lady. If you'll allow me to go out for an hour or two. Tom... the lad I told you about... will do anything I ask."

Adelaide rose to her feet. "In that case I'm coming too. Get out my warmest winter clothes, Molly, "It will be better if we walk."

*

As they set off briskly towards the naval part of the town, Molly admired Lady Adelaide's resolution and good sense. If she'd sent for the mistress' carriage there would have been no way to prevent the coachman from telling the mistress where they'd been.

All the same, she was worried. Gently bred ladies weren't accustomed to walking for miles, especially in the bitter December cold. And, it was all very well for Lady Adelaide to be on foot here, in the quiet, tree-lined lanes of Angleseyville, but when they reached the busy, rougher part of town she could be subjected to lewd comments. Even in the early afternoon some sailors were roaring drunk. Molly felt grateful that although Lady Adelaide's clothes were of fine quality and elegant cut, they were sober in colour and style because of her widowed state.

"If you please, m'lady, you ought to let me summon a hansom cab," she said, as one of these useful vehicles approached.

"Very well."

Molly waved at the driver and he brought his horse to a halt.

"Where to, Missy?" She saw with relief that he looked sober and respectable and, although his cab was shabby it seemed reasonably clean and his horse looked strong and fit.

"Weevil Lane. You can put us down before we reach the Victualling Yard." There was no point in risking running into Pa. The less he heard about this business the better.

She helped her mistress into the vehicle and climbed in to sit beside her, glad of the privacy the two-seater cab provided. Once in motion, the driver, seated outside and at the back of the hansom cab, would not be able to hear what they said. In an open, four-wheel carriage the driver could listen to every word.

She saw Lady Adelaide looking at the worn seats and was about to apologise for the roughness of the vehicle when Lady Adelaide said, "Molly, why is the place you live in called Weevil?"

To Molly's annoyance, she felt herself blush. She was embarrassed to explain to Lady Adelaide about the lowly origins of her home. "Over twenty years ago, before the Victualling Yards were built, it was where most of the beer was brewed and some people say that all the grain that was stored here attracted a lot of weevils. But others say it was no such thing and the place was named after Mr Weovil who used to manage the brewery. Even so, it's not a posh reason for naming a place, not like Angleseyville."

"It's certainly a lot less pretentious," said Lady Adelaide. She giggled. "It seems Mr Weovil was aptly named for his profession. Don't look so uncomfortable, Molly. This is quite an adventure for me."

Chapter 15

The short journey was swiftly accomplished and Molly rapped on the roof to remind the driver to set them down before they reached the Royal Clarence Yard. As they walked along the rough, cobbled streets, she realised she'd grown accustomed to the quiet, gracious houses of the rich. From the first moment she'd arrived at The Crescent she had loved the peaceful roads with their clean, well-made pavements. The trees had all been in new leaf and everything smelled green and fresh and she'd heard birds singing.

Lady Adelaide asked, "What will you tell your father?"

"As little as possible, m'lady. I hope he'll still be at work in the Victualling Yard and we won't run into him."

"I went to see the outside of the Royal Clarence Yard," said Lady Adelaide. "It was the day when we first met... when my carriage lost its wheel. My aunt had asked me to order new caps and aprons for the female servants from Mr Upfield's drapery store and, when I had done so, I realised I was near the Victualling Yard and I was curious to see where the Naval stores were prepared. My father accompanied the Queen's party when she visited it, when she was just a girl. He told me it was an impressive building. Indeed, from the outside, I thought it looked magnificent and wished I could have explored it."

That answered one question that Molly had never dared to ask. She had often wondered what Lady Adelaide had been doing driving through the far from genteel district of Weevil.

The Royal Clarence Yard had been named after King William IV when he was still Duke of Clarence. It had been constructed to feed the Navy around the time that Molly had been born. When she was younger, Pa had asked permission for her to visit it, proud to show her the place where he worked. It had none of the elegance of The Crescent, but when she remembered the powerful, well-proportioned buildings, she had to admit it had its own magnificence. Pa had shown her over the Granary, an immense building, four storeys high and raised from the quayside by powerful iron pillars.

"Pa took me into the Victualling Yard, m'lady. He wouldn't let me visit the Slaughterhouse but, as well as the Cooper's building, I saw the Granary and the Bakehouse. I was given one of the biscuits baked in Mr Grant's wonderful machine. Do you know they can bake ten thousand biscuits in an hour in that machine?"

"I believe the Queen, when she was Princess Victoria, sampled one. Tell me, what are they like?"

Molly pulled a face. "Hard. I don't think sailors can afford to be too fussy about what they eat."

Lady Adelaide laughed. "For all your complaints, I think you have had an interesting life."

That astonished Molly. "But I've never been anywhere, m'lady, hardly out of Gosport, apart from staying on my great-aunt's farm. I've never even been on a train."

She had been twelve years old when the railway came to Gosport and often she had waited near the station just to see the trains pull in. Most people said they were dirty, noisy things but Molly thought they were splendid. Their power, strength and speed were magnificent, and the hissing clouds of steam, the smell of smoke and hot oil and the black smuts that made most travellers mutter complaints, to her seemed wonderful. She thought they were like some great monsters, not from mythology but of the new industrial age. She loved the fact that they travelled to the distant corners of Britain and reached ports that imported goods from the whole Empire. In the last few years, Gosport's shops had held more exciting wares than ever before. Molly's purse was not plump enough to buy much but she loved to stare in the shop windows and admire.

"We'll have to see what we can do about that. But Molly, there's one thing I don't understand. You speak of your father working at the Royal Clarence Yard but surely he has his own cooperage yard?"

"Yes, m'lady. He's got an old man there who keeps an eye on things and oversees any apprentices Pa doesn't need with him at the Victualling Yard. If he can, Pa spends a day at his own yard every week and makes barrels to supply the local people, but most of the time he works for the navy in the Victualling yard. The navy always wants barrels, nearly every scrap of food and drink they take on board ship is stored in them."

"Would it not be more profitable for him to put all his resources into working for the navy?" asked Lady Adelaide.

"It might be, m'lady, but his father and grandfather had the cooperage yard before him and he wouldn't want to let it go. Anyway, Pa says, with the navy you never know where you are. One day some admiral will decide he wants things different and they'll up stakes and move all the work elsewhere."

She paused a moment beside a hot pie stall. "If you don't mind waiting a moment, m'lady, I'll buy a pie for Tom." If she hadn't been in company with Lady Adelaide she'd have bought a pie for herself as well.

"They smell good," said Lady Adelaide.

"They are, m'lady. Mrs Partridge makes tasty pies, with decent meat in them."

"I'm hungry, aren't you, Molly?" Lady Adelaide handed her a florin. "Is that enough to purchase three pies?"

"More than enough, m'lady." Molly thought Lady Adelaide had changed. It was as if she'd broken free and was intent on enjoying every morsel of her stolen freedom.

As she led Lady Adelaide into Pa's cooperage yard, she noted with relief that fortune had favoured her. Pa must have taken the older apprentices with him, because there was only Tom, sweeping up the yard, his face was pinched and his fingers blue with cold.

He turned and saw them and his face lit up in a welcoming grin. "Mistress!"

"Where's Walter?" The old overseer had known her all her life, which meant he'd think he had a right to interfere if he didn't like her plans.

"At home in his bed. His chest's real bad again. And Master's over to the Victualling Yard."

"So it's just you here? There's no-one else around?"

Tom nodded. "Master said I couldn't do much damage tidying up the yard. There's not much to do here but he didn't want me with him. I cast up me accounts again after breakfast. He told me to sit in the hut when I finished. There's a fire going in there."

Molly thought, not for the first time, that for all his gruff ways, her father was a good master to his apprentices, treating them with a kindness that few other masters showed. She saw that Lady Adelaide looked puzzled and prayed she didn't ask for a translation of Tom's words.

Molly led her mistress and Tom into the workman's hut and set a stool for Lady Adelaide.

"Tom, I've got an errand for you. Are you feeling better? Well enough to run?"

"I'm all right now, Mistress. What is it you want me to do?"

"I want you to get a message to one of the Turkish sailors on the training ship, the Mirat-y Zafer. His name is Kemal. Can you manage to speak to him?"

"I'll try, Mistress, but it may take a while."

"Kemal is a common Turkish name," said Lady Adelaide. "Make sure you contact the Christian sailor who attended St Mark's Church."

"Yes Madam." Tom's eyes were on the meat pies that Molly had placed on the hearth to keep warm. "Mistress, I'm fair gutfoundered. I ain't had a bite all day, not since..."

"That's enough, Tom." Molly interrupted before Tom could say anything else to offend Lady Adelaide's genteel ears. "Make sure you eat slowly."

She handed Tom a pie then turned to Lady Adelaide. "Would you care to come into the house, m'lady?"

"I'm quite comfortable here, Molly." Lady Adelaide watched as Tom bit into his pie and gravy squirted down his chin. She smiled as he licked it off. "But plates and cutlery would be a good idea."

Molly sped into the house and gathered up the things they required. Again luck was with her, the girl who came in to help Grandmama with the rough work had gone for the day.

Molly returned to the shed and discovered her mistress chatting pleasantly to Tom.

Lady Adelaide ate her pie daintily, her plate supported on a workbench. Molly poured three glasses of milk from the jug she had taken from the pantry. She'd have preferred ale but that wasn't fitting to offer to Lady Adelaide. Her duties as a hostess done, she sat down and ate her own meal.

"Molly, I've been thinking," said Lady Adelaide. "It might be an excellent idea for us to go across to Portsmouth on the Floating Bridge."

Molly felt puzzled. She loved the magnificent ferry that hauled itself across the harbour on vast chains but why should Lady Adelaide think that crossing on it would be a good idea?

"It is a public conveyance and it would not be our fault if some foreign naval officers were crossing at the same time," explained Lady Adelaide. "I left a message for my aunt that I was going shopping and there is a milliner's shop in Broad Street that I have been intending to visit for some time."

Molly thought Mrs Tate would probably enquire why Lady Adelaide had gone across as a foot passenger, rather than taking the carriage across on the Floating Bridge but it was not her place to argue, especially when she had no better plan. Lady Adelaide was right, on the Floating Bridge, no-one could blame them for the company they kept, one could not choose one's fellow passengers.

She gave a sharp look at Tom, trying to assess whether he had his wits about him and could run. The Press Gangs were no longer the danger they'd been when Grandmama was young, but taking men for naval service was still part of the law. Pa had lost an apprentice to them, about three years ago. Craftsmen and their apprentices had special passes that gave them exemption from being pressed and Pa had protested to the authorities but he hadn't got Billy back. Like some great sea monster, the naval fleet had gobbled him up. Perhaps one day he'd return, a hardened sailor with a store of tales, but it was more likely he was dead.

Tom met her gaze and said, "I'm ready to take your message, Mistress."

Chapter 16

Molly thought that Tom and Kemal were only two people in the world that called her 'mistress' and she wanted to protect them both. And yet she was endangering them both. It would be no light task for Tom to contact a foreign sailor on his ship, and, by asking for help, she might draw Kemal further into this tangled web.

She took out the half-sheet of paper she had written the message on and re-read it to check its meaning was clear. '*Kemal. Meet me at the ferry known as the Floating Bridge as soon as possible this afternoon. Set the time with my messenger. May the angel that watches over strangers protect you. M.*'

She twisted the paper into a tight spill and handed it to Tom. "You'll need to wait for an answer. Listen very carefully to what he says and repeat it back to me, word for word. Can you do that?"

"I'll do my best, Mistress."

"Don't let anyone else see the note and if you can't get back here before four o'clock we'll meet you where the Floating Bridge docks at four." Tom didn't possess a timepiece but down on the dockside there was always someone to ask.

"I'll be there, mistress."

"And Tom, promise me you'll take care."

"I promise." He sidled out of the door and was gone.

Lady Adelaide looked anxious. "Will he be safe?"

"I hope so, m'lady."

"How will he get the message to Kemal?"

"I don't know, but if anyone can do it Tom can."

"Tell me about him," said Lady Adelaide.

"He's an orphan, brought up in the workhouse. When he was ten, he was given to an innkeeper down on the docks. They called him an apprentice but it was more like slavery. They treated him terribly." Molly knew this was not the sort of thing you told a lady, but if the people with power were left in ignorance how could anything change? "He ran away but the parish constable picked him up. They beat him and sent him back to the workhouse. Pa was looking for a new apprentice and Grandmama and I had gone with him. Grandmama said it was time I understood about the evil people inflicted on each other in the name of Charity. Tom wasn't the boy Pa would have chosen but I picked him and Grandmama agreed."

Molly remembered the dirty, battered boy she had picked out that day. His face had been cunning but his eyes were full of fear. She could no more have ignored him than she could have walked past a puppy that had been kicked into the gutter to die.

"That was kind, Molly," said Lady Adelaide.

Molly shook her head. "It's not as simple as that. I know Tom would do anything for me and that's why I shouldn't ask him to take risks. I'll clear up these things, m'lady, then we'd best be on our way."

She washed and dried the dishes and put them away, careful to leave no sign that she'd been there. As she led Lady Adelaide out of the yard her spirits plummeted. A laden farm cart had stopped outside her father's house and the burly driver got down to help his female passenger to alight.

Molly's first instinct was to slip away and run, but she couldn't ask Lady Adelaide to do anything so undignified. The woman saw Molly and her companion. For a moment her surprise was obvious, then she gave a curtsey that was beautifully graded, low enough to show respect for a member of the aristocracy, dignified enough to reveal awareness of her own worth. "Good afternoon, Lady Adelaide. Hello Molly."

"Grandmama," said Molly nervously. "I didn't expect you to be home so soon."

*

Adelaide felt embarrassed. She had not been in Mrs Dorrington's house since the day her carriage had lost its wheel and Molly's grandmother had invited her inside. It was ill bred of her to come here uninvited in such a way.

"My sister's husband had to send a man into Gosport with a cartload of carrots and turnips to provision the Star Inn," said Mrs Dorrington. "I thought it wise to travel home with him in case the weather worsened. Don't just stand there, Molly, take the baskets inside. My dear sister has been most generous."

"Yes Grandmama." Obediently Molly bent to pick up two of the baskets of fruit and vegetables the farm labourer was unloading from his cart.

Adelaide stepped forward and picked up a wicker basket full of rosy apples.

"No, m'lady," protested Molly, "it's not seemly."

"I'd like to help." Adelaide thought how sweet the apples smelled.

Mrs Dorrington gave her an assessing look, then her stern face relaxed into a smile. "Thank you, Lady Adelaide." She turned to the farm labourer. "Thank you Jed. Do you want to wait while we empty the baskets or call back for them?"

"I won't wait, Missus. The mistress said she's got plenty of baskets. Next time you visit will do. She wanted me back in case the weather turns."

"You'd better go then. Thank you for bringing me home." She reached up and gave him two silver sixpences. "Give those to your children."

The man looked covetously at the coins but said, "There's no need for that, Missus. It's always a pleasure to help you."

She smiled at him. "Take it as a Christmas gift for your two boys."

"Thank you Missus." He pocketed the money, tugged his forelock and drove away.

Mrs Dorrington got out her key and opened the front door, then she picked up her valise and briskly entered. "Won't you come in, Lady Adelaide?"

"Thank you."

In the narrow hallway Mrs Dorrington set down her valise and turned to take the basket from Adelaide. "If you'd like to go into the parlour, Molly will kindle the fire. I'll bring refreshments as soon as I've brought the kettle to boil. Molly, is the range still alight?"

"Yes Grandmama, but damped down, the way Pa left it this morning."

"Please, I'd rather go to the kitchen with you." Adelaide could not endure the thought of sitting alone in the chilly formal room.

Mrs Dorrington's finely arched eyebrows lifted. "As you wish, Lady Adelaide."

Adelaide wished Mrs Dorrington would not mention her name and rank whenever she spoke to her. She wondered if it was deliberate; a reminder of her position and the folly of stepping out of it. Then Mrs Dorrington smiled at her. It was a warm smile, with a sparkle of mischief that reminded Adelaide of Molly.

"Please sit down." She ushered Adelaide to a chair beside the scrubbed, pine table. "Molly, put the kettle on for tea."

As she spoke she looked appraisingly around her small domain. Adelaide thought she should be well satisfied. Everything looked spotlessly clean and on the softwood dresser, pale from years of scrubbing, copper jelly moulds gleamed and the white dinner plates were neatly stacked.

"I was here yesterday, Grandmama. I tidied up and made sure Sally had scrubbed the kitchen floor," said Molly, her tone still uncharacteristically meek.

Mrs Dorrington sat down on the opposite side of the table to Adelaide. "Leave emptying the baskets until later, Molly. Now tell me exactly what's going on."

Adelaide listened in silence as Molly told the story yet again. She sounded subdued but she told her grandmother everything that she had told Adelaide.

Mrs Dorrington showed remarkably little emotion as the story unfolded. The only time she frowned was when she discovered that she had sent Tom to try to contact Kemal. "I fear that could prove dangerous."

Molly hung her head. "I know, Grandmama, but I could think of no other way. I am worried that I might have endangered Tom and perhaps Kemal as well."

Mrs Dorrington leaned forward and laid a hand on top of Molly's twisting fingers. "There's a possibility you must consider."

"What?"

Adelaide watched as Molly's blue eyes stared at her grandmother in innocent enquiry that slowly turned to understanding and sparkling indignation. She jerked her hands away. "No! Kemal didn't kill Miss Berry."

Mrs Dorrington's tone remained gravely reasonable. "I pray you are right."

"I am right. Kemal is a good man!"

"But, Molly, you know very little about Kemal."

Adelaide saw Molly consider this, then raise her chin defiantly. "You're right, Grandmama. I don't know much about him. It's possible he could do something rash. But one thing I'm sure of, if Kemal did such a dreadful thing, he wouldn't plot and plan to involve me."

Adelaide realised, with relief, that Molly was thinking with her head not just her heart.

As her mind cleared she thought of another, equally powerful argument. "And, if Kemal is guilty, who was it that hit him on the head?" she demanded. "And why should anyone do so if he was part of some dark plot?"

"How severe was this head wound?" asked Mrs Dorrington.

"It was a cruel blow," said Adelaide.

Molly gave her a look that glowed with gratitude but before she could speak they heard a soft scratching on the kitchen door. Molly ran to open it and Tom stood there, looking none the worse for his adventure. "I delivered your message, mistress. The sailor says he'll meet you at the Floating Bridge at four."

"Were those his exact words?" Tom had never met Kemal and she had to be sure he hadn't spoken with an impostor.

"No, he said this really silly thing." Tom looked scornful.

"Tell me." Then, as he still looked unwilling, she leaned forward and hissed in his ear, "It's a secret code."

"Oh I see!" Tom brightened immediately. "He said the stranger thanked the angel for guardin' him." Looking past Molly he became aware of Mrs Dorrington. "Oh lawks!"

"Lord have mercy indeed, Tom," she agreed dryly. "Come in, boy, and warm yourself by the range."

"I'm sorry, mistress," he said.

"You have no reason to apologise, Tom. You merely did what Mistress Molly required of you. Now I have another errand for you."

"Yes mistress, but the master will be angry if he comes home and finds I'm out the yard."

"The master will not be angry because I'll tell him I told you to take a message for me. You need not mention visiting the Turkish ship."

"Grandmama, where do you want Tom to go?" demanded Molly.

Adelaide was startled by her forthright question but Mrs Dorrington seemed unoffended. "I am sending a note to my old friend, Lady Dewsbury, requesting permission to pay a call on her. And then, I think, we should be on our way."

"Our way, Grandmama?"

Mrs Dorrington smiled. "Of course, my girl. Did you really think I would allow you to go off on this wild venture alone?"

By the time they reached the landing quay for the Floating Bridge the steel grey sky was turning darker but there was enough light to see that the great vessel had already docked and the passengers from Portsmouth had disembarked. Now the crew were overseeing the loading of the two large decks that flanked the engine and the passenger accommodation. Molly noted they were taking care with the disposition of carriages and carts, making sure the vessel was well balanced for the journey across the rough water of the harbour.

On the shore the foot passengers were waiting their turn to go aboard.

Grandmama said quietly, "Can you see him, Molly?"

"Not yet. I'm sure he'll come if he can." She struggled to keep her voice confident.

"It's hard to see at this distance. Go nearer. I'll wait here until you have warned him of my presence. I don't wish to alarm the boy."

Keeping close together, they walked towards the queuing passengers. Adelaide was a head taller than Molly and it was she who first spotted Kemal and his companion. She gripped Molly's arm and pointed. The two young men were standing slightly aloof from the crowd. They were both tall, dark-haired and wrapped in heavy boat cloaks.

Kemal saw Molly and hurried towards her. He looked pale and haggard and someone had fastened a grubby bandage around his forehead. "Mistress Molly, is all well with you?" He grasped her hands and squeezed them.

"Yes. Are you all right, Kemal?"

"It is well, at the moment."

Adelaide stared at Kemal's companion. Molly had to admit he was a remarkably handsome man; older than Kemal and taller, his features more strongly marked, his expression formidable. As he approached them he continued to frown, then he met Adelaide's eyes. Abruptly he smiled. It transformed his face. "Your servant, Madame," he said.

Chapter 17

Molly saw Lady Adelaide blush. The bright colour made her look younger and even lovelier, as did the sweet half-smile that curved her lips. A swift glance at the lieutenant showed Molly that he too was looking moonstruck. The hunger in his gaze made her uneasy.

Kemal released Molly's hands.

She said quietly, "They didn't harm you, Kemal?"

"No. The gentleman drove me to my ship and he made the policeman ask questions. Hasan and others in my crew bore witness for me."

"I'm glad you're safe." Even as she spoke, she knew, despite Kemal's calm manner, he was deeply afraid. "But you don't feel safe, do you?"

He shook his head. "I do not think I will be truly safe unless they find who harmed that poor lady."

And, if the investigation were left to the likes of Jeremy Bray, the truth would never be discovered. In two months' time, if Kemal were still under suspicion, would they let him sail home with the rest of his crew? What would happen if they made him stay here? He'd make an easy scapegoat once his comrades had gone.

"My Grandmama is here. She wanted to meet you."

Kemal looked surprised, then he smiled. "She has come to see that you are safe? I am glad. It is most gracious of her to permit you to meet me in this way."

Grandmama was walking slowly towards them but Molly was sure her keen ears had caught his words. She was glad he'd said something so appropriate. She wanted Grandmama to like Kemal.

"Madam." Kemal greeted her with a bow. "I have to thank you for your granddaughter's great kindness. Without her I would be dead."

Molly felt her cheeks burn. It wasn't the sort of thing an English man would say. She watched, in acute embarrassment, as her grandmother's cool grey eyes looked Kemal over, assessing him from head to toe. She smiled. "That would have been a great pity," she said. And, to Molly's satisfaction, she saw Kemal blush as well.

Lady Adelaide and the lieutenant were talking to each other in a language Molly guessed must be French. Their voices sounded soft and intimate. Lady Adelaide turned away from the lieutenant, the smile still lingering on her lips. "The lieutenant speaks little English but his French is excellent."

Grandmama nodded. "It is many years since I had cause to speak any foreign tongue but I am sure it will swiftly return to me."

She turned to the lieutenant and said something in French and, the next moment, to Molly's dismay, they were all jabbering away and she couldn't understand a word.

At last Lady Adelaide turned to her and said, "As we discussed earlier, we've decided to go over to Portsmouth on the Floating Bridge."

"Yes, m'lady." The more Molly thought about it the more she prayed that none of Lady Adelaide's acquaintances saw them and reported back to Mrs Tate. For that matter, she hoped none of Pa's drinking cronies were travelling at this time. She hated to think of Pa's reaction if her name was bandied about in the alehouse when he went in for his customary heavy wet. She shrugged the thought aside. Talking paid no toll and they had to get a translation of these letters as soon as possible.

"Don't look so worried, Molly," murmured Grandmama in her ear. She smiled mischievously.

"Pretend you're gentry and carry it off with a high hand."

Molly drew her grandmother to one side. "Are you crossing with us, Grandmama?"

"Not unless you wish me to, my dear. I would prefer to get home before your father returns and questions Tom too closely."

That must mean Grandmama considered her safe in her present company. "Then you understand why I had to help Kemal?"

"Of course I do." The mischievous look deepened. "With looks and a smile like that you'd be a very strange young woman if you had not succumbed."

"Grandmama! It's not like that!"

"If you say so, my dear. But if I'd been forty years younger, I'd be tempted to throw my cap over the windmill for him too."

"It's not because he's handsome," protested Molly. "He's not as good looking as the lieutenant, and I don't even like him."

"But that's different. The lieutenant wasn't smiling for you."

Molly felt mortified. Did her grandmother really think her such a shallow, frivolous creature? "Please, if you're teasing me I wish you wouldn't. You make me feel ashamed."

Immediately, her grandmother was penitent. "I'm sorry, Molly, I didn't mean to distress you. It's such a novel experience to see my sensible girl so swept away. But I must tell you, from the little I've seen of him, as well as being handsome and charming, your Kemal seems to me to be a good young man."

"Thank you, Grandmama." Molly felt as if a great weight had lifted from her. "What do you think of the lieutenant?"

"Ah, that's a different matter." She looked across to where the lieutenant, Lady Adelaide and Kemal were standing. Kemal stood aloof and watchful, but, despite the dangers of being observed, his lieutenant was talking animatedly to Lady Adelaide. "A young man of great arrogance and overwhelming passions," said Grandmama.

"My lady looks so happy."

"Yes, my dear. We must pray that it lasts." She bent and kissed Molly's cheek. "You'd better hurry. The foot passengers are embarking."

Even after such a dreadful day, Molly felt a thrill of pleasure as she approached the ticket office.

"Kemal, have you got money to pay your fare?" She felt shy but she had to be practical and Lady Adelaide had given her a generous sum to cover their expenses.

He smiled at her. "Yes. Do not be concerned Molly, we have been ashore in Gosport many times. A lot of people have been welcoming."

Molly said nothing. Despite Pa's efforts to shelter her, she'd heard rumours of the sort of welcome the residents of a seaport town offered sailors with plump purses, but a good woman didn't speak of such things.

Tickets bought they walked carefully along the slippery iron slope that led to the deck. Lady Adelaide said, "The lieutenant and I will go into the cabin and you two can stay out here. Bring me the letters when you have finished consulting Kemal."

Without waiting for a reply, she moved towards the more expensive cabin accommodation. Molly stared after her in dismay. They had bought four tickets for the cabin and she could hardly believe her gentle, well-bred mistress had ordered her and Kemal to travel in the bitter cold of the deck so she could continue her flirtation with a man she had only just met.

The ferry was not crowded. The Victualling Yard had not yet turned out and, since Portsmouth had gained their own railway, there were fewer consignments of goods travelling by train to Gosport and across on the Floating Bridge to stock Portsmouth's shops. Few people chose to travel across the harbour for pleasure in December at dusk, so Molly's wish that they would not meet any of Lady Adelaide's acquaintances seemed likely to come true. She found a secluded, sheltered corner and sat down. She felt cold and tired. The Floating Bridge would never seem quite so much fun again. Or maybe it would if she could see it through Kemal's eyes. She loved the lively interest with which he prowled the deck, clearly considering how the mechanics of the ferry worked, as, with a creak and clanking of the giant chains and the throb of the two great steam engines, they chugged away from the shore. And yet when they were underway and he came to join her, he sat down with a weary sigh and his smile could not conceal his exhaustion. She thought, if this day had been hard for her, it must have been monstrous for him.

"Could you translate these, please Kemal? It is Turkish, isn't it?" She opened her reticule and passed him the top letter, careful not to allow it to get damp.

He nodded and, squinting in the flickering light of the boat deck, he started to read, "My beloved and adored Nasimah, your news has filled me with great joy..." He broke off. "Mistress Molly, we should not be reading this. It is a private letter of love."

"I know. I don't like it either, but we must know what's in these letters. They belonged to Miss Berry. Somewhere in them could be the reason she was killed."

"But where did you get them?"

She had hoped Kemal would not ask that. It sounded so dishonourable to admit she'd stolen them from the dead lady's room. With eyes cast down she told him what she had done.

To her relief Kemal took her confession calmly. "It is not nice to take the property of the dead, but it would be a greater wickedness to leave the lady unavenged."

Unfortunately, as he translated the contents of the letters, it became clear they were unlikely to be of help. They were love letters to a woman called Nasimah from a man who signed himself Habib. There was not even any proof that Nasimah was Miss Berry, apart from the veiled references to the woman's 'news' and a promise to stand by her. Molly soon realised that if there was a clue concealed within them it remained well hidden.

Chapter 18

"Does it help you to know who killed the poor lady?" asked Kemal, as he returned the letters to her.

"I'm afraid not. Wait here a moment." Molly stood up and, moving cautiously on the slippery deck, went to the passenger cabin. Lady Adelaide was deep in conversation with the lieutenant and Molly had to go right inside to hand her the letters. It was much warmer in the cabin and as Molly returned to Kemal the chill struck her anew and she started to shiver.

"You are cold." Kemal leapt up and started to remove his coat.

"No. You'll take a chill." She had her good, woollen cloak, even if it wasn't as thick and waterproof as Kemal's coat.

"That is of no importance. I am a sailor. I am used to hardship. You are a lady." A thin trail of blood was seeping from under his bandage and trickling down his face. He wiped it away with his fingers.

"That bandage is too thin and it's dirty. Sit down." She undid the bandage and placed her own lace-trimmed linen handkerchief as a pad before retying it. "That's the best I can do but I wish I had clean water and some of Grandmama's herbs to wash the cut."

"It is good. Thank you. Please do not worry about washing it. I am..."

"I know, you're a sailor. That means you like being cold and damp and having your wounds dressed with filthy cloths."

To her surprise he understood her gentle sarcasm and grinned. "No, I do not like it but it is a life where a man has to become accustomed to many things. Now, may I lend you my coat?" He already had it undone.

"No, but if we sit close together we can share it."

Snuggled against Kemal she soon felt warmer, but it was a strange sensation. In all her life she'd never been so close to any man, except for sitting on Pa's lap when she was a little girl. Kemal's clothes smelled slightly musty, with a trace of exotic spices. He shifted a little and his face brushed against her ear. It was rough with the day's growth of beard. It brought it home to her that he was not like Tom, a boy in need of her protection. He was a man; a voyager and a fighter, who had seen battle and death.

The Floating Bridge was making slow progress and creaking and groaning more than usual. They were more than halfway over the harbour. In front of them the lights of Portsmouth twinkled and, looking back, the lights of Gosport glowed. To their right, she caught a flicker that she thought might come from the lighthouse on the Isle of Wight, or perhaps from a large vessel heading out to sea. A ferryboat, also bound for Portsmouth, overtook them, cutting across their bows. It looked very small and frail, tossed by the rough, black water. On her way back from the cabin Molly had heard the crew complaining about the bitter weather. She prayed they didn't shut down the Bridge after this trip. Some of the men who owned the small ferryboats might venture out when the weather was dangerous if they were offered enough silver but they wouldn't be decent, careful men and the risk would be too great. Even if Lady Adelaide could hire a carriage in Portsmouth, the journey by land was over ten miles and many of the roads were poor. She shuddered at the thought of being marooned on the wrong side of the harbour. She was sure Lady Adelaide had not considered this.

"You are cold still?" said Kemal.

"No. I'm worried we might get stuck in Portsmouth because of the bad weather. There'll be a lot of trouble if Lady Adelaide isn't back by dinnertime."

"That will not happen." She squirmed round a little to look into his face. He looked confident and amused. "The sailors they like to grumble but the weather is not so very bad." He stared across the harbour at the great ships, scarcely visible against the black sea and darkening sky. "It is a fine navy."

"Have you been across to Portsmouth to do your training?"

"We will go there to train in ordnance, but we will be rowed over in a naval boat. I may not get the opportunity to travel on this ferry again."

That made Molly sad. There were so many things she wanted to show Kemal and share with him and so much she wanted to ask about his native land. But none of that was as important as clearing him of murder.

"Kemal, do you remember your mother and father?"

"My mother no. She died on the day that I was born. She was not spoken of by my patron. Of my father I have some memories but they are clouded. I was young when he died and it is possible that what I remember is not true."

"What was your mother's name?"

"Elif."

Molly was silent. Elif bore a worrying likeness to the English Ellen.

After a moment Kemal continued, "It is sad to know so little of my mother."

That tugged at Molly's heart. She had many good memories as well as sad. She could remember her pretty, dark-haired mother, dancing around the room and laughing joyously. That was before she grew heavy with child, the baby that would have been Molly's little brother had he been born alive. Mama had only lived for a few hours after her infant son.

The Floating Bridge was docking. Hastily she pushed her dark thoughts away and sought for more information, "Was the man who adopted you a relative?"

"No. He was an English soldier but, for many years, he did not fight for your country. He was what you call a soldier of fortune. We of his household call him the Captain. He had gained much wealth in prize money. He and my father were comrades. He told me my father was the bravest soldier he had ever known."

"That's good to know," said Molly softly.

"When my father died the Captain took me in. He said my father had been his friend. He gave me a good education and managed to arrange for me to enter our navy. That was not easy, dhimmi are not usually allowed to serve our Empire in such a way, but I have always loved ships and travel. I think the Captain hoped I would achieve greatness. He was pleased when my knowledge of your language meant that I was selected for this mission. It is not easy to gain promotion when one is not of the faith of the country one serves." His voice trembled slightly. "I pray, if I cannot return to my country, my comrades do not tell the Captain what has befallen me. I would be saddened to know he had heard bad things of me."

Molly took his cold hand and squeezed it comfortingly. "I know you're innocent and we'll prove it." She prayed this promise would come true.

"Thank you." He raised her hand to his lips and kissed it.

Molly stared at him, struggling to order her tumbled thoughts. It was only a kiss on the hand, but it had stirred something in her that she'd never felt before. The apprentices in Pa's yard had always been friendly to her but they knew their place and she'd never been one to encourage men's attentions. She'd always known she wanted to do more than get married and keep house and breed children.

She searched for something casual to say but her mind stayed blank. In the end it was Kemal who spoke, "Why did you show me those letters?"

"I needed you to translate them."

"You showed me these letters and then you asked about my mother. What is her history, this Mademoiselle Berry? What was her connection with my country?"

"She travelled there when she was a young woman."

"And what befell her?" There was no escaping his penetrating gaze.

"There was... a scandal."

In the silence that followed she felt as if something precious and fragile was balanced between them and she feared it might fall and smash.

"When was this scandal?"

"I don't know exactly. Many years ago."

He spoke very quietly, "You think Mademoiselle Berry was my mother, do you not?" His voice sharpened, "Do you also believe I murdered her?"

Chapter 19

"No!" Molly gripped his hand. "Kemal, I promise you I never thought that. I don't know who is doing this to you and none of it makes sense, but I trust you."

"Thank you." She could feel his fingers trembling but his voice was controlled as he continued, "There is another thing that is strange about the letters."

"What's that?" She spoke urgently, the Floating Bridge had reached Portsmouth and they had little time left to talk.

"Mademoiselle Berry was a Christian, was she not?"

"Of course she was... at least I think so... she was in Church with Lady Dewsbury every Sunday," Molly racked her memory, "and she took Holy Communion."

"But if she was the woman called Nasimah it makes no sense. It is a Muslim name. It means a gentle breeze."

"And Habib?"

"That too is Muslim. It means beloved. Of course they may be names bestowed upon each other as a secret symbol of their love."

"But you told me your parents were both Christians. Surely they wouldn't have taken Muslim names as love symbols?" She blushed as she said the last two words.

She saw Lady Adelaide approaching, closely followed by the lieutenant. Disentangling herself from Kemal's coat, she stood up.

Lady Adelaide seemed to be in excellent spirits. She smiled at the Turkish officers. "Thank you for your escort, gentlemen. We will not detain you longer. Come Molly. I wish to visit that milliner's shop my aunt recommended."

Molly ventured a protest, "We must take care not to miss the ferry back, m'lady."

"Don't fuss, Molly, there will be many ferries returning before I need to be home."

"Only if the weather permits, m'lady."

"Nonsense, it's not so very cold." She set off at a brisk pace.

As Molly followed behind her mistress, she thought that if Lady Adelaide considered it not so very cold she ought to try travelling on the deck.

*

Adelaide knew that Molly was not happy. She told herself it was no part of her maid's duties to criticise her behaviour but, in her heart, she knew Molly had reason to be upset. They had walked some distance and were clear of the public houses that lined the ferry docking place. Adelaide signalled to Molly to walk alongside her and offered an olive branch. "I hope you were not too cold on the deck, Molly?"

"No m'lady." Molly's voice was stiff. "It's not my place to feel cold, m'lady."

Adelaide resisted the impulse to box her ears.

"I thought it better to take Hasan and Kemal to separate places to translate the letters. In that way it seemed more likely we would know if either gentleman was not telling the truth."

"Oh I see. I didn't think of that. Kemal said they were love letters, m'lady. They spoke of the woman's news and that the man would stand by her."

"That's what Hasan said also. I wish we could know if 'Nasimah' was indeed Miss Berry. I should have asked Lady Dewsbury whether she could read Turkish."

"If she couldn't there'd be no point in keeping those letters," said Molly. "But there's one thing that's strange. Kemal said the names Nasimah and Habib were Muslim names, but Miss Berry was a Christian."

"Perhaps, if Habib was of the Muslim faith, Nasimah was a... love name," suggested Adelaide. Less than an hour ago Hasan had declared, 'I shall give you a name of my country. I shall call you Durrah, for you are pale like a pearl.' "Ah, here we are." They had reached Broad Street and discovered the milliner's shop.

Before they entered, Adelaide removed the letters from her muff and passed them to Molly. "Tuck them away safely until we decide what's best to do with them." She pushed the door open, hesitated, then added softly, "I did not mean to exclude you, Molly."

She said no more, for the milliner was surging towards them, uttering words of welcome and beaming delight at the advent of a customer on a December afternoon.

*

The next few minutes were devoted to frivolity as Lady Adelaide tried on several hats. "It's time I came fully out of mourning," she said to Molly, "But I must spend wisely."

Molly said nothing. She knew Lady Adelaide received an allowance from her father but she wondered if it was enough to meet the cost of these fashionable bonnets. They were more expensive than she had ever dreamed of and this wasn't even a fine London milliner. She wondered whether her mistress' decision to brighten her wardrobe had anything to do with Hasan and feared it did.

Lady Adelaide purchased a bonnet in dark blue velvet, trimmed with a sky blue ribbon that matched her eyes. It was very beautiful and very expensive and, as they walked back towards the ferry, Molly carried the bulky hatbox carefully.

Before they reached The Floating Bridge, Lady Adelaide made her way into a confectioner's shop and purchased a selection of sugared fruits. "For Tom," she said. "I hope they will not disagree with him."

To her surprise, standing quietly at the corner of the dock, Kemal was waiting. Lady Adelaide nodded permission and Molly hurried over to speak to him. "I thought you'd have taken the earlier ferry back."

"Hasan has done so. He has duties to perform, but he has relieved me of my duties for today. I waited because I knew you were concerned about the journey back. I did not wish you to be left with no protector if, by chance, the great ferry ceased to run."

"Thank you. Kemal, if I gave you the letters, would you make a written translation of them? Then we could study them. In case there's something to give us a clue."

"I could do that and would most willingly."

"Perhaps we could meet soon and talk again?" That prospect lifted her spirits.

"I would like that. I remember our special words." She handed him the letters and he slid them into his coat pocket.

"Lady Adelaide! What good fortune to see you here." The hearty male voice startled Molly. She suppressed a squeak and sidled back to join Lady Adelaide. A glance over her shoulder assured her that Kemal had disappeared into the shadows.

Chapter 20

When Molly recognised the bombastic gentleman who had hailed Lady Adelaide as Mr Henry Russell, several of the rough words that she had heard in her father's yard flitted through her mind. Of all the mischances, encountering Dr and Mrs Russell's son on their homeward journey was one of the most unfortunate. Even worse was the prospect that his parents might be accompanying him.

"Good afternoon, Mr Russell. This is an unexpected pleasure." Outwardly Lady Adelaide retained her composure. "Are Doctor and Mrs Russell with you?"

"My mother came over the water to meet me. She's already gone on board." He smiled at Adelaide. "I'm returning home for Christmas and, to be honest, I was feeling pretty bored until I saw you, then I knew my luck had changed. Allow me to escort you aboard, Lady Adelaide." He offered a confident arm. "Father is meeting us with the carriage and we'll be able to take you up with us. Unless, of course, your aunt is sending her carriage to collect you."

Molly saw Lady Adelaide surrender to the inevitable. It was no use pretending her aunt's carriage was awaiting her when she was certain to be caught out in a lie.

Molly followed meekly as he ushered Lady Adelaide on board the vessel. She could sense her mistress' reluctance. The last time Henry Russell had honoured his parents with a visit he had pursued Lady Adelaide with a persistence that would have been flattering if she'd had the least desire for his attentions. Molly wondered how a lady as high in the instep as Mrs Tate could encourage a man like him to dangle after her niece. Of course Mrs Tate and Mrs Russell were bosom bows and it was common knowledge that Mrs Russell was wealthy, although she dressed like a dowd.

"Come into the cabin, Bowman. It's too cold for you on deck."

"Yes, m'lady." She wondered whether her mistress was trying to curb any indiscreet meeting with Kemal or if she wanted support when dealing with Mrs Russell and her son.

The cabin was crowded. It smelled of warm leather and damp wool and of too many people huddled into a small space. Obedient to Lady Adelaide's signal Molly sat down beside her.

"Good evening Adelaide. I see you have been jauntering to Portsmouth to buy frivolities." Mrs Russell's sharp blue eyes fixed on the hatbox.

Lady Adelaide flushed but, to Molly's amazement, she didn't pass off the impertinence with her usual docility. "Good evening, Mrs Russell. I see you have also been jauntering to the town to purchase fripperies." She looked with meaning at the parcel of haberdashery Mrs Russell was clutching.

Her son gave a shout of laughter. "That's trumped your ace, Mother."

Mrs Russell compressed her colourless lips until they were as thin and straight as a pencil line. "Pray do not be vulgar, Henry." And then, to Lady Adelaide, "I had to collect some silks. I have been so occupied with my work with the lower orders that I have got behind with my domestic duties but, if I apply myself, there is still time. I intend to embroider my men folk new slippers as a Christmas gift."

"Don't put yourself about for me, Mother. I haven't worn the last two pairs you made me." Molly saw tears in Mrs Russell's eyes and looked away. She didn't want to feel sorry for Mrs Russell, she was too accustomed to loathing her. The doctor's wife had always been well known in Gosport, her skinny, poking figure inclining forward as she bustled along, as if following her long, pointed, quivering nose. When Molly was a child Mrs Russell had been forever preaching to the destitute sinners down by the docks. When she'd tired of that, she'd taken to interfering with the private concerns of respectable working people and claiming it was for their own good. Molly remembered overhearing Grandmama telling Pa that Mrs Russell was a malicious creature, capable of almost anything to serve her own ends. Unfortunately, at that point, Grandmama had become aware of Molly, lurking in the next room, and had sent her to do her chores.

"You are a very accomplished needlewoman, Mrs Russell," said Lady Adelaide.

Mrs Russell nodded acknowledgement of this tribute but the stricken look did not fade. She dabbed at her lips with a handkerchief.

"Are you unwell, ma'am?" enquired Lady Adelaide.

"Today has been very trying."

"Everyone must be upset about that poor woman," said Henry. "It's strange, until my last visit I wouldn't have known who she was. I only met her a few weeks ago."

"Indeed?" said Adelaide. "I did not realise you were on visiting terms with Lady Dewsbury?"

"Oh I'm not. I met her in the garden, when I was last staying with my parents. The wheel came off the old lady's chair. She was nearly thrown out but the companion managed to hold on and I ran to the rescue. I carried the old lady home."

"That was kind of you," said Lady Adelaide.

Henry shrugged. "It's no bad thing to be on terms with someone as well connected as Lady Dewsbury. She may be old but she's still got influence. She was very grateful. Especially as her companion must have hurt herself when the chair collapsed. She looked so white I was afraid I might be left with a swooning woman on my hands as well as the old lady." He turned towards his mother. "I took the broken chair back to our house and Father said he'd get it mended. Did he do so?"

"I believe so, but Lady Dewsbury said there was no need to hurry. The weather is too cold for her to venture out." Mrs Russell turned her attention to Molly, "And how is your grandmother, Bowman?"

"Very well, thank you, Mrs Russell." Molly knew that Mrs Russell was unsure what tone to take in her dealings with her grandmother. She wished to despise a woman who had moved down in society so grievously but Grandmama's quiet dignity did not allow anyone to despise or pity her.

Mrs Russell sniffed. "I'm sure she will be most displeased with you, bringing shame on your family, arranging assignations with that heathen savage. It's your just punishment to be dragged through a common Court of Law."

Before Molly could speak Lady Adelaide intervened, "Whatever do you mean?"

Mrs Russell looked triumphant. "Reason has prevailed. My husband has convinced the local police officers to do their duty. Before I left Gosport they were heading for the Turkish ship to arrest that young savage and imprison him."

*

Chapter 21

Adelaide saw Molly's colour drain. For a moment she feared she was going to swoon, then she noted the blazing anger in her eyes. She couldn't imagine what would happen if Molly struck Mrs Russell, but she looked capable of doing so. Behind the cover of the hatbox, Adelaide gripped Molly's arm, pinching hard. She watched as Molly shivered and visibly regained self-restraint. She still looked at Mrs Russell with hatred but her hands remained clenched on the hatbox and her lips stayed firmly shut.

Adelaide sympathised with Molly. She too would have been glad to slap that thin-lipped, self-righteous face. But there were other ways of dealing out punishment. She smiled at Mrs Russell. "How public spirited of you. So worthy not to consider the implications for your son."

"My son! What do you mean? This matter has nothing to do with him!" Adelaide had achieved a greater effect than she'd anticipated. Mrs Russell's shrill voice caused many of their fellow passengers to turn and stare.

"Be quiet Mother. No need to make a scene." Henry Russell turned to Adelaide. "What the devil do you mean by implications?" He looked bewildered and uneasy.

"Mr Russell! Your language please! It's not what I'm accustomed to." In truth Adelaide had heard far worse than 'the devil' on her husband's tongue, but Mrs Russell was a stickler for propriety, so let the same rules apply to her beloved son.

Henry looked sullen. "Well I apologise, but what do you mean by implications?"

In her years in her father's household Adelaide had taken pains to cultivate her look of innocence. She used the expression now. "The political ramifications of arresting that young Turk. Just this morning Mr Corfield was counselling your father to be cautious. I understand our relationship with the Ottoman Empire is in a delicate state and if it were to be disrupted over such a matter as this... well I am a mere woman and know little of political affairs. As an employee of the government you must know better than I how such matters work, but surely when you're at the start of your career there must be a danger of losing preferment because of your father's zeal."

She stopped, having run out of breath, but she had the satisfaction of seeing Henry's alarm.

"Mother, I wish you and Father would be less busy. It would be wiser if you paused to consider my interests. You know full well that I hope to be seconded to the Foreign Office. If I'm passed over I'll know who I must thank."

"Oh Henry! How can you say that? You know how much your advancement means to me."

Adelaide had intended to stir up dissent in the Russell household but she was astonished at how successful she had been.

Mrs Russell became aware of Adelaide's gaze. Her eyes glared hatred as she raised her handkerchief to her lips. "I am unwell. My husband tells me that I wear myself out with my good works."

"There was no reason for you to come and meet me," said her son. "I wish you'd remember that I'm a man full-grown." He turned back to Adelaide and smiled, "My mother frets about me. Perhaps when I'm married she will worry less."

Adelaide did not respond to this blatant reference to his attempts to gain her interest. There was nothing in him to attract a woman of refinement. Her aunt frequently said how tall and handsome Henry was but Adelaide thought him too heavily built and swarthy. She had to admit his features were strong and his dark eyes were striking, but his wide, sensual mouth reminded her of her late husband, and she thought he could also be like Bernard in his insensitivity, arrogance and selfishness.

"We're here," said Henry, stating the obvious as the ferry docked. "Mother, I've offered Lady Adelaide a place in our carriage."

"Of course." Mrs Russell had recovered her composure. As they disembarked she gave her acid smile. "My husband will be with our carriage, so I fear we will not have room for your maid, Adelaide, but, after all, she is accustomed to walking the streets."

From close beside her, Adelaide heard Molly snarl. It was a soft noise, trapped in her throat, but it made her feelings clear.

"In that case I will not trouble you. We will summon a hansom cab." Adelaide knew there was sufficient room in the carriage if Mrs Russell wished. It was early evening but she had no wish to expose Molly to the dangers of a walk through Gosport alone in the dusk. Apart from anything else there was no knowing what she'd get up to. Adelaide was certain, given the opportunity, she'd try to warn Kemal. She felt sorry for the young Turk and sympathised with Molly's wish to help him, but Molly was too impetuous. It would be better to argue his case through the proper channels

"Nonsense, Adelaide. Bowman's perfectly capable of getting herself back. If you spoil your servants they get ideas above their station."

Molly took matters into her own hands. "If you please, m'lady, I'd rather make my own way. I can go to my father's yard and ask him to send one of his apprentices with me. I don't want to push in where I'm not wanted and I wouldn't like to crush Mrs Russell's fine gown."

Adelaide was torn between amusement and dismay. Mrs Russell was well known for her tight-fisted dowdiness, but Aunt Susan's patience had already been tried to the limit and now was not the time for her to receive a complaint from Mrs Russell about Molly's impertinence. "Very well, Molly," she said, "but be careful. Have you sufficient money to hire a vehicle? I don't wish you to walk these streets alone."

"Yes, m'lady. Don't worry, I won't be alone."

"Hoity-toity little minx," growled Mrs Russell as Molly sped away. "I wonder that you tolerate her impertinence, Adelaide."

When it came to discourtesy, Adelaide wished, as she had so many times before, that Mrs Russell would not presume upon her friendship with Aunt Susan to call Adelaide by her given name. She said quietly, "I do not find her impertinent, ma'am," and allowed Henry Russell to guide her towards the carriage that had just drawn up.

As they drove back to The Crescent Adelaide knew Henry was staring at her. To avoid meeting his eyes she kept her gaze fixed on the dark streets outside. They passed a group of rough-looking men. It was clear by their demeanour that they were drunk. Adelaide thought that there was a brutality about them and felt afraid for Molly's safety. She should not have yielded to Mrs Russell's importunities and left Molly behind.

"Henry, the blinds," said Mrs Russell sharply.

Obediently he reached across, pulled down and fastened all the window blinds, isolating them from the threatening world outside.

*

Chapter 22

Molly stood pressed into the prickly bushes that edged the entrance to the jetty and watched until the carriage drove away. She felt light-headed with exhaustion and very much alone. Her mistress was doing her best but she couldn't understand how desperate the situation was. Lady Adelaide had no idea that the authorities would use mobs of drunken oafs to hunt down a wanted man, but Molly had already seen groups of men lurking, like they were waiting to be told where to go.

As Molly scanned the shadows for Kemal her imagination pictured the scum of the dockyard fired with ale and the pleasure of violence. Kemal boxed in, bewildered and lost. They'd corner him and force him into submission with boots and cudgels. Nobody would care if they beat him to death.

It was no use cowering here in the near darkness. She was afraid for her own safety but terrified for Kemal. She tugged her skirt free of a spiky bush and stepped out into the light of a street lamp. If she couldn't see Kemal, at least she could make it easy for him to see her. She prayed that no enterprising townsman took her for a doxy looking for passing trade.

At last, as hope was fading, she saw him. When she first became aware of him it was as a deeper patch of black in the darkness where the street lamps didn't reach. For a moment she was filled with dread, fearing it was some predatory male circling her before he closed in, but then, with a rush of relief, she knew it was Kemal. Even after so short an acquaintance she knew the way he moved. He was walking softly but confidently, drawing nearer all the time, and she was sure he'd seen her.

She turned, meaning to go to him, but some instinct held her back. She hesitated, certain she was being watched. Then she heard the tread of heavy boots and a familiar voice, "Molly? What're you doing standing in the dark all on your lone?"

"Jeremy!" Her heart plummeted. "What are you doing here?"

"Keeping a watch on the ferry for that Turk o' yourn. Word is he was seen boarding it this afternoon and he'll have to come back sometime." His voice sharpened, "You haven't been meeting him, have you?"

"How dare you! What sort of girl do you think I am?" She flounced angrily and raised her voice to a penetrating peal. "I'm not the sort of girl who makes assignations with a man the police officers are going to arrest and drag to the lock up. And, if that's what you think of me, I'll thank you to go away."

"No. I don't think that. I didn't mean to offend you," said Jeremy hastily. "It's just you seemed mightily taken with that Turk."

"You don't have to be taken with a man to want him to be treated fairly. I told you, Kemal didn't kill that poor lady." Out of the corner of her eye she saw the shadows shift slightly as Kemal moved silently away.

"It's not for you or me to judge who should be arrested. Dr Russell and the other nobs say he's guilty and it's not for us to argue."

"Mr Corfield doesn't think Kemal's guilty."

"Well your precious Mr Corfield should keep his opinions to himself. Them Londoners should stay in their own place, not start interfering with us men who've got a right to be here. And that's even more true when it comes to filthy Turks. You never told me what you're up to, standing here in the dark. I been watching you from the hillock over there. I thought maybe you was planning to meet that Turk."

If she'd run straight to Kemal, Jeremy would have cornered him and Kemal's capture would have been her fault. Molly felt sick but there was anger simmering under the surface and that put an edge to her voice, "I don't know where Kemal is, but if I did I wouldn't tell you. Go away and leave me alone or I'll tell my pa you've been bothering me again."

Jeremy took a step backwards. "I didn't bother you. I wanted to marry you."

Molly reigned in her temper. If she angered Jeremy it would be the worse for Kemal. "I didn't mean to shout at you, Jeremy. I was feeling nervous, standing here alone in the dark. I'm glad you showed yourself when you did."

That had the desired effect. "Of course I'll look after you. But why are you here?"

"Lady Adelaide had to leave me to make my own way back. The Russells insisted on taking her home but they don't want to share their carriage with the likes of me."

"It seems your Lady Adelaide's not much better, leaving you here on your own."

"She made sure I'd got money for a hansom but she had no choice about leaving me. Mrs Russell pinched and pried and was so nasty. You know what she's like."

"Yes. Always was a tart old biddy, ever since we was kids. Lord, we used to run when we saw her coming, didn't we Moll?"

"It was worse for me. At least you boys were allowed to go off fishing or berrying. If she saw me with a torn dress or my bonnet hanging by its strings she used to call me a slattern and box my ears."

"It wasn't much better for us lads. Once, when I was running past her, I tripped over her umbrella and it snapped in two. She called me a clumsy clodhopper and hit me over the head with the broken bits. She's got a temper for all her prissy ways."

They grinned at each other, briefly united by their memories.

"Often makes me chuckle," said Jeremy. "Her so set against sin and that son of hers down the dockyard taverns with his trull when his ma don't even know he's in the town. He was chasing the doxies before he was seventeen and we've had him drunk in the lock up more times than I can count."

"Really?" asked Molly, her interest caught.

It was clear Jeremy regretted letting his tongue run away with him. "None of your business, Molly. A young lass like you don't need to know such things."

Molly knew he wouldn't tell her any more and she wanted to keep him sweet. "Mrs Russell's a cruel woman, for all she claims to be so full of good works."

Jeremy's face darkened. "She wasn't so fond of her good works two years back, when the pestilence was raging. Kept close in her fine house then didn't she? It was your grandmother who was out all hours helping folk."

Molly shivered as she remembered that dark time when cholera, a constant enemy, had grown to epidemic proportions. Over six hundred people had died of it in Gosport alone. They had all lived in constant fear, scanning the faces of those they loved, searching for the first signs of disease.

"My ma says it was your grandmother's herbal drinks that saved my life," continued Jeremy.

Molly smiled. "And Grandmama says it was the way your mother nursed you."

"She'd already lost my three brothers. She weren't going to lose me too."

"Dr Russell didn't come near, either," said Molly.

"We don't have money do we? He wouldn't risk himself or take the chance of carrying the pestilence back to his fine patients."

"Perhaps you should have remembered that when you were taking his side today."

"Just because he's too purse-proud to treat common folks don't mean he's wrong about that Turk."

That banished the goodwill their shared memories had roused. Molly glared at him. "I must get back to The Crescent, my mistress will be needing me."

"So why were you standing here, instead of heading straight back?" asked Jeremy.

It occurred to Molly, if she was wily, she could divert Jeremy and give Kemal more time to get clear. "I was scared, out here in the dark alone. It was only this morning I found poor Miss Berry. It upset me."

He patted her arm. "You don't have to worry about that, Molly. I'll hail a hansom for you and put you safely in it."

She grasped his arm. "Please, come with me to the Crescent, I'm scared to go alone."

"I wish I could but I've got a gang of good lads waiting for me to lead them on the hunt."

Molly had listened to the apprentices gossiping in her father's yard and she knew what sort of men turned out on a manhunt. Again she raised her voice, "If you had any regard for me, the manhunt for the sailor could wait until you'd seen me safely back to my mistress. If you come with me, I'll pay for you to take the hansom back."

He hesitated. She clung tighter to his arm and he yielded. "Come on then. We'll have to be quick. I've got my duty to do."

As he handed her into the hansom cab she succumbed to weakness and said words she knew were unwise, "Jeremy, if you take Kemal, promise me you won't hurt him."

He smiled at her. "Of course Molly. What sort of man do you think I am?"

'A liar, toadeater and bully,' she thought but she didn't say it. Provoking him could only harm Kemal and she knew she'd already said too much.

Across the road, lurking on the street corner, a gang of drunken yahoos had congregated, awaiting Jeremy's commands.

*

Chapter 23

"I'm sorry, m'lady, but I've got to find out what's happened to Kemal."

Adelaide sighed. For the second morning in succession she'd been awakened by an overwrought maid. "Don't be absurd, Molly. You have no idea where to look for him."

"I've got to try."

The stubbornness in her voice warned Adelaide that she'd have to take some action, otherwise Molly would branch out on her own to find Kemal. "Take the tray, Molly."

With her breakfast dishes safely disposed of she pushed back the bedclothes and stood up. "My new dress. The lavender with the deep, scalloped trim." This half-mourning dress was the prettiest she possessed and, despite the serious situation, she felt her spirits lift.

"Yes, m'lady." Molly moved obediently towards the wardrobe but her reproachful look made her disapproval clear.

Adelaide bit back a rebuke and explained, "At the moment we know nothing, Molly. We have no idea whether those men captured Kemal last night and, if so, where he is being held. We cannot act until we know."

"Are we going to the lock up to find out?" As if by magic Molly transformed from sulky despair to eagerness.

"No. I don't think it's wise for us to question the police officers directly."

"Because it's not ladylike you mean?"

"Because they wouldn't tell us anything. We need a gentleman to act for us. Yesterday evening, I sent my aunt's footman with a note to Mr Corfield's hotel, requesting him to meet me at the Reading Room as soon as it opens its doors. It's fortunate we can reach it without going through the garden."

"And he wrote back to say he would, m'lady?" asked Molly anxiously.

"No. I requested him not to do so. My aunt is already exceedingly distressed." Adelaide felt embarrassed. Ladies of quality did not seek clandestine rendezvous with single gentlemen. Still less did they suborn their aunt's footman, by the gift of a silver coin, to keep silent about the messages they had sent.

Adelaide dressed with great care. She told herself it was important to make a good impression on Mr Corfield, then, when Molly wasn't looking, she pulled a wry face at her hypocrisy. It was foolish to think she might again encounter Hasan and even greater folly to wish to.

Molly dressed Adelaide's hair beautifully, with coils twirled over her ears in the style made fashionable by the Queen. Only when Adelaide demanded her new bonnet did she protest, "It's raining, m'lady, and velvet marks so badly."

"Very well." Regretfully Adelaide watched as Molly selected a more practical hat.

The Reading Room had only just opened its doors but the staff knew their duty and a fire had been kindled at an early hour to warm the room. Adelaide seated herself in one of the comfortable, leather armchairs, sipped hot chocolate and turned over the periodicals and newspapers. No other patrons were using the Reading Room and she gave Molly permission to look around the shelves to see if she could find a novel that took her fancy. The small fee for borrowing a book would be well spent if it distracted Molly's mind from her worry about Kemal.

"Have you read any of the novels of Miss Austen?" she enquired.

"No, m'lady."

"I think you might enjoy them. They are very engaging. They are well represented here because her brother lived in The Crescent soon after it was built."

Molly took out a copy of *Sense and Sensibility* and opened it, then shut it again. "I'm sorry, m'lady, I can't think of anything but Kemal."

"Be patient, Molly. I trust that Mr Corfield will arrive soon." Adelaide tried to sound confident but, after they'd waited for nearly an hour, she felt despondent and conspicuous. The Reading Room attendants must have realised she was waiting to meet someone and, if Mr Corfield arrived it would be obvious she had planned an assignation with a gentleman. However, she thought it unlikely that he would appear. It seemed she'd over-estimated her influence with Mr Corfield and he wasn't going to come.

"Perhaps he didn't get your message, m'lady," said Molly when, at last, they left the Reading Room. "Please, let us ask at his hotel."

"I'm not sure that's wise," said Adelaide. If she presented herself at the Anglesey Hotel the news was likely to get back to her aunt.

"I think he'd have come to meet you if he could," urged Molly.

"Very well." Adelaide yielded to her own wishes as well as Molly's persuasion. When she had her maid with her there was no real harm in visiting the public rooms of a respectable hotel.

However, in the magnificent reception area they met with a setback. Mr Corfield, they were informed, had departed in haste yesterday afternoon and Adelaide's note lay undelivered at the hotel desk.

As they left the hotel Adelaide stopped, uncertain where to go or what to do. She saw Molly staring at her impatiently, waiting for their next move. "I'm sorry, Molly. I don't know what else to do. It would be wise for us to return home. I left another note for Mr Corfield at the hotel and I'm sure he'll contact me when he returns."

"But who's to say he will return? Maybe he'll be gone for days, or perhaps he's sloped off for good."

"Do you think so?" Adelaide's pride was stung. Edwin Corfield had been striving to fix his interest with her for weeks. Surely he would not abandon his endeavours so easily?

"I don't mean to talk out of turn, m'lady, but he's a funny one. I can't make out why he'd stick his nose into police business the way he did."

"I'm sure he had his reasons." Adelaide turned to walk back to her aunt's house.

From her position, just behind Adelaide, Molly continued defiantly, "Yes, I'm sure he does have his reasons but that doesn't mean they do him credit. He never said what he was doing out at that time yesterday morning." Molly's tone sharpened, "As if we haven't got enough trouble! What's he doing here?"

Startled Adelaide followed the direction of her gaze and saw Hasan approaching, striding along The Crescent as if he owned every house.

Chapter 24

"Durrah! My Pearl!" At the intimacy of this greeting she felt herself blush. He stepped close to her and spoke rapidly in French. "This is great good fortune. I came to seek you out but I did not know the number of your dwelling. So many houses, all so alike. I knocked upon the door of the first house but the manservant who opened the door did not speak French."

"It's not customary." Adelaide felt a twinge of annoyance. Were all the servants in Hasan's country so highly educated? She thought of the exceedingly respectable family that lived at the end of The Crescent and had a nightmare vision of the gossip and speculation Hasan's attempt to visit her would stir up.

"You are angry with me, my Pearl? You did not wish me to visit your abode? Forgive me. I do not understand the customs of your country."

His apology disarmed her. "I'm happy to see you but I do not wish people to talk about us."

"Forgive me," he repeated. To emphasise his penitence he took her hands and raised them to his lips.

Adelaide was unable to escape. She was aware of eyes upon her from drawing rooms all along The Crescent. She didn't know what to do. If she snatched her hands away it would cause even more gossip. Anyway she didn't wish to offend Hasan.

"People are watching you, m'lady." Molly spoke sharply.

Hasan might not have understood Molly's words but he must have interpreted her tone. He released Adelaide's hands and took a pace backwards.

"Why have you come to see me, Hasan?" she asked.

"I came to see Mistress Molly." Adelaide thought he gave a sarcastic twist to the respectful title. "I wished to speak with her if you will be my interpreter."

"What do you want with her? Does Kemal need her?"

"Kemal did not return to his ship last night. I came to see if he had spent the night with her."

"I beg your pardon?" Adelaide drew herself up to her full height and glared at Hasan. "Your manner and your question are offensive."

For a moment he met her eyes and then hastened to retreat, "I meant nothing improper. I thought she might have offered him shelter. The officers of the Law have been seeking him."

"We have no knowledge of his whereabouts."

His gaze flicked towards Molly. "Forgive me, my Pearl, but would your servant tell you if she had helped Kemal to hide?"

"Yes." Adelaide knew that Molly would not pretend to search so desperately for Kemal if she knew where he was.

"Then I must seek elsewhere. I am your most devoted servant."

He moved towards her as if he would kiss her hands again but she kept them firmly plunged into her muff. He bowed, turned on his heel and strode away. She stared after him, embarrassed, uncomfortable and strangely dissatisfied.

"What did he want, m'lady?" demanded Molly.

"He was looking for Kemal. He didn't return to his ship last night and the police officers have been searching for him."

Molly abandoned mistress and servant decorum and fell into step beside her. "I'm sorry, m'lady. I can't wait for Mr Corfield to turn up. I can't stay here, dilly-dallying, when Kemal could be being beaten and maybe killed."

Adelaide stopped dead and stared at her. "What do you mean? Surely Kemal won't be harmed unless he resists arrest?"

Molly's expression made her feel naïve and ignorant. "It's not like that, m'lady, not for ordinary folks. When there's a manhunt they send the yahoos out to scour the rougher parts of town. A local man might have a chance to disappear into the courts around the tenements and get taken in but a foreigner like Kemal would have everybody against him."

"I don't understand. What are yahoos?"

"Ruffians who hang round the pubs waiting for a chance to cadge a free drink or an excuse to get into a fight. Some of them think it's good sport to kick a man to death. Even better when the Law says it's all right."

Adelaide felt sick. "I didn't realise. You should have told me how urgent the situation was. What can we do?"

"I'll walk you home, m'lady, and then, with your permission I'll go and talk to Jeremy Bray."

"Who's Jeremy Bray?" The name sounded familiar but Adelaide couldn't place it.

"The police officer who came to the house yesterday. I should be able to get him to tell me whether they've captured Kemal. Like I told you, Jeremy's always had a liking for me but I've tried not to encourage him until now."

"And you're still not going to encourage him," said Adelaide firmly. "I will accompany you."

"Thank you, m'lady. I had thought of asking Grandmama to go with me but she may not be at home."

"And there's no time to waste." The rain was heavy and the cold wind was pinching at Adelaide's nose but she said, "We'll walk until we can hail a hansom cab."

*

No empty vehicles passed them and they had to walk all the way. Molly felt guilty. Lady Adelaide wasn't used to doing things like this. Her fashionable caped jacket and ermine muff were warmer than Molly's cloak but high born ladies were brought up to be delicate. Molly prayed Lady Adelaide didn't contract an inflammation of the lungs.

Jeremy still lived with his widowed mother not far from Molly's home. The best thing she knew about him was his kindness to his ma. As they passed the cooper's yard Molly moved discreetly, wary of encountering her father. To her dismay, when she thought they were safely past, she heard the sound of running feet slipping and sliding on the wet cobbles but still making good time. A glance confirmed that Tom was gaining on them. If Pa had seen her and sent Tom to summon her back it would be useless to try and escape.

Tom caught up with them. He was hot and breathless but managed to gasp, "Mistress. Lady Adelaide, ma'am." He gave Molly his gap toothed grin but Lady Adelaide received an ungainly bow.

"What do you want, Tom? Did my father see us and wish to speak to us?"

"Oh no, Mistress. The master's down to the Victualling Yard again. It was the mistress that sent me... I mean my other mistress..."

"I understand. You mean my grandmother." Molly tried to curb her impatience, Tom's tongue tied itself in knots when he was shouted at.

"Yes Mistress. She told me to go to the harbour and find out what's happenin'. There's been an accident. Body fished out of the water. She told me to see if there's anything' she could do. Not that there's anythin' you can do for them that's been drowned, just dry them out and lay them out, poor coves."

Molly felt as if the sound of the sea was thundering in her ears. It matched the frantic pounding of her heart. The world swayed around her in sickening arcs.

"Molly." Lady Adelaide's grip was firm upon her arm and a sharp smell under her nose made her gasp.

She turned her head aside and took a deep, shuddering breath, then gently pushed Lady Adelaide's vinaigrette away. "Thank you, m'lady. I'm not going to swoon."

"This may be nothing to do with Kemal."

"I know, but what if he tried to swim back to his ship?"

"There's only one way that we can know. If you feel well enough, let us go."

"Of course." She was humiliated that her weakness had delayed them.

It was easy to identify the fatal spot by the crowd of fishermen and sailors, and other people, both men and women, that Molly recognised as local residents. They were in a half-circle, gazing down at something lying on the ground. It was clear from the fearful, edgy silence that they were looking at death.

Molly abandoned her companions and forced her way through the crowd. The stench of stale sea water, strong liquor and unwashed bodies made her feel sick.

The dead man lay in a pool of water that darkened the ground and puddled under him. Some Christian soul had covered his corpse with a dark, woollen cloak. The victim was a tall man and sparely built, that was clear from the outline under the covering. On the left side a crooked elbow protruded from beneath the cloak and the skirt of his coat was also visible. From the pocket trailed a linen handkerchief, lace trimmed and embroidered with the initials M.B. Despite its soaking in the sea, the handkerchief still retained the pale, straggling remnants of a pinkish stain. Yesterday Molly had used her handkerchief to tend Kemal's head wound.

Sobbing, she fell to her knees and pulled the cloak aside to look at the dead face.

Chapter 25

It wasn't Kemal. That shock almost took Molly's wits away, but there was no doubting it. Even in death Kemal couldn't be so pale. And this man's face was a different shape, longer and heavy jowled. Recognition dawned. "Jeremy!"

Fighting the urge to scream, she pressed her hand against her mouth. She tried to rise but her legs were too weak and her skirts too cumbersome. Tangled in them she tripped and sprawled upon the ground. Her bonnet skewed round, covering her eyes.

"I'm here, Molly." Lady Adelaide was beside her, her hand on her arm. "Tom, come and help us."

Still blinded by her bonnet, Molly heard Tom shuffle forward but it was another hand, larger and stronger, that grasped her arm and hoisted her to her feet. She heard a quiet voice that throbbed with anger, "Adelaide, what in hell's name are you doing here?"

Molly regained her balance and pulled her bonnet free. At any time now they'd be taking her off to Bedlam because she must be mad. Jeremy Bray was lying dead at her feet and Mr Corfield was standing beside her, using the sort of language he'd never use to Lady Adelaide.

Even more remarkable, Lady Adelaide didn't reprove him, instead she murmured, "Edwin!" as if she were glad to see him.

"Take Molly and go home. It's not a fitting sight for either of you." His tone was gentler now.

"No! I want to stay!" Molly spoke vehemently. "But you go, m'lady, please."

"Nonsense. If you stay I must."

"There's no need for either of you to stay. I promise I'll tell you all you need to know," insisted Mr Corfield.

Molly's brain started working again. "That would be best, m'lady."

There was no use making a fuss. A new dread had replaced her earlier fear, not Kemal dead but Kemal truly a killer. How else could Jeremy have come by her handkerchief? As she followed Lady Adelaide back through the crowd she tried to weave a story about how she'd met Jeremy at the ferry port yesterday evening, that at least was true and could be confirmed, and how he'd had a nosebleed and she'd lent him her handkerchief.

Tom squirmed his way through the crowd and came to join them. "It's a rum go, Mistress. The flash cove turned him over and had a look. His head's been bashed in."

Molly nodded, tight-lipped but unsurprised. She knew Jeremy would have to be incapacitated to drown in the roughest seas the harbour could produce. Jeremy was a clumsy lummox on land but he could out swim any fish.

"Are you well now, Mistress?" asked Tom anxiously. "I ought to be getting' back to tell your grandmother what's happened. She'll want to go to his ma and see what she can do to help. It's a hard thing for a widder woman to lose their only son. But I don't like to leave you, not when you look so pale."

"I'm quite well, Tom. Thank you."

"I'll look after Mistress Molly, Tom," said Lady Adelaide.

He flashed her a grateful smile and sped away.

Molly's emotions threatened to overcome her as she thought of Jeremy's mother. She'd known Mrs Bray all her life, and pitied her, although never so deeply before. She was an elderly woman who'd already lost six children, three in their infancy, three to the cholera. Jeremy had been the youngest of her brood. He was all she'd had left in the world, and she adored him and took great pride in him. Now, with nobody to support her in her old age, it seemed likely she'd end her days in the workhouse. Molly thought, even if Kemal had struck Jeremy in order to save himself, he shouldn't have tipped him into the harbour. That was a cowardly, villainous thing to do. For all his stupidity and boorish ways, Jeremy had not deserved to die like that. And yet the thought of Kemal being tried and hung was unbearable. If he'd drowned Jeremy it must have been in a moment of panic.

A police constable arrived in haste and approached the body. He looked shocked and flustered and Molly guessed he'd been informed the victim was a police constable like himself. The crowd moved aside to allow him access and Mr Corfield drew back and walked across to join Lady Adelaide and Molly.

"Have you not gone yet?" he said.

"We will leave as soon as Molly is fit to walk." Lady Adelaide's voice was cold.

Mr Corfield frowned. "You came on foot? What are you doing here?"

Molly thought this was a question they should be asking him. He seemed to be in the habit of turning up wherever there were dead bodies. But she had to admit, so did she.

Lady Adelaide said, "Molly's family live not far from here. We wished to speak with her Grandmama and we heard a fatal accident had occurred."

"And so you came to look, the way well-bred ladies do?" His voice was laced with sarcasm.

"We were concerned and hoped that we could help." Lady Adelaide's haughty answer made it clear she was not influenced by his opinion of her actions.

"Do I understand that you've identified the unfortunate drowned man?"

Startled, Molly realised Lady Adelaide hadn't heard when she'd gasped Jeremy's name. She must have glimpsed enough to know it was not Kemal but the dead look different to the living and she'd only once encountered Jeremy.

"Has Molly not told you? He was a police constable. The one who came to your aunt's kitchen yesterday. The one that Molly's friend, Kemal, threatened with a knife. He may have drowned but not until he'd had his skull cracked by a vicious blow."

Molly heard her mistress' sharply indrawn breath. What had come over Mr Corfield that he could speak to Lady Adelaide in such a way?

"I beg your pardon if I've distressed you, ma'am, but I'd prefer you not to dabble in such sordid matters."

"Indeed sir? And have I given you the right to dictate my conduct?"

He stared at her in silence, his pale face inscrutable, then he bowed slightly. "You haven't, madam, and I apologise for my presumption in caring for your well-being." He turned his attention to Molly, "The young police officer has a handkerchief trailing from his pocket. It's a lady's handkerchief and the initials match your own."

The moment of decision had come. The lie was on the tip of her tongue, but she couldn't utter it. "I don't know how my handkerchief came into Jeremy's possession. I gave it to Kemal to bind his head."

He sighed and his shoulders slumped slightly. Then he smiled at her and, to her surprise, she thought he seemed relieved. "Thank you, Molly. I thought that was what must have occurred."

"But I don't believe Kemal did this. Jeremy's death must have been an accident."

"Perhaps so. It may be hard to prove whether the unfortunate officer fell into the water, knocked himself unconscious on some debris and then drowned, or was attacked and thrown into the water. One thing is certain, Kemal did not attack him."

She stared at him. "I don't understand?"

"Kemal was captured last night, long before Jeremy Bray died. Indeed Bray was one of the men who... apprehended him. I presume it was then he took your handkerchief from Kemal."

She found it hard to cope with the bewildering array of feelings that were bombarding her. She realised Mr Corfield had been testing her truthfulness and felt glad she had not lied, but, more important, she'd noted Mr Corfield's hesitation over the word 'apprehended.'

"Did they hurt Kemal when they captured him?" she asked.

"He was badly beaten. This morning, it was considered a wise precaution to remove him to the Royal Naval Hospital."

"You made them do that, didn't you?" said Adelaide. "You made them obtain medical treatment for him."

"I have no power to command the police, Lady Adelaide." He smiled. "But I do have several useful acquaintances, including the Chief Constable. Captain Harris is not a man who allows lax behaviour in his men. I paid him a visit last night when I heard of Kemal had been apprehended and he has assured me there will be an enquiry into the matter."

"Jeremy was one of the men who beat Kemal, wasn't he?" said Molly.

Mr Corfield nodded. "The battered state of his knuckles indicates that."

"I want to see Kemal."

"It would be wiser to keep your distance. He's being well cared for."

"I want to see him."

"Don't fret, Molly," said Lady Adelaide. "If Mr Corfield cannot help you, we'll see what my influence can do. I may not have as many 'useful acquaintances' as Mr Corfield but I think I have sufficient to deal with this."

Molly watched as Lady Adelaide's blue eyes met Mr Corfield's paler, colder gaze. She felt she was observing a silent duel. It was Mr Corfield who gave way. "If I refuse my assistance, you will probably storm the hospital. Very well, Molly, I'll do what I can to arrange for permission for you to visit him."

"For us both to visit him," said Lady Adelaide.

This time he didn't even pause before answering. Molly thought he was a rare creature, a man who knew when he'd met his match. He bowed slightly. "As you wish, ma'am. Now, may I beg you to return home and await my word?"

Lady Adelaide smiled and inclined her head. "Of course, sir," she said demurely.

*

Chapter 26

Despite her brave front for Mr Corfield, Adelaide felt nervous. She'd never been in a hospital before. Any ailments that had afflicted her family had been nursed at home. She walked with Molly along the busy corridors, glad they'd heeded Mr Corfield's advice and changed into plain bonnets and dark-coloured, unassuming clothes, with only one petticoat each. It had been fortunate her aunt had not been home and their departure had escaped her usual vigilance. Adelaide shuddered to think what Aunt Susan would have said if she'd seen her niece's unfashionable attire.

In the carriage, on the way to the hospital, Mr Corfield had spoken the merest civilities and she knew he was still annoyed with her for her unladylike foray into the affairs of men. When they'd arrived at the hospital, he'd escorted them past the sentry gate, helped them out of the carriage, bowed and promised to return for them within the half-hour. She was glad he didn't intend to stand over them while they spoke to Kemal but she felt uncomfortable that he disapproved of her.

A seaman had been designated to show them the way, which was a mercy, as otherwise they would certainly have got lost. Adelaide recalled that, when it was built, a hundred years ago, it had been the largest hospital in Europe. Some of the nurses who passed them looked rough and reeked of strong beverages, while others appeared quite respectable.

"This is where they've put Kemal, m'lady." Molly broke in on her thoughts. Her voice was trembling. Impulsively, Adelaide reached out and squeezed her hand.

It was a long room with narrowly spaced rows of beds. It smelled of men and sickness although it appeared reasonably clean. A lot of the seamen turned to stare at them and Adelaide felt embarrassed but Molly didn't appear to notice the other men. She ran straight to Kemal's bed. "Oh Kemal, what have they done to you?"

Adelaide was shocked by Kemal's appearance. His face was bruised and his swollen eyes were closed. He was propped up in bed, his chest bandaged and his breathing shallow.

His eyes opened. "Mistress Molly. How goes it with you?"

"Never mind about me! They've hurt you so terribly!"

"Not so very badly. I have been hurt far worse."

"But that was in battle. These men are meant to be officers of the Queen's Justice."

Kemal made a dismissive gesture. "I think this was not about justice. It was a matter more personal. The man who kicked me was the man who came to your lady's house to take me this morning... no... I mean the morning before... time is growing muddled in my head. He was angry. He said that I had stolen his woman. Mistress Molly, is it true you are his woman?"

Molly blushed. "Of course I'm not. He had no right to say that."

"I am glad."

"Kemal, that police officer was killed last night. Someone hit him on the head and threw him in the sea."

To Adelaide, watching intently, it seemed Kemal's horror and astonishment were completely genuine. "But who would do such a thing?"

"I don't know."

"Mistress Molly, he took the letters from me and your handkerchief."

"Oh!" Molly bit her lip. "The handkerchief was found in his pocket, but I don't know what he's done with the letters. Perhaps they're still at the lock up."

Adelaide moved nearer to the bed. "If they're in the possession of the police, sooner or later they'll come to the attention of someone in a senior position. If that happens, you must tell them the letters came from us. Otherwise they'll think you lied when you said you were not acquainted with Miss Berry."

"We can say I stole them," said Molly. "There's no need to involve you, m'lady."

Adelaide would have liked to step clear of the potential scandal but if she did she'd despise herself. "I'm afraid there is a good reason, Molly. Being an Earl's daughter carries a certain amount of power. If necessary I will go to Lady Dewsbury and beg her to tell the police officers she gave me the letters and commissioned me to find someone fluent in Turkish to translate them for her."

"No," said Kemal. "It is not right that you should be brought into danger and distress to aid me. I beg you, do not involve yourselves further."

Molly's lips quivered. She leaned over to stroke Kemal's cheek. As a conscientious mistress, Adelaide knew she should intervene but, to her dismay, she felt not anger or outrage but an aching envy. It must be sweet not to feel afraid of affection.

From the next bed a thin, dark-haired young man said something in a tongue Adelaide could not understand. Kemal replied in a sharp tone. The young man laughed.

"Who is that?" asked Molly.

"His name is Ahmet. He is also a sailor on our training mission. He had a fall and was hurt, but now he is almost well. Soon he will return to our ship but while he is here he is glad that I am too."

"It must be lonely for him, in hospital in a foreign country, not able to speak the language." Molly's voice was warm with sympathy.

Kemal smiled. "Ahmet is one that is never lonely. He does not need language. He will make himself a home in any place. But he is glad I am here because he is always hungry and I have little appetite."

Molly had a strong suspicion that hospital victuals would not tempt anyone to eat. She called to a nurse. "Are we allowed to send food in for the patients?"

"Why yes, Missie. I'll see he gets anything you care to send, as long as you sees fit to grease me palm."

Adelaide had no idea what the woman meant but Molly nodded briskly. "Of course." She turned back to Kemal, "I'll send you some of Grandmama's broth. You won't get well without proper victuals. And, if you promise to eat it, I'll send enough for Ahmet as well. Does he eat mutton?"

"Yes. He will be grateful." Kemal turned his head and said something to Ahmet, who laughed again and replied. Kemal looked embarrassed.

"What did he say?" asked Molly.

"It was nothing. Just Ahmet's foolishness."

Adelaide was aware that Mr Corfield had promised to return for them and it was a long walk through the hospital. "Come Molly. It's time we left."

"Yes, m'lady. I'll see you tomorrow, Kemal."

"No," said Kemal. "I beg you, do not ever come again."

*

Chapter 27

Molly stared at him in aching disbelief. "You don't wish to see me again?"

"It would be better so." He kept his eyes lowered and his voice muted and she tried in vain to read his thoughts.

"You don't care for me?"

"Molly!" Lady Adelaide's tone made it clear she'd offended against the rules of decorous behaviour.

Molly ignored her. This mattered too much for her to retreat now. "Don't you care for me, Kemal? I care for you." In those few words she'd thrown away her pride and independence and all she could do was wait for his reply.

For a moment she thought he wouldn't answer but then he said quietly, "You asked me what Ahmet had said to me. He said that I was a most fortunate man to have a lady who is so beautiful and so kind."

Molly heart was thudding. "And what did you say to him?"

Kemal raised his eyes and looked at Molly. "I said if you would consent to be my lady I would indeed be the most fortunate of men."

Molly felt herself blush. "Then why did you try to send me away from you?"

His voice was filled with pain. "Because I wish you to be happy and safe and prosperous. It is not right that you should be with a man who will soon be hanged."

"No! They can't! I won't let them." Even to her own ears the protest sounded childish. What could she do? She had no power or influence.

Kemal shrugged. "It is the way of the world. People are afraid of that they do not understand." He smiled suddenly. "Apart from you, dear Molly."

"But it's not fair."

"You must face the truth, no-one with power will speak out for me."

"Perhaps my lady..." Molly's voice trailed away, aware she had presumed. She turned to look at Lady Adelaide, silently begging for her aid.

"I have no power with the men who make decisions."

"Mr Corfield does, m'lady. If you were to ask him, he might help Kemal."

Her mistress met her gaze, her face so severe and still it seemed as though she was carved out of stone. Like a marble angel, a churchyard effigy. "I have no influence with Mr Corfield. You forget yourself, Molly. Come now, it is time to leave." She nodded to Kemal. "I hope you and your friend are soon restored to health." She turned and walked away, moving sharply, with less than her usual elegance.

Molly looked at Kemal and forced a smile. "I'll come back tomorrow," she said, "even if m'lady forbids it I will come." Then fiercely, "I won't let them hang you."

When they emerged from the hospital, Mr Corfield was waiting. His manner was civil but forbidding and Lady Adelaide responded with equal coolness. Molly was still smarting about her mistress' refusal to ask for aid for Kemal and she thought they were well suited, two icebergs who would crush a vessel between them and scarcely notice it.

"Are you satisfied with your mission?" enquired Mr Corfield.

"Yes, thank you, sir," said Lady Adelaide.

"I am glad to hear it. I trust you will not request me to assist you in repeating such an expedition?"

Lady Adelaide regarded him with disdain. "Have no fear, sir, I will not ask you to escort us here again."

The carriage drew up in The Crescent and Mr Corfield helped Lady Adelaide to alight. He accompanied her to her aunt's door but refused her invitation to come in.

As Mr Corfield took his leave, Molly looked towards the Garden. The police officer was no longer stationed at the gate and she thought the Garden had been reopened for the residents. She wondered how she'd feel when she had to go through that gate again. Her gaze travelled from the gate to the nearby Reading Room. In its pillared porch she caught sight of a surreptitious movement and recognised Hasan.

She cast a wary glance at Mr Corfield. The footman had opened the front door and Mr Corfield appeared fully engaged in ushering Lady Adelaide inside. Molly looked towards Hasan and cautiously raised her hand. His answering signal was equally guarded but she was satisfied he'd wait until she could find an opportunity to speak to him. She was grateful for his discretion but she recalled the arrogant way he had sought out her mistress this morning and felt frightened that he now found it wise to approach so secretively.

As soon as they entered Lady Adelaide's bedchamber, her mistress said, "Molly, you must never again suggest I approach a gentleman to ask him to intervene in such a matter."

"Yes, m'lady." Then, immediately disobeying this command, "I saw Hasan outside in the road. He was keeping back, as if he didn't want anyone to see him. He signalled to me. I think he's waiting to speak to you, m'lady." Despite her earlier reservations, she wanted Lady Adelaide to see Hasan and discover what he knew.

"Why should you assume he wishes to talk to me?"

"Well it's no good him talking to me, m'lady. He doesn't speak English." Molly realised she was in danger of offending her mistress again. Quality folk made a fuss about the strangest things and there was no use fighting it. "Maybe Hasan knows something that could help."

Lady Adelaide nodded. "Very well. I'll go and talk to him."

*

With Molly decorously behind her, Adelaide held her head high and walked towards the Garden. Within her muff she held her aunt's key for the gate and even through her gloves, it felt cold. Nervousness made her clumsy and she fumbled turning the key in the lock.

As they entered Adelaide heard Molly's ragged breathing and saw her eyes were fixed on a spot just inside the gate. This must have been where Miss Berry's body had lain. Adelaide repressed a shudder. She grasped Molly by the arm and urged her onwards, gently but firmly, as if she were guiding a nervous horse.

"Thank you, m'lady." Molly sounded breathless. "It's foolish of me, I know. Especially when I was the one who wanted you to come."

"You were right to press me to come. Kemal deserves justice." To herself she admitted her less worthy motives, curiosity and a desire to see Hasan.

"Durrah, my Pearl." As the thought came, he was there beside her. As they had expected, he had followed them through the open gate. "Thank you for making this rendezvous."

"I am glad to see you," Adelaide felt embarrassed, 'rendezvous' seemed so much more intimate than 'meeting.'

He stood looking around the garden. "This place is strange to me. I know the central building is for reading books but what are the buildings on either side?"

"They are Bath Houses, one for men and one for women." She saw his puzzled look. "Just around the corner there is a Pump House and water is pumped from the sea to the Bath Houses for people to bathe in it. It is very popular. It is supposed to improve health."

"The English are a truly strange nation. And this is the place where the English woman was killed?"

"It's where her body was found. Where she died is still unknown." Conscious of Molly beside her, listening anxiously to a conversation she could not understand, Adelaide turned to more important matters, "Hasan, we wished to consult you about Kemal. I do not know how much you have been told but he is in a most unfortunate predicament."

Hasan looked angry. "All my Captain has been told is that he is in custody. I wish my Captain to complain to our diplomats. It is not right that one of our Company should be treated in such a way, even though he is an outsider amongst us."

Adelaide felt a stab of pity for Kemal, doomed to be a stranger everywhere. Aware that they were visible to any visitor to the Garden, Adelaide guided Hasan to a more sheltered spot and said, "Kemal is in the Royal Naval Hospital at Haslar Creek and he is being well cared for." She was tempted to encourage Hasan to urge his Captain to complain but she was uncertain that it would help Kemal if he became the centre of a diplomatic incident. She suspected that he was of no importance to either side, save as a pawn in their political power games. With this is mind, she skimmed over Kemal's rough treatment and hurried on to describe their visit to Kemal in hospital and their promise to go again and to send him food. Despite her tact, she was aware of Hasan's simmering anger.

"It is an outrage. An affront to our country." He raised his voice in protest.

"M'lady, we'll be heard," warned Molly. "There are people over by the gate."

Impulsively Adelaide laid her hand on Hasan's arm to silence him. "Are they coming this way, Molly?"

"I think not. They're just standing gawping at where she was found."

"How strange." Adelaide spoke at random, distracted by the hard muscled strength of Hasan's arm beneath her hand. He had a musky, masculine smell, overlaid with the damp saltiness of the sea and a scent reminiscent of the exotic spices her mother's cook sometimes used to flavour puddings. She found it strange and exciting.

"It's the way folks are," said Molly. "They're always curious about death. Especially when it's sudden or violent. They've gone now, m'lady. There's no need for you to keep hold of him any longer." The sharpness of her tone penetrated Adelaide's preoccupation. Hastily she released Hasan's arm and stepped back.

Chapter 28

"I still do not understand," Hasan said gravely. "This woman who was killed, she was English. What connection could she have with Kemal?"

Adelaide was silent. If Kemal had not seen fit to confide in Hasan, it was not her place to reveal their suspicions of his parentage.

"I see! You think we are savages who kill for no reason. That Kemal encountered this woman by chance and decided to slit her throat?"

Adelaide was startled by his rage, but irritated rather than afraid. "Don't be absurd. We don't think Kemal is a savage and I'm sure the Authorities don't think so either. If they believed him a felon they'd have him held in closer confinement than an open ward in a naval hospital. Such foolish allegations will not aid Kemal."

She stopped, embarrassed by her outburst. Hasan looked outraged. She thought that he had taken umbrage. That amused her. It seemed such a ladylike term to apply to a dashing young man.

Her laughter was swiftly suppressed but he must have seen it. He flushed and spoke stiffly, "You are a woman of spirit, Madame. One who is not afraid to speak her mind."

Adelaide half-expected him to turn and walk away, which wouldn't help the situation or Kemal. It was time to make amends. "I apologise if I spoke too vehemently. I am concerned that Kemal is given fair treatment and Miss Berry receives the justice she deserves."

"You are right, Madame. In what way can I serve you?"

"I don't know." Now she had his co-operation Adelaide did not know how to proceed without betraying the secrets of Miss Berry's past. "Could you tell me what you know of Kemal's background? I know he had an English sponsor. Is that usual in your country?"

Hasan looked surprised but answered readily, "It is not a situation one would encounter every day, but it is not so very rare. In our Empire we are tolerant of the dhimmi, those of the Christian or Jewish faith who settle amongst us and work. It is not rare for a dhimmi of fortune to take in a child of their own faith but it is unusual for such a person to be accepted into our navy. Kemal's sponsor must be a man of influence."

"Do you know anything about his family?"

"Very little. You think it is connected to his troubles here?"

"It may be. There must be some reason why Kemal has been singled out."

Hasan frowned, clearly searching his memory. "I think our Captain made some remark about Kemal being of use to us because he had some English connection, but whether he meant his English sponsor I do not know. We assumed it was because Kemal spoke good English. Most of my fellow officers speak French, as I do, but there is less knowledge of your language."

"Perhaps you can ask your Captain what he meant by Kemal's English connection? But please be tactful. I would prefer not to appear in the matter."

"Of course. I will do my best to discover what I can. There may be others on the training ships that know more about Kemal than I do."

"Thank you." Adelaide smiled at him, glad he was not offended. To ask a man to probe into the background of his comrade seemed distasteful if not dishonourable.

"But do not raise your hopes too high, Durrah. Kemal has always been a private man. Perhaps it would be more effective if you were to speak to your Monsieur Corfield? He came to our ship and it was clear he is a man of influence, who I think knows a great deal."

Adelaide felt her face burn. "He is not my Mr Corfield. I cannot and will not ask any favour of him."

Hasan greeted her refusal with a smile. "I am happy to hear that. I will make the opportunity for another rendezvous very soon. Until then, au revoir."

Adelaide held out her hand for him to shake. This time she was not surprised when he raised it to his lips. He released his grasp and turned and walked away.

"We'd better wait a minute to let him get clear," said Molly. "It's a miracle we haven't been spotted talking to him already."

"You're quite right, Molly." Adelaide answered with unusual docility.

She saw Molly looking at her enquiringly. "M'lady, is that Turkish manners? I mean do Turkish men always kiss a lady's hand to say goodbye?"

"I don't know." Adelaide thought she'd be interested in discovering the answer to that question herself.

*

Sitting in private with her mistress in her bedchamber, Molly listened to her account of her conversation with Hasan. She was bitterly disappointed. Her first thought was there seemed remarkably little meat amongst a lot of fiddle-faddle.

"You were talking about Mr Corfield. I heard his name. Did Hasan want you to talk to him about Kemal?"

She expected another reprimand but Lady Adelaide answered quietly, "Yes. He thought Mr Corfield had knowledge and influence and, if I asked, he might use them to aid Kemal."

"And you said you wouldn't do so?"

"You don't understand, Molly. It's not just that I'm unwilling to place myself in his debt. It was you who pointed out how much interest he has taken in this matter. Think how much he seems to know and the influence he seems to have. Then there's the way he turns up without reason where he's least expected, especially when somebody has died."

"You mean you don't trust him?"

"I don't know. We know so little about him. He's admitted to good houses but I cannot discover his background or where he gets his income."

Molly knew little of the higher levels of Society but she was sure there could be other reasons for a man's secrecy about his origins. "Perhaps he's in Trade, m'lady. If he made his money that way it's not likely he'd boast about it."

Lady Adelaide shook her head. "I'm sure he's not a tradesman. He is in every way a gentleman."

"Well his father or grandfather might have been the ones who made the fortune," insisted Molly. "He'd still want to keep quiet about it if he was set on acting like part of the gentry. Especially if he was set on courting a high-born lady."

Lady Adelaide blushed. "You could be right, Molly, but I'm still uneasy."

"He was the one who got Kemal taken to the hospital, and he stopped Kemal from running away and took him back to his ship."

"I know. I've told myself that he acted for the best but then I wondered if it was because he wished to keep Kemal where he could put his hand on him."

Molly could not deny this. The same distrustful thoughts had worried her. "Then what's his lay, m'lady?"

"I don't know but I've spent some time in company with Edwin Corfield since he came to Angleseyville. He's clever and I think he could be ruthless."

There was a knock on the door. "Answer that, Molly." Molly obeyed. To her surprise the housekeeper stood there, bearing an envelope on a silver tray. She surged past Molly into the room and curtsied ponderously to Lady Adelaide. "There's a letter come for you, m'lady. I thought I'd better bring it to you myself as it's from your father. And m'lady, the mistress is holding a tea party and she said she'd like you to attend."

"Oh yes! I fear I'd forgotten. I'll go down in just a moment, thank you, Bradbury." She spoke briskly but the hand that took the letter was shaking.

The housekeeper departed and she said, "Go and rest, Molly."

Molly was very tired but there was something she needed more than her bed. She longed to see her grandmother, to talk with her and tell her what had happened and how confused and afraid she felt. If anyone could make sense of her bewilderment it was Grandmama. "Please, m'lady, I don't need to rest. Could I go and visit my Grandmother?"

"Very well. Make sure you're back to help me dress for dinner. Now leave me."

It seemed to Molly that her mistress was distracted and impatient for her to leave. "Thank you, m'lady."

As Molly closed the door, she saw Lady Adelaide, sitting, turning her father's letter over and over as if she feared to open it.

*

Chapter 29

Molly left and Adelaide sat staring at the letter. It was in her father's hand. That worried her. Usually he delegated his correspondence to his secretary. Reluctantly she opened it and read:

My dear daughter,
Your aunt has informed your mother that you have put off full mourning and have begun to go about in Society, at least such society as your present abode offers. Your aunt confided in your mother that you have attracted the interest of a prospective suitor. She says that Mr Henry Russell is a young man of good character and excellent prospects, whose family is much respected locally.
I considered it wise to institute my own enquiries into Mr Russell's background and prospects. I am pleased to inform you that my agent reports that your aunt is correct. Mr Russell's birth is not noble but it may be considered respectable; his career as a Civil Servant could well lead to higher political rank, and, if that should fail, his mother has a satisfactory fortune, the income from which is available for her use but the capital will remain intact and pass to her only son on her demise. As you will appreciate, the unfortunate circumstances surrounding your late husband's death make it essential that you re-establish yourself by a judicious marriage. Therefore you

have my permission to encourage Mr Russell's advances. I trust I need not remind you to act with the discretion and breeding you owe to your Family.

I have informed your aunt that if Mr Russell wishes to ask my permission to approach you I will look favourably upon his suit.

I remain your affectionate Father.

Adelaide tore the letter into pieces, which was no easy task, for the writing paper was of the highest quality and very thick.

As Adelaide took tea with her aunt and her aunt's two guests she found the conversation tedious. It followed a common pattern, that of perennial complaints about the difficulty of discovering good servants and, having found them, not having them enticed away by some upstart who bribed them with higher wages or longer holidays. Aunt Susan spoke with displeasure about her butler and parlour maid, who had left her three weeks previously, giving inadequate notice, in order to get married and to take up work under the bride's father at the inn he owned in Sussex.

"Such a pity you have been unable to replace them." Mrs Russell smiled acidly at her hostess. "Perhaps you should promote your footman to the butler's room, although he's rather young and heedless for such responsibility. But then, I've always said that footmen are a foolish extravagance, especially if your income is limited. Before you know it your housekeeper will complain that she is overworked and leave you."

Adelaide wondered how her aunt could possibly believe that marriage into the Russell family could be conducive to her happiness or status in the world. She was certain Mrs Russell knew that Aunt Susan had inherited from her late husband a sufficient legacy to command some of the elegancies of life but not its extravagances. To comment on her limited income was malicious and ill bred.

She intervened. "Bradbury has been with my aunt for many years and, before that, she was with my mother. She was born and bred on my father's estates and would not dream of leaving my aunt's employ."

"Yes, indeed," said her aunt's other guest, Mrs Boyle, "my cook has been with me since she was a kitchen maid and I couldn't dismiss her if I wanted to. Not that I wish to, she's got a wonderfully light hand with pastry."

After that, the conversation returned to purely domestic matters, concerning the best place to purchase oysters. Adelaide found her attention drifting and forced herself to concentrate. These ladies were three of the most formidable gossips in all of Angleseyville, skilled in garnering news as well as purveying it. It seemed to Adelaide that they were able to pluck the thoughts out of their victim's mind.

On no account must she let them suspect what she had been doing today. She didn't wish her aunt to know of her visit to Haslar hospital to see Kemal and nobody must ever hear of the meeting with Hasan. Of course the moment she thought of Hasan his image was vivid in her memory. She banished him. He was unsuitable for her in every way. She remembered a poem, learned in the nursery, about a high born lady who'd run away with a gypsy and slept under the stars. She smiled at the absurdity of her thoughts.

"Pray, Adelaide, tell us what is so amusing?" Mrs Russell's sharp voice jerked her back to reality.

"A foolish fancy. Nothing of importance."

"Indeed?" Mrs Russell gave her humourless smile. "Well we won't pry. You must be tired. I understand you visited the naval hospital today?"

"Why yes." Adelaide tried not to sound guilty. "How did you know that?"

"Oh I have my sources."

Rescue came from Mrs Boyle. She smiled at Adelaide and said, "Mrs Russell is a frequent visitor to the hospital. She goes to preach to the sailors or some such thing and always comes back with something to tell us."

Adelaide smiled back at her, grateful for her intervention. Mrs Boyle was a plump, cheerful woman, a well-to-do widow with a large family. She was a great gatherer of gossip but less malicious than Aunt Susan or Mrs Russell.

Mrs Russell bridled, clearly resenting Mrs Boyle's dismissive tone. "It is true I deem it my duty to spread the Lord's word amongst the unredeemed."

Aunt Susan forced her way into the conversation, "My dear Lydia, whatever a woman of your years and character chooses to do, it is most improper for Adelaide to be visiting such places."

"In that case I suggest you watch her more closely, Susan." Mrs Russell sniffed. "You would be wise to dismiss that impertinent maid who is such a bad influence. It is a mistake to choose one's servants without due care."

"If you're talking about young Molly Bowman, she seems a nice enough girl," said Mrs Boyle. "And her family are well respected in the town."

"I don't boast of numbering tradesmen amongst my acquaintances," snapped Mrs Russell. This was a deliberate insult. Mrs Boyle's father had made his fortune from Trade.

Mrs Boyle swelled with indignation and her florid colour deepened. "It's strange for you to talk about picking one's servants with care when you give house room to a half-wit you took from the gutter. We all know the trade his mother was engaged in."

"Charlotte! Lydia! Please!" exclaimed Mrs Tate.

Adelaide was finding the quarrel entertaining. In fact she was enjoying it far more than a gentlewoman should. But she felt sorry for her aunt. A good hostess should be able to prevent her guests from coming to blows over the cakes and sandwiches. Adelaide's mother had taught her how to quash pretentious upstarts and she decided that now would be a good time to practise the art of the well-administered snub.

She spoke haughtily, "I appreciate your interest, Mrs Russell, but there is no reason for anyone to feel concerned on my behalf. My mother, the Countess, taught her daughters to do their duty to their dependants. That is why I made a duty visit to ensure the welfare of a young man for whom I felt some small measure of responsibility. He is a stranger in this land and has been harshly treated. I was well chaperoned and protected and took no harm."

Aunt Susan said, "That is quite proper."

"And that ends your involvement with this Turk?" demanded Mrs Russell.

"I believe my maid intends to ask her grandmother to send the boy and his compatriot some broth." Adelaide spoke with studied indifference but she decided that tomorrow she would accompany Molly to deliver the broth. She would not allow Mrs Russell to dictate her conduct.

"Broth indeed! They should have him in leg irons until they hang him for the murdering scoundrel he is!" Mrs Russell's vehemence startled her listeners.

"Please Lydia," protested Aunt Susan, "I do not care for such conversation in my drawing room."

"My apologies, Susan. I will not say another word." Mrs Russell sat straight backed and tight-lipped.

Mrs Boyle broke the uncomfortable silence, "It's not surprising we're all distressed. Such a terrible crime and so near to us."

"Yes indeed, poor woman." Aunt Susan leaned forward and lowered her voice confidentially, "I've heard that she had some dark secret in her past."

"We all have things in our past we'd rather not dwell on," said Adelaide, hoping to bring the matter to a close.

"Some more than others." Mrs Russell accompanied the sharp words with a sniff. Her meaningful glance made it clear she was referring to Adelaide's own misfortunes.

"It's strange you should say that," Mrs Boyle reclaimed the conversation. "I encountered poor Miss Berry not that long ago. She was coming away from St Mark's. I could see she'd been crying so I stopped her and said 'my dear, are you unwell?'" She paused, awaiting the questions she knew would come.

"And what did she say?" demanded Aunt Susan.

"She said something I didn't understand," admitted Mrs Boyle. "She said, 'Thank you, I am quite well but I've had a shock. I saw my past standing there in front of me. I can't believe I recognised him but there's no doubt in my mind. Like seeing a ghost.'"

"When was this?" asked Adelaide.

"A few weeks ago. I don't recall the date. If I'd realised how important it was I'd have taken more note of it." Mrs Boyle shook her head, censuring her own lack of foresight.

"Whoever was she talking about?" demanded Aunt Susan.

Adelaide thought she could answer that. The Turkish ships had docked here in November. Perhaps Kemal had gone to St Mark's to introduce himself to the vicar, although he'd not immediately attended the Church.

"I can't answer that." Mrs Boyle sounded regretful. "I said, 'Really? Who are you speaking of?' but she didn't answer me. She just said, 'I didn't say anything to him. I need time to think.' Then she hurried off." Mrs Boyle sighed. "I'd have pressed her harder if I'd known I'd never get another chance."

*

Chapter 30

When Molly reached Pa's house she discovered that the workmen had returned in good time from the Victualling Yard and were tidying the premises.

"Master's in house," said the senior apprentice. "He'll be pleased to see you. Especially as he's alone tonight." He spoke respectfully in front of the other lads then turned his back on them to wink at her and grin. They were much of an age and he'd known her since she was a mischievous girl, sneaking away from Grandmama's lessons to play in Pa's yard.

"Is my grandmother not at home?" She picked up on his warning.

"The Mistress is tending the Widow Bray. She's taking her loss cruel hard."

Molly found her father in the kitchen. He'd given up waiting for Grandmama's return and was getting his own victuals. He didn't hear Molly enter and she stood for a moment observing him. He'd put off his coopers' apron and had his shirtsleeves rolled up as he cut cold beef to lay on slabs of bread. His arms were sinewy and strong and his large, capable hands were pocked with small scars, the legacy of a lifetime of hard work. In repose his heavy-featured face looked dour, then he turned and saw her and smiled. "Why Molly love, you've been in my thoughts today. It's good to see you, girl."

He held his arms open wide. Molly ran to him and hugged him. The rough cloth of his shirt rubbed against her cheek and she could smell tobacco mingled with the hint of wood shavings from his day's work. She was taken back to the days when she was a little girl and his strong arms had been her fortress, shielding her from the dangers of the world.

"Now what's wrong, my girl?"

She pushed away slightly to look up at him. "Nothing Pa. It just came over me, Jeremy dying and his poor ma left all alone."

"Aye. I've been thinking of him. It's not right when your children are taken first." Molly knew it was not just Jeremy who was heavy in Pa's mind. He'd been brooding on his baby son, who had scarce drawn breath before he went to Heaven.

"You're not fretting for Jeremy Bray now he's gone, are you, Molly? I know he had a fancy for you but I always thought it went the one way?"

"It did Pa." Molly made haste to reassure him, "I'm not grieving for him, no more than for any other lad taken before his time."

"I'm glad of that. Like I said, I've been thinking a lot about you today, my girl, and how I'd feel if I was to lose you." He pulled up a chair, sat down and drew her to sit on his lap, disregarding the crushing of her dress. "I know you think I've been a harsh parent these last few years, pushing you to wed a good, solid craftsman who could keep you safe, but it's a worry to me that I might die and leave you without a man to look after you. Your Grandmother's a fine woman but she's getting on in years. I want to see you settled with a family of your own."

"I know Pa, but I can't marry a man I don't care for." She wriggled round to smile up at him. "Grandmama told me that your Pa wanted you to wed and there were lots of girls who would have liked to marry you but you'd got your heart set on Mama and wouldn't have anyone else."

"That's another matter. It's different for a man. Anyway you haven't got a man of your choice in mind." He looked at her sharply. "Have you?"

"No Pa." To tell him about Kemal could only do harm and it was pointless when her own feelings were so confused.

"Well, whatever I want for you, I'll never force you into marriage." Deep down she'd always known that but it was good to hear it. His constant introduction of prospective suitors was irritating but not intolerable.

"You mentioned inviting some Turkish lad for Christmas." That made her jump. She'd suggested it casually after she'd first met Kemal but she hadn't thought Pa had taken it on board. "It seems strange one of them Turks being a Christian, but as long as he speaks some English I don't mind offering him a meal."

"He speaks very good English." Molly recovered her wits and thanked her good fortune that Pa was the last man in the world to listen to dockyard gossip. She wondered how long it would be before he heard about Kemal. "At the moment he's in the naval hospital. He had an accident. I was going to ask Grandmama if she'd send some broth to the hospital for Kemal and his shipmate."

"You'd think my pockets were bottomless the way you and your Grandmother give good food away," grumbled Pa, "but I dare say we can manage a jug of broth. You'd better leave a note for your Grandmother in case it slips my mind."

"Thanks Pa." Molly reached up and kissed him on the cheek.

"No need for thanks. It's a hard thing to be young and alone and away from your own country, especially when you're sick. You know, them over the harbour are calling us Turk Town, but I'm glad we've treated those boys more charitably than them."

Molly thought wryly that there was little charity in the way Kemal had been treated last night. "It's not the fault of the boys in the training ships that the people of Portsmouth are calling us rude names."

Pa shrugged. "A few rough words won't harm us. From all I've heard most of those Turkish boys seem decent enough lads but when it comes to the crew of any ship there's bound to be a few bad apples in the barrel. They say one of the Turkish boys has been thrown in prison today."

"Really?" So Pa had heard the rumours, he just hadn't tied them to the sailor that Molly had befriended. She struggled to keep her voice casual. "What did he do?"

"They say he stabbed a woman. Probably a trull who lifted his purse." Molly saw him recall who he was talking to. "But that's no matter. When trouble comes it moves thick and fast. The next time you see him, you tell that Church-going lad to tread carefully."

The sound of the front door opening made her jump off of Pa's lap and flounce out her crushed skirts. She heard Grandmama's voice thanking somebody and bidding them goodnight. The front door closed and a few moments later Grandmama joined them in the kitchen. She looked very tired and Molly hurried to put the kettle on.

"Don't bother with tea," said Pa, "a glass of brandy will put more heart in her. I got some in for Christmas." He went off to the front room and returned with a glass containing the clear amber fluid, which he handed to Grandmama.

"Thank you. It has been a sad day."

"You didn't walk back alone did you? As soon as I'd eaten, I'd planned to step down for you and bring you home. Charity's all well and good but there's no need to do all of the caring yourself, let some of the poor woman's neighbours take their turn."

"They are, and I was not alone. Mr Corfield conveyed me in his carriage."

"Mr Corfield!" exclaimed Molly.

"Who's Mr Corfield?" asked Pa.

"He's a gentleman who's taking an interest in this matter," explained Grandmama. "Mrs Bray has gone to stay with neighbours. She was afraid to stay in the house after what has occurred."

"Grief takes people strange ways," said Molly's father, "but I don't understand why she should feel like that. She stayed there when the cholera took her other sons and they died in that house."

"Early today, before Jeremy's death was known, his mother was out buying the food for their evening meal, and some villain broke into the house. He ransacked Jeremy's room."

Molly felt as if someone had placed a cold hand on her neck. Icy shivers went through her.

"But why?" said Pa. "The Brays had nothing of value. What did Jeremy ever own that was worth robbing and killing for?"

*

"Miss Berry's letters," said Adelaide. "I can think of no other reason. Whoever pillaged that poor woman's house must have been looking for them."

"But how would they know Jeremy had them?" objected Molly as she bustled around Adelaide's bedchamber, laying out her clothes for dinner.

"I don't know and surely it was a great risk to break into the house? They could not know that Mrs Bray would be out at that time."

"It's common knowledge she'd be out at that hour," said Molly. "She's regular in her habits and always does her marketing early."

"So that gets us no further." Adelaide felt despondent.

"At least we know it wasn't Kemal. He was already in the lock up."

"But it must have been Kemal that Miss Berry was referring to when she spoke of seeing a ghost," insisted Adelaide. "He must be her child. I assume she recognised him because he resembles his father."

"Kemal said he'd never met Miss Berry," objected Molly.

"If he was frightened he might lie."

"Kemal said he'd never met her," repeated Molly.

Adelaide curbed her irritation. "There's no-one else she could have been speaking of. Kemal's the only Christian in the two training ships and the only stranger who has visited St Mark's for many months."

"Maybe, whoever he was, they didn't meet at the Church. Even if Miss Berry's child was half-Turkish, there's no proof he was raised as an English speaking Christian. That's assuming she was right about seeing her son at all."

"But if she did not see her child, why was she killed?" Adelaide felt as if they were talking round in circles.

"I don't know," admitted Molly. "But somebody lured Kemal to the garden and hit him over the head."

"That's true," admitted Adelaide.

"M'lady, what are we going to do?"

Adelaide faced the inevitable. "The only thing we can do. I'll go to Lady Dewsbury and confess we took the letters, but not until after Miss Berry's funeral tomorrow. Make sure my black silk and my ostrich feather fan are in good repair."

"Are you sure that's wise, m'lady? Ladies don't usually attend funeral services."

"It isn't customary, but it is Lady Dewsbury's wish that Miss Berry should be shown honour and dignity. She is going to attend and I will be there to support her."

*

Chapter 31

The funeral passed without incident, although Molly, in dutiful attendance on Lady Adelaide, thought there were more people present to revel in the excitement than to mourn. As one man remarked in a hoarse whisper to his friend, 'you don't get a murdered woman buried every day.'

At Lady Dewsbury's request, Miss Berry's corpse had been returned to her home the previous day and the whole household had been put into deep mourning, clocks stopped and black crepe wrapped around the door knocker, in a manner more appropriate to a member of the family than a servant. Lady Dewsbury had ordered that everything should be of the best. The funeral was conducted with all ceremony and black-plumed horses pulled the shining black hearse bearing the coffin, which was covered with flowers.

Lady Dewsbury was a shrunken figure of immense dignity, determinedly upright in her wheeled chair, newly repaired and returned by order of Dr Russell. It was pushed by one of her footmen, while the other footman walked alongside to help lift it over the grass that led to the newly dug grave. The wheels of the chair cut deep patterns on the icy paths. The jerky movements must have been painful for Lady Dewsbury but she did not let her discomfort show. She was attended by Molly's Grandmama, who wore her shabby black clothes with a stateliness that transformed them into elegance. They were escorted by an elderly, ruddy-faced man, who, Lady Adelaide told Molly, was a retired admiral.

Of the fashionable local residents only Mrs Tate was missing. She had protested that gentlewomen should not attend funerals and certainly should never witness the interment. In fact there were more ladies present than Molly had expected and they stayed for the whole ceremony. Mrs Boyle was escorted by her eldest son. Dr and Mrs Russell and their son also attended. Mr Corfield was there, immaculate and watchful.

The service over, they followed the coffin across the small churchyard. It was a grey, chill December afternoon. The whole thing seemed so bleak and Miss Berry's death so pointless. Molly felt like howling, screaming, cursing, anything to break the reverent silence of hypocrisy. She stood mute and obedient, the perfect lady's maid.

After the interment Lady Dewsbury bade a general farewell to the other mourners but said, "I understand that Lady Adelaide is here?"

"Yes, ma'am." Adelaide came forward and bent over the wheeled chair. Molly accompanied her and was not rebuked.

Lady Dewsbury lowered her voice and spoke intimately, "I am not inviting these people back to my house. They had no interest in Ellen when she lived, why should they poke through her memory now she's gone?" She nodded to Molly's grandmother. "Elizabeth says she has unfortunates to visit but Admiral Daley is dining with me. I don't invite you to join us, dear child. We're too old to amuse you, but I have a favour to ask of you. Please come and visit me soon."

"Tomorrow if that is convenient for you, ma'am," promised Lady Adelaide.

"I'd be grateful. Elizabeth tells me there was a good turn out, but she could not put a name to everyone. Tell me who's here."

Dutifully Adelaide listed the mourners. When she mentioned Mr Corfield Lady Dewsbury smiled. "He's a charming young man and a deep one."

"I didn't realise you knew him, ma'am?"

"He came to visit me when he first arrived in Gosport. He brought letters of introduction from a cousin of my late husband. And he paid me a visit of condolence. He asked strange questions and yet I think his sympathy was sincere."

"What sort of strange questions?"

"Questions about Ellen, but everyone has been asking me those. He was also asking about my household, especially my footmen, how long they had been in my service and what I knew of them, and whether I kept my servants well confined."

"How odd. I mustn't keep you out here in the cold, ma'am." Adelaide signalled to the footmen who lifted Lady Dewsbury into her carriage.

When Molly's Grandmama had settled her comfortably and seated herself beside her, the elderly admiral climbed in. Grandmama leaned out of the carriage and said, "I will see Lady Dewsbury home and then go down to Haslar Hospital with the broth. Lady Dewsbury has kindly lent me the use of her carriage to go to the hospital."

"May I come with you to see Kemal?" begged Molly.

"If Lady Adelaide permits."

"Willingly. I would like to accompany you as well."

"We will have to take a hired vehicle home, your ladyship," warned Grandmama. "I must not keep Lady Dewsbury's horses standing in the cold."

"Of course."

Molly wondered why Lady Adelaide had changed her attitude to visiting the hospital. She feared it had some connection with Hasan.

"I will return for you here as soon as Lady Dewsbury is safely within doors." Grandmama climbed into the carriage, which moved away as Mr Corfield and the Russell family approached.

"Lady Adelaide, may I escort you back to your aunt's house?" Mr Corfield's offer was so formal and colourless that Molly could not decide whether he wished to walk with her mistress or was merely being polite.

"Thank you, sir, but I am not immediately returning to The Crescent. I have errands to complete, which must not be delayed."

"Your servant, ma'am." He bowed and walked away.

"Errands? Surely you can send your maid off to do anything like that." Henry Russell strode up to Adelaide, ebullient and demanding. "I'm taking my mother back to visit your aunt. You can't just go off when I was planning to talk to you. Now come on, what do you say?"

"I say I have errands to fulfil." Lady Adelaide spoke with calm good humour, as though responding to a troublesome child.

"So what are these errands? If it's library books I can be of great service to you. I can reach books from the tallest shelves and I promise to dust them with my handkerchief rather than let them soil your ladyship's fair hands."

"I do not require your company on my errands, thank you, sir."

His colour darkened and he scowled at her. "So what are you up to? Taking soup to the hospital for that dirty Turk?" He turned on his heel and marched away.

Despite her annoyance, Molly wondered how he knew about their errand. He must have heard of it from his mother who poked her nose in everywhere.

Having rebuffed both her admirers, Lady Adelaide seemed perfectly composed as she exchanged platitudes with Dr and Mrs Russell and Mrs Boyle.

Molly stood quietly in the background, wearing the cloak of invisibility that servants don when they are not required. She noted how old and grey Dr Russell looked, and how unusually quiet he was. By contrast his wife seemed brighter and brisker than usual. The Russells departed and Mrs Boyle and her son left as well. Lady Adelaide spent some time reassuring the vicar that he'd said everything appropriate, considering the very difficult circumstances surrounding Miss Berry's death, until Lady Dewsbury's carriage returned for them.

Once they were settled in the carriage, Molly's grandmother indicated a large, covered jug. "The broth."

"Thank you, Grandmama." Molly looked doubtfully at the size of the jug. "There's more here than I expected."

"That's because you don't know the way of hospitals. For every mouthful the patient gets there'll be a dozen nurses demanding their share."

"Are you acquainted with the hospital, ma'am?" asked Lady Adelaide.

"I have visited patients there. Occasionally, when there have been great casualties, I have nursed there. Both soldiers and sailors have been tended there, you know."

This time, without Mr Corfield's influence to smooth the way, they had to deal with the toll bridge and sentries themselves. Molly felt uncomfortable when she saw the way the guards ogled Lady Adelaide, so elegant in her fine funeral clothes, but her mistress seemed unworried by their stares.

*

Once again a seaman was detailed to escort them to Kemal's ward. As they drew near, they heard a man shouting, it was a foreign language but Adelaide knew the voice immediately. She pushed past their guide. "Hasan!"

He was outside the door that led to Kemal's ward, confronting the guard who barred his way. As Adelaide approached he turned and broke into a volley of French.

At his words Adelaide felt her throat tighten and her senses swim. She rallied and said sharply to the guard, "This gentleman is an officer on the Mirat-y Zafer. You must allow him access."

The guard drew back and Hasan plunged into the ward.

Lady Adelaide turned to Molly. "Hasan was angry because they didn't understand and wouldn't let him enter, even though those in charge had sent for him." She took Molly's hand. "He says he was summoned because a Turkish sailor is near to death."

Molly gave a whimpering cry of protest. She pushed past the guard and ran into the room.

*

Chapter 32

Kemal wasn't dying! He was sitting upright on his bed, Molly halted, unable to believe her eyes. The pain she'd suffered didn't ease into relief, instead she felt confused and tearful. She wondered how many more times she could bear to live through the fear of Kemal's death.

Her grandmother's hand on her arm steered her forwards so that she and Lady Adelaide could get past. Scolding herself back into calmness Molly followed them to where Kemal was sitting, anxiously watching the doctor at work on the occupant of the neighbouring bed.

Ahmet lay on his back, unconscious. His face was still and grey. His breathing was slow and shallow, with long pauses when it seemed as though those who listened also held their breath, willing him to struggle on.

Molly paused beside Kemal's bed, as did Lady Adelaide, but Grandmama moved into the group surrounding Ahmet. So assured was her manner that no-one questioned her right to lay her fingers on the patient's wrist and, having counted his pulse, to lift his eyelid. "This boy has been poisoned. I would think with an opiate."

"That is my opinion, Madam. May I enquire who you are and your business here?" The doctor spoke stiffly from the other side of the bed.

"She is Mrs Dorrington, a local nurse, much respected for her work in the town." Mr Corfield made his way through the on-lookers. He was carrying a tray. "The other ladies are Lady Adelaide Talridge and her maid, Miss Bowman. I fear I cannot enlighten you as to what they are doing here. I have brought the coffee, as you directed, Doctor. Strong and black."

"Thank you sir."

"May I ask, Doctor, have you administered a purgative?" Grandmama spoke to the doctor with the quiet assurance of one professional to another.

"Indeed ma'am. I did so as soon as I realised the reason for his collapse. Now we have to get this stimulant into him. No easy matter I fear."

"With your permission, Doctor, may I administer the coffee?"

"Please do, ma'am. Because of the unfortunate circumstances, we have no skilled nurses available for this ward." He spoke sharply to the orderlies who were standing looking bewildered in the corner of the room, "You two, raise the patient to a sitting position for the nurse. Look lively about it." They jumped to obey.

"What is the patient's name?" asked Grandmama.

"Ahmet." Molly and Kemal answered at the same time.

Grandmama gave them a brief, comforting smile. "Perhaps it would be better if you waited elsewhere."

"No!" Again they spoke in unison.

"I have been cooling a little coffee in this saucer, ma'am. No need to scald his mouth," said Mr Corfield.

"Thank you. And you've brought a spoon. You think of everything, sir." She held the liquid to Ahmet's slack lips. "Ahmet, swallow this."

There was no response. The liquid trickled down Ahmet's chin.

Molly remembered something. "He doesn't speak English, Grandmama."

"Of course, how foolish of me. Kemal, can you tell him, please?"

Kemal spoke to Ahmet. On the third plea Ahmet accepted a spoonful of coffee.

"He's taking it," said Molly hopefully.

"Not quickly enough," said the doctor. "He needs a lot for it to take effect."

Hasan moved to the foot of the bed and said something in Turkish. He spoke in the tone of a martinet officer rapping out commands. Ahmet took the coffee into his mouth, and with Grandmama's gentle fingers at his throat, he swallowed. Again and again it happened, until on the sixth spoonful he swallowed without aid.

"A good sign," said Grandmama and held the cup of cooling coffee to his mouth.

Halfway down his second cup he sighed and turned his head away. Hasan spoke firmly and he turned back again to drink.

Molly saw Kemal was smiling. "What are you thinking?" she whispered.

"That the good sailor knows an officer by the way he speaks and a good sailor always obeys his officer. I rejoice that Ahmet is a good sailor."

By the time Ahmet had drunk three cups of coffee he was half-conscious and muttering words that only Kemal and Hasan could understand. Molly thought that might be a good thing if the words he was saying were as rude as she suspected.

Grandmama looked enquiringly at the doctor. "Is it time to get him on his feet?"

"Let us try, ma'am." He looked along the ward and spoke to the other patients, "Stay in your beds and keep out of the way. We need the space to walk him." He eyed the more fashionable and influential part of his audience and Molly could see he was trying to find a suitably civil way to tell them to sling their hooks.

"Perhaps we might wait in your office?" suggested Mr Corfield.

The doctor looked relieved. "Of course. Please escort the ladies there, sir."

Mr Corfield turned to Lady Adelaide, "If you please, madam." Molly was shocked at the coldness of his tone.

"Kindly lead the way, sir." Lady Adelaide's ice matched Mr Corfield's.

Grandmama said gently, "Kemal, go with Molly. I will explain to Hasan what is needed and he will stay here to translate for Ahmet." Kemal clambered painfully from the bed. Dressed in an inadequate nightshirt, issued by the hospital, he looked young and vulnerable. His feet were bare and Molly was worried about how cold he must be. She stripped the blanket from his bed and bundled it up to take with her.

The doctor's office was warmed by a small fire. Molly urged Kemal towards it and settled him in a chair, tucking the blanket around him and making sure his feet were resting on the fireside rug. She sat down on a footstool next to him, tucking her skirts in to keep them clear of flying sparks.

*

Adelaide stood facing Mr Corfield in the centre of the room. She felt profoundly grateful that Hasan had stayed in the ward with Ahmet. She felt embarrassed and vulnerable enough as it was.

"I believe, Madam, you gave me your word that you would not come here again." Mr Corfield's voice retained its icy formality.

"I assured you, sir, that I would not ask you to escort me here."

"I see that your bond must be read very carefully, Lady Adelaide."

"And what of you? What is your business here? Or will you tell me you arrived by chance at such a moment?"

His hesitation was barely perceptible. "I requested to be informed of any untoward incidents involving the Turkish sailors."

"Why was that, sir? And who informed you of what had happened to Ahmet? Was it the officer in command of this establishment?"

He did not reply but his silence gave consent.

Adelaide became aware that anger had overtaken her without warning. Her voice was cold and stubborn as she persisted, "You have influential friends. Why do you use your power to intervene in such an affair?"

This time his silence lasted longer. "I fear I cannot tell you that. I can only ask you to trust me and meddle no more in this affair."

"It seems, sir, with you trust only travels one way."

Nobody spoke again until the doctor entered. "I have left him in the care of that good lady. He should do now, God willing. A strange business. He was due to return to his ship this week. Do you think some villain was trying to prevent him?"

Kemal spoke from the depths of his armchair. "I know of no reason anyone would wish to harm Ahmet."

"Well it's a dark business. There will have to be a formal enquiry."

Adelaide was surprised that the Navy was taking an attack on a Turkish seaman so seriously. These diplomatic waters must run deep.

"I must arrange for some replacement nurses for that ward," said the doctor, "then I must report to the

Admiral. Of course the families will have to be informed."

That made no sense. "Forgive me, Doctor, but I don't understand. What families are you referring to?" she asked.

The doctor frowned. "I apologise, Lady Adelaide. I presumed Mr Corfield would have told you of the tragic deaths. As well as that young seaman, two nurses were poisoned but unfortunately they died."

"But how?" demanded Lady Adelaide.

This time Mr Corfield chose to answer. His voice was cool and expressionless, "I have been questioning the orderlies who were working with the unfortunate nurses and it appears that they were poisoned by the broth Molly sent in for Kemal."

*

Chapter 33

"No!" Molly leapt to her feet.

"It's impossible!" agreed Lady Adelaide. She glared at Mr Corfield. "You are mistaken, sir. The broth only entered the hospital a few minutes ago. Ahmet was poisoned before we arrived."

"It is true that the unfortunate victims died from poisoned broth sent in by Molly," he insisted. "If you will not believe me you may ask Kemal."

Molly swung round to stare at him. "Kemal, I didn't!"

"Kemal, tell them what you told me," commanded Mr Corfield.

Kemal hesitated then spoke reluctantly, "The nurse came to me and gave me a bowl of broth. She said my lady friend had sent it for me. They had warmed it and said I was to drink it while it was hot."

"But this is nonsense," exclaimed Lady Adelaide. "We brought the broth with us." She looked around, unable to locate it.

"Grandmama left it in the ward," said Molly. "She set it down on the floor when she went to tend Ahmet."

Lady Adelaide glared at Mr Corfield. "Do you really believe that Molly would send Kemal poisoned broth? She, above all others, has been trying to preserve his life."

"Mistress Molly would never harm me," said Kemal.

Molly reached out to take his hand but she directed her words to Mr Corfield. "I swear that I sent no broth to Kemal other than that which we brought with us today. I would never willingly harm Kemal."

Mr Corfield considered at her and she felt as if he could read her every thought. At last he said, "I believe you Molly." He gave a rueful smile. "Now we have to discover who did try to kill Kemal. No easy task I fear."

*

"Where did the poisoned broth come from?" said Adelaide. "Kemal, do you know who delivered it?"

He shook his head.

Mr Corfield frowned. "You saw no-one you recognised or who looked familiar?"

"No. There are many people here. Too many strangers to remember or recognise."

"Molly's Grandmother told us that when food is sent in for the patients the nurses take a share," said Adelaide. "The person who sent in the poison cannot have known that."

"Possibly they didn't know," replied Mr Corfield. "Or they didn't care who else they harmed. The jug they left with the nurses is not large. Enough for two or three servings. I have no idea whether that was to limit the number of victims or to make sure the opium was strong enough."

Adelaide repressed a shudder at his forthright words. He was talking to her with respect, like a person with intelligence who could follow his reasoning and she was not going to throw away his regard by displaying squeamishness.

"Kemal, why did you not drink the broth?" she asked.

Kemal didn't answer. He looked so guilty it would be easy to believe he'd caused his friend's injury through malice not accident.

"Kemal, please answer. I know you did nothing wrong," begged Molly.

"I did not intend harm but I have caused it all the same. I am sorry, Molly. I promised I would drink the broth you sent but Ahmet was disappointed that the nurse only brought one bowl, and that was but half full, so I gave it to him."

"That's all right." Molly spoke in a small, gruff voice and Adelaide knew she was struggling to hold back her tears.

"I must report to my superiors," said the doctor. "Although I'm uncertain what I can say. This whole dark business makes no sense at all. Perhaps Mr Corfield you would care to accompany me?"

"Of course, sir. I will join you in a moment." The doctor bustled out of the room but Mr Corfield lingered, "Lady Adelaide, did anyone else know of Molly's promise to supply broth for Kemal?"

"Yes. Mrs Russell, Mrs Boyle and my aunt all knew of it, and Mr Henry Russell referred to it after the funeral." And Hasan. She'd mentioned it to him when they'd met yesterday, but she couldn't bear to disclose this to Mr Corfield.

He sighed. "I feared as much. If those three ladies were discussing the matter it is unlikely that there was a person of Quality or their servants who didn't know."

"At your convenience sir." The doctor's voice came from the corridor.

"One moment only." Mr Corfield turned back to Adelaide, "I have no idea how long this business will take but I would like to escort you home. You will be quite safe here in the doctor's room."

Give the man an inch and he tried to rule her life. "Thank you for your concern sir, but there is no need." She smiled at him. "And remember, I gave you an assurance."

She saw a glint of humour in his blue eyes. "I do remember very clearly, ma'am. You said you would not again ask me to escort you here, but nothing was said about escorting you home again." He bowed and left before Adelaide could reply.

Adelaide stood in the centre of the room, her hands pressed against her burning cheeks. She was uncertain whether she was affronted or pleased that they were moving back to friendly terms. One thing she was sure of, Edwin Corfield knew a great deal about what was going on. If she waited for his escort she could charm him into confiding in her. Good sense cut in. He was more likely to gain possession of all her secrets before the carriage had travelled half a mile.

"M'lady, what can we do?" Molly's voice cut across her thoughts. "Somebody wants to kill Kemal and we don't know who it is or why. We can't protect him."

"I can protect myself," protested Kemal.

"What are you going to do? Never eat in case someone poisons you? For that matter you won't be able to sleep in case someone smothers you. You're already as weak as a cat. And if you cut up rough they'll say you're queer in the upper storey and clap you up."

"I am sorry, Molly, what is it you say that they will do to me?" Adelaide could not blame Kemal for his confusion, she'd noted before that the more agitated Molly became the more colourful her language.

"Perhaps you could explain in English for us, Molly?" she said.

"If Kemal doesn't do as he's bid the doctors will decide he's mad and put him in an asylum." Adelaide's breath caught in her throat. This was a very real fear for anyone who was within another's power. One of her late husband's friends had confined his wife in an institution for the insane. Her only fault had been protesting against her husband consorting with prostitutes then forcing his diseased body upon her. Bernard had told her the story as a threat. When such memories intruded she could hardly believe that she had escaped her marriage unharmed.

"It's true, m'lady." Molly's voice recalled her. "There's a special bit of the hospital for sailors who are insane. If they put Kemal in there he wouldn't stand a chance. We've got to do something. Kemal is in danger all the time he's in this place."

"I agree, but if they discharge him from hospital I cannot believe they will return him to his ship. He will not be safe in prison. I wish there was one man we could trust and who would act for us."

"Well we can't trust Mr Corfield," said Molly. "You were right, m'lady. That cove's too clever by half and whenever anyone croaks he's always on the spot. Sorry m'lady, by croaks I mean..."

"It's all right, Molly, I know what you mean. Although I suppose Mr Corfield might point out that we also seem to be present at a lot of deaths."

"Hasan might help us," said Molly.

Adelaide wondered why Molly had suddenly decided that Hasan was worthy of trust. "I admit it is impossible that a man of Hasan's rigid honour would stoop to poison."

"If you say so m'lady. I was thinking it wouldn't be easy for him to find the means to poison anybody in the hospital. Kemal, what sort of broth was it?"

He looked surprised. "It was an English broth, with vegetables and sheep's meat. I remember that because Ahmet asked the nurse. He would not have eaten pig's meat."

"I doubt they cook that sort of food on the Mirat-y Zafer?" said Molly, looking enquiringly at Kemal.

Kemal shook his head. "No, we do not have such food. But what madness are you thinking of Hasan?"

Molly ignored his question. "He could have bought it from a food vendor but it seems a chancy way for him to kill Kemal."

"It's unreliable for anyone," said Adelaide, "and it didn't work."

"But Hasan is Kemal's friend. It's much easier to harm someone who trusts you. He could find a surer way."

"Hasan is not treacherous," insisted Kemal. "He would not act with dishonour." Adelaide was glad to hear him say this and wanted to believe that he was right.

"In this country is it easy to get opium?" asked Kemal.

Adelaide knew the answer to this from bitter experience. "If one has money it is not hard to buy opium. There are places in London where many men spend their time smoking it and there must be such places in a dockyard town as well." Her late husband had frequented such haunts and taken pleasure in describing to her what took place there.

The door opened and Molly's grandmother entered. She looked weary but serene. "I think the worst is past now and he will survive. I have been thinking, I fear it is not safe for Kemal to remain in this place, we must remove him from here without delay."

Chapter 34

Adelaide felt tempted to burst into hysterical laughter. Mrs Dorrington sounded so matter of fact. She controlled herself and said, "We are aware of that, ma'am, but there is nothing we can do. The only alternative is the lock up and he will be no safer there."

Mrs Dorrington looked surprised. "But surely the solution is clear? We must smuggle him out of this establishment. Then we can keep him concealed until we discover who is behind this attempt to discredit him and make sure it is safe for him to resume his place in the world."

"But Grandmama how could we?" said Molly. "There are guards on the gate."

"We would have to outwit them." She gave a sparkling smile. "Surely no great problem for three resourceful women. If Fortune favours us, they may spend many hours searching the hospital for Kemal before they realise he has escaped."

"Is that likely, Grandmama?" Molly sounded dubious.

"It is quite possible. This is a vast and complex building."

"But how can we smuggle Kemal out of the hospital?" demanded Molly.

"We must act promptly," said her grandmother. "I will go to the nurse's room. I saw dresses and aprons hanging there. I will change into one of them. If anyone questions my actions I will explain that my dress became soiled during my ministrations to Ahmet, and I'll say I wish to stay here a little longer to ensure his return to health."

"And we'll dress Kemal in your clothes and walk out of the hospital with him," said Molly. "Grandmama you're incomparable."

"Nonsense child. It is fortunate I'm wearing my black hat with the heavy veil. I only wear that for funerals."

Kemal had been listening intently, now he said, "If you please, there is something I must say."

Adelaide expected an argument. A dashing young man like Kemal would never accept the idea of masquerading in women's clothes. She was sure that Hasan would rather die than submit to such an indignity.

To her surprise he said, "This is a plan that has many risks. It would be better if m'lady and Molly do not leave with me. I will go first and they will follow. In that way, if I am taken, I can say I stole your clothing and they can disown my company and will not be brought to shame."

Mrs Dorrington smiled at him. "Thank you, Kemal."

"And if it doesn't work, we're free to try something else," said Molly.

"I will go and change," said Mrs Dorrington.

She hurried away. Adelaide prayed she would be swift. She dreaded that Mr Corfield would return and catch them in the midst of this masquerade. "Where can we hide Kemal once we have got him out of the hospital?" she said.

"Would he not be safe back on his ship?" asked Molly.

"I think not," said Adelaide. "From the little I've heard about the political situation, if his Captain refuses to return Kemal to our authorities it could cause a major diplomatic incident." On the other hand it was quite possible the English diplomats would not claim Kemal for fear of offending the Turks. Her father interested himself in politics, which meant that Adelaide had known many diplomats and had learned how untrustworthy they could be. This felt too much like a gamble with Kemal's life. "Perhaps Hasan could hide him on board," she said.

"No," said Kemal. "You must not tell Hasan what we have planned."

"Why?" demanded Molly. "You said he's your friend?"

"He is a man of the most rigid honour. He will not lie." Adelaide thought such honour was a fine thing but in everyday life it might be impossible to live with.

Mrs Dorrington returned, looking old and humble in her plain grey hospital dress and grubby apron. As Molly helped Kemal to don her grandmother's clothes she told her what they had been discussing. "We daren't take him home," said Molly. "Even if Pa would consent to let him stay it's the first place they'd look for him."

"I will not allow your father to be put in jeopardy of the Law," said her grandmother firmly. "But there's an old, derelict warehouse that he bought in the summer. No-one could blame your father if a fugitive took refuge there unbeknownst to him."

"Of course!" said Molly. She explained to Adelaide and Kemal, "Pa plans to rebuild it and use it for storage but at the moment nobody but Tom goes next or nigh the place. Tom told me there's a small upstairs room that's still dry and not too cold."

"So that's where the rascal has been sneaking off to," said Mrs Dorrington. "Your father will make him smart if he finds out."

"Hush!" Adelaide had been standing by the door, holding it slightly ajar and listening for Mr Corfield and the doctor to return. She heard the sound of approaching footsteps. "Someone's coming!"

"Quickly Kemal, we must not be seen like this." Mrs Dorrington signalled him towards the door.

Adelaide watched as they crossed the corridor and disappeared into what she suspected was a cupboard. Then she crossed the room and sat down by the fire, adopting a pose of bored elegance although her heart was pounding.

The footsteps drew nearer, stopped, turned round and retreated again.

At Molly's summons, Mrs Dorrington and Kemal reappeared.

"Are you all right, Grandmama?" asked Molly, as her Grandmother arranged Kemal's bonnet, tying the ribbons firmly and straightening the veil to conceal his face.

"Of course I am. A most exciting afternoon. It is not often a woman of my years is shut in a broom cupboard with a handsome young man."

"Your gloves won't fit Kemal, Grandmama."

"Force them on. No matter if you split the seams. His seaman's hands are our biggest danger. Here Kemal, hold my handkerchief. That should conceal the damage to my gloves. Go quickly now and God bless you all." Mrs Dorrington ushered them towards the door.

They made their way along the corridors, trying to move with assurance. Walking behind Kemal, Adelaide thought he was hobbling like an arthritic old woman. She realised he was forcing himself onwards through the pain of his injured body and prayed he didn't need to run.

At last they achieved the gate. Kemal was ten yards ahead of them. The guards today were casual and bored, hardly bothering to look as the visitors passed through. Adelaide's heart was thumping. Could Kemal carry it off?

Kemal was past the guards when a white muslin square fluttered to the ground. One of the guards shouted, "Oy Missus, yer 'andkerchief."

Kemal kept on moving.

The guard bent to pick up the handkerchief. Molly hastened forward and grasped it. "I think she's deaf. I'll run after her."

"It's all right Missy, I'll catch her. Don't want you slipping on these damp stones."

"No I'll take it." Molly kept hold of the handkerchief.

Adelaide hurried to join them, fearing that at any moment there would be a most unseemly and conspicuous tug of war. There was nothing else for it. Adelaide's mother had ensured that her daughters were well trained in all of a gentlewoman's arts and Adelaide knew the time had come to deploy the most effective weapon in a lady's armoury. With a swift glance to ensure the guard was within range she slumped into his arms in a most artistic and convincing faint.

Chapter 35

One disadvantage of pretending to have swooned is that one has to keep one's eyes closed. Adelaide was tortured by her desire to know what was happening. Listening as well as she could when pressed against the guard's vile smelling coat, she could hear no sounds of outcry or pursuit. That gave her hope her diversion had worked. She could hear a buzz of men's voices, rough but not unkindly. The one holding her was explaining how she'd fallen down in a swoon and another saying he'd summon a doctor from the hospital to tend her. Then Molly's voice, "There's no need to call a doctor. She's just overcome by the sights she's seen in there. Gentle born ladies aren't used to such things."

There was a mumble of agreement and one man said, "Gentry folk should stay where they belong and not go messing with things not fit for them."

"Aye," said the man who was holding Adelaide, "But you know what flash coves are like, poking their noses into everything. I've heard tell they even go round Bedlam to watch the antics of them dicked in the nob."

"Don't stand there insulting your betters," commanded Molly. "Set a chair for my mistress. Bring it out here, that guardroom smells like a midden."

Adelaide could well believe that. She was most uncomfortably situated with her face pressed against the rough cloth of the guard's coat, one of his buttons digging sharply into her cheek. She feared she'd soon be overpowered by the mingled smells of damp wool, rum and unwashed man and would swoon in earnest.

She felt herself placed on a chair, heard the rustle of Molly's petticoats and smelled her fresh, flowery scent, then a sharper smell as Molly wafted her vinaigrette under her nose. She opened her eyes. "What happened?"

"You fainted mistress," said Molly. "This guard caught you as you swooned."

"How foolish of me." She turned to the guard, "Thank you for your help. You've been so kind. I was fortunate you were so quick-witted and saved me from a nasty fall." Adelaide's mother had also told her that, next to fainting, flattery and a smile would usually bring a man in line and certainly the guard looked most gratified.

"I could offer you a mouthful of something, ma'am. It'd put the heart back in you."

The thought of quaffing strong beverages with these rough although respectful men made Adelaide shudder. Even more dreadful was the thought that Mr Corfield could appear at any time and find her in such a predicament.

"Thank you, but I am quite recovered and must go home." She stood up. "Molly, pray give me your arm."

Molly supported her and they walked across the bridge, using the slow steps of a recovering invalid. The guard, who seemed to consider Adelaide his protégée, accompanied them a short distance.

"There now," he said, "I never did catch up with that old dame. I'll put her 'andkerchief in the guardroom and she can claim it if she recalls where she dropped it. That's if she came by it 'onest. Nice bit o' linen. Quality make."

He turned it over in his hands and Adelaide noted, with relief, that it bore no embroidered name or initials to reveal the owner's identity. She rummaged in her reticule and produced a few small silver coins. "Please take this for you and your friends to buy a drink. And thank you for your kindness."

"Thank you ma'am." He made a strange gesture, a cross between doffing his cap and saluting, and returned to his post.

"M'lady, you were wonderful," said Molly.

"And lucky," said Adelaide. "Let us get away from here before our good fortune runs out." A new problem occurred to her. "I hadn't considered before, but how can we find Kemal again?"

"Don't worry about that. I told him where I'd meet him. I knew there was a chance we'd get split up."

"You think of everything, Molly."

"I wish I did. We don't seem any further on than we were. If you please, m'lady, I'll see you home then I'll go and find Kemal. A lady like you is too noticeable round places like the dockyard. You'd be remembered."

"We'll discuss that in a minute. Summon that hansom, Molly. I wish to be well away from here before Mr ... before the naval authorities discover Kemal has fled."

Molly did as she was bid. The hansom cab drew up and Adelaide said, "There's no need for you to accompany me, Molly, but I have every intention of driving with you to where you need to go. I will not leave the vehicle. You are right that I would be too conspicuous. Once I've seen you safely to your destination I will go home and see you at my aunt's house when you have finished."

"You can't travel alone in an old wreck like this, m'lady." Molly eyed the dirty old vehicle with disgust. "And the area I'm heading to is rough."

"All the more reason that I should ensure your safety." Adelaide smiled. "I assure you I am not in the least afraid. When you consider the number of improper and illegal activities I have been embroiled in during the past few days, riding alone in a hired vehicle is quite tame."

"But with any luck your aunt won't find out about any of those other goings on. She's bound to know if you pull up outside her house in that."

"A good point. I will be sure to tell the driver to stop outside St Mark's Church. Don't argue, Molly. Take this." She handed her two guineas. "You will need to buy Kemal clothes and food. I hope that is sufficient."

"It's plenty, m'lady, thank you. We don't need him dressed up like a flash cove, we want him to blend in." She gave a sudden, mischievous smile. "If the dibs aren't in tune I can always send Tom out on the nick from someone's washing line."

Adelaide interpreted the last remark then pretended she had not. She climbed into the carriage, hoping fervently that Molly was joking and, if not, that none of the miscreants got caught.

Sitting well back in the corner of the vehicle, Adelaide had not noticed the area that they were travelling through until Molly had rapped on the cab roof and commanded the driver to set her down, telling him to drive on to St Mark's Church, Angleseyville, before she walked briskly away.

Left alone, Adelaide took stock of her surroundings. She had spoken the truth when she said she was not afraid to travel by herself, but she did feel conspicuous. Soon she understood what Molly had meant about it being a rough area and she was grateful for her dark, concealing veil.

The streets were full of rough looking seamen. They emerged from low, dirty taverns, lurching drunkenly. Several times the driver had to check his horses as foolish men meandered carelessly into the road, intent on reaching the many houses of ill-repute. Adelaide knew they must be bawdy houses. What other establishment would have grubby, scantily clad women standing in the doorways and leaning out of windows? They screeched invitations to the passing men in terms that Adelaide did not fully understand but nevertheless brought a blush to her cheeks. One hussy thrust her naked leg out of the window and waggled it provocatively.

It was then she recognised Henry Russell, standing in the street, laughing raucously at the woman's uncouth antics. Adelaide averted her face and prayed he would not see her. What would his sanctimonious mother make of his behaviour? And Aunt Susan, who had urged her to encourage his attentions? Perhaps they'd say it didn't matter what a man did but it was the duty of women to stay above reproach. Adelaide felt sick. The thought of allying herself to another such man repulsed her.

As they drove into quieter areas her discomfort took a different turn and she prayed none of her aunt's acquaintances would see her riding in such a vehicle. She felt relieved when they arrived at St Mark's Church. From here it was only a minute's walk to The Crescent and, with good fortune, she'd be unobserved.

She felt in need of a period of quiet reflection and, instead of going straight to her aunt's house, she turned her steps towards the church. Her thoughts were troubled. They had smuggled Kemal to safety but what if they never discovered Miss Berry's killer or who was trying to harm Kemal? They could not keep him concealed forever and when he was captured his punishment would be harsh. Even if the English authorities did not hang him for murder, his own navy might execute him for desertion. Adelaide didn't know how the Turkish Navy punished deserters, and she preferred not to dwell on it.

Chapter 36

The church was empty. She was glad of that. It was a small, modest church, built six years ago. It had none of the magnificence of the great parish church of St Mary's in Alverstoke, but St Mark's reminded Adelaide of the village church near her childhood home and she felt comfortable there.

She took her usual place and knelt to pray, begging for Divine mercy and comfort for all those who were tangled in this web of suffering and sin. She prayed for Molly and Kemal; for Mrs Dorrington, Lady Dewsbury and young Tom; for the mother of the dead policeman and the families of the murdered nurses. She prayed for Hasan and Ahmet and then prayed that they and God would forgive her for petitioning a God who wasn't theirs. She prayed for her mother, whose lessons had proved so valuable today, and for her young brother, and her sisters because she was fond of them and hoped their experiences would be better than hers had been. And for Aunt Susan, who did not mean to be unkind. She didn't pray for her father. She did pray for Edwin Corfield. She wasn't sure why, except it seemed unkind and rather rude to leave him out.

Above all she prayed for Miss Berry, that justice was done and the truth revealed.

She had not heard the vicar enter the church but when she opened her eyes she saw him sitting patiently, as if he had been there for a long time.

"I'm sorry. I didn't realise you were waiting for me." She rose hastily.

"I did not wish to disturb your prayers."

"Thank you. Miss Berry was much in my thoughts and I find it a great comfort to come here and pray."

"So did she," said the vicar. "When she was troubled she came here every day."

Adelaide was conscious of the need to tread carefully. The vicar had spoken openly of Miss Berry using the church as her spiritual retreat but he would never willingly breach her confidence, still less betray the secrets of her soul.

"I have been praying that Miss Berry will receive justice and the truth about her death will be brought to light."

The vicar looked wary. "If it is God's Will I am sure the Truth will be revealed." His cautious tone confirmed Adelaide's suspicion that he knew more about Miss Berry than he thought it right to reveal.

"Sometimes God shows his will by giving those with knowledge the opportunity to speak out."

"I fear it would be a breach of my sacred trust to tell what passed between myself and my parishioner."

"I think it is God's Will," she said boldly. "That is why he brought us together in this holy place to speak of Miss Berry."

"A compelling argument. You would make a theologian, Lady Adelaide." Adelaide ignored the hint of humorous patronage in his voice. "I know Miss Berry was brooding about something that happened a long time in her past. It was a very private affair." She put slight emphasis on the last two words.

She saw the vicar relax. "If you know that, you know as much as I. All she told me was that she felt as if she had been speaking with the departed. She said it felt as though she had been in company with a ghost. I am glad the poor lady had a friend like you to confide in."

Adelaide felt guilty. She had not deliberately misled the vicar but she did not repudiate his assumption that Miss Berry had told her the secret of her youthful folly. This was as good as lying, and she had done so in the House of God.

The memory of Kemal's danger held her back from telling the truth. "One thing I must know or an innocent man may be put to death. Did Miss Berry ever indicate in any way the identity of the person who had reappeared from her past?"

He stared at her in frowning silence. The wait went on for so long she felt uncomfortable. At last he said, "It is growing late. Your good aunt will be distressed by your absence, unaccompanied and after dark. I will escort you home."

She accepted the unspoken rebuke meekly and rose obediently to her feet, but then, as if she received Guidance, a final question came into her mind. "One last thing, I beg of you. Can you recall when it was that Miss Berry spoke to you about seeing this person that brought back memories of her past?"

*

Before seeking out Kemal, Molly made a swift detour to her father's house, although she hoped Pa wouldn't yet be home. Grandmama always washed, mended and stored Pa's old clothes and those of the apprentice boys, so they could be reused. With luck she would find something suitable for Kemal to wear and certainly she would be able to take some food. If Kemal had to leave for good, Lady Adelaide's guineas would be needed and Molly planned to save them for that. It might never be safe for him to live openly. She pushed that thought away. There would be time to think about the future when she'd got him safely stowed.

Both yard and house were empty, apart from Pa's dog that guarded the premises. He was a fierce brute but he knew her and obeyed her command to keep quiet. In the garret she found a goodly store of her father's clothes, packed up with lavender to keep the moths at bay. They'd been abandoned a few years ago when middle age had started to take its toll and Pa had put on weight. Not that he was fat but he said a working man needed to be comfortable. The trousers would be too big for Kemal but with a belt and the ankles rolled they'd do tonight in the dark. She packed one bundle with clothes for him to wear now and another for her to take back to The Crescent to alter in the privacy of her room. If Kemal had to flee the town he'd need clothes that fitted properly so he didn't stand out from the crowd.

She pillaged the larder. Grandmama would be glad for her to take anything she needed and would cover its loss as soon as she got home. She wondered if Grandmama was still at the hospital. She prayed she was all right and they were still treating her with respect. By now they must have missed Kemal and she was sure that Mr Corfield would suspect who'd helped him disappear.

Her last job was to go to her own room and change into the simplest of the dresses she'd worn before Lady Adelaide took an interest in her. Staring at her reflection in her small looking glass she thought she looked ordinary and rather plain. Fine clothes did make a difference. She wondered if Kemal would still think she was beautiful when she was dressed like this, then told herself not to be a ninny. She wasn't trying to impress Kemal, she was trying to save his life.

On her way through the yard she saw one of the apprentices had left a small hammer lying on the ground. They'd be in trouble when Pa found out, carelessness with tools was something he couldn't abide. She felt sorry for the culprit but she picked it up and stowed it in her reticule. Its solid weight was comforting.

She'd arranged to meet Kemal in the garden near the docking place for the Floating Bridge. It was a place he knew how to get to and safe enough unless they'd missed him from the hospital and had started the hue and cry. She waited, her senses strained to breaking point. She felt a surge of relief when she saw him limping towards her, his hat veil down to conceal his face. He joined her, then, when the coast was clear, he ducked into the bushes. She passed him the clothes she'd brought with her and he passed her Grandmama's dress and bonnet, which she stowed in the marketing basket she'd brought for that purpose. It would take much sponging and pressing before Grandmama could wear them again. Molly resolved to do the job on her next day out.

The Floating Bridge was ready to depart. Molly felt an impulse to hand Kemal the guineas and tell him to catch it and get clear before word came from the hospital that a suspected felon had escaped. Once free of the Portsmouth docks he could disappear.

As he stepped clear of the bushes, she knew that was a foolish idea. He was staggering from weakness and clearly in pain. It would be all he could do to walk a mile to the warehouse.

They walked openly along the streets, although, in all but the darkest lanes, she kept her lantern shaded. Kemal staggered and she moved close beside him, draping his arm round her shoulders. If anyone glanced at them she met their eyes boldly. She was just a long-suffering young woman helping her husband home after he'd taken a drop too much. Her spirits rose. They were going to make it.

It was as if the thought cursed them. A burly man stepped into their path. "Now my fine fellow, I want a word with you."

Chapter 37

"What do you want?" Molly spoke sharply trying to conceal her fear.

The impertinent fellow ignored her. He stepped closer to Kemal, "Now you seem a likely looking lad. The sort that might be up for adventure."

Molly squeezed Kemal's arm to warn him to keep silent. "I don't know what you want but you can leave my man alone."

The man directed his words at Kemal. "Why don't you send your good woman home and come along to have a drink with me and I'll tell you what I've got in mind. My moniker's Jeremiah Crockshaw." He held out his hand.

Molly stared at the large, callused hand, proffered so insistently for Kemal to shake. Reason told her they should humour the fellow and slide tactfully away, but despite the smell of rum that hung about him, she didn't think he was drunk. Instinct overcame good sense. Through her reticule she gripped the handle of the hammer and cracked it down on the stranger's hand just before it made contact with Kemal's.

He yelped and swore at her. Onto the pavement tinkled a silver shilling.

The man raised his uninjured hand as if to strike her but Kemal gripped his arm. "You will not do that," he said. He released the man and pushed him away. "Molly, I do not understand?"

"He's part of the Press Gang," said Molly breathlessly. "He'd have put the Queen's shilling into your hand and called up the rest of his men to take you to the Fleet. They say they don't take men by force these days but they still need to keep up their numbers and I'd heard they'd taken to dirty tricks."

The man glared at her and nursed his hand but he spoke to Kemal, "You missed your chance. If you'd enlisted you'd have escaped that termagant. I wouldn't have your head tomorrow or your wife. She'll make you suffer." He turned and sloped off. From the way he walked Molly knew she'd been right, he wasn't drunk.

"Let's go," she said and led Kemal a cunning way down several twisting back alleys so she could be sure they weren't being pursued.

"Molly, thank you," he said quietly, "again you saved me."

"And you stopped him from hitting me, that paid me back."

By the flickering light of the lantern she saw him smile. "Dear Molly, you know that is not true." She smiled back at him, turned one last corner and said, "We're here."

Tom had told her he got into the warehouse by prising loose rotten boards and slithering through the gap but neither she nor Kemal were undersized workhouse waifs. With that in mind she'd taken the door key from its hook in the scullery. It seemed unlikely her father would notice its loss. He'd bought the old warehouse to get hold of the land and intended to pull down the derelict building and put up a new one when he felt the time was right.

Once inside the building she moved her lantern around cautiously, afraid its gleam might be seen through the missing boards. Her heart sank. It was cold, damp and draughty, not fit to house a stray dog, much less a sick man.

"It will suit me well." It seemed Kemal had read her thoughts.

"But it's so cold."

He smiled at her. "I am not so delicate. I have slept in many places worse than this. Now where is this room without holes that you spoke of?"

"Up here." She led him up the rickety wooden stairs to the upper floor. Part of it had been partitioned into a small room, not cosy but a lot better than the rest of the storehouse. "Oh good, Tom's left some blankets. I could only carry one." Tom's blankets were grubby and in one or two places so thin that they had worn into holes. Next to them stood two toy soldiers made of tin. They were chipped and battered but Molly knew they were Tom's pride and joy.

"He comes here a lot to play, this boy?" asked Kemal.

"I think he must do. The other apprentices can be a bit rough with him." When Molly had lived at home she'd made sure the horseplay had stopped short of bullying but she knew some of the other lads resented Tom because he'd come from the workhouse and she, the Master's daughter, had chosen him.

She laid out the blankets and made the small room as comfortable as she could. "If I see Tom when I sneak back to Pa's house I'll tell him to bring more blankets and a straw pallet out to you." She realised he was about to protest. "Tom will like to do it. He loves adventure. And no-one will see him. He moves like a shadow."

"Then he will make a good fighting man one day."

"Perhaps he will." She'd never considered that. "I'll leave you the lantern and there are candle stubs and a tinder box as well. Be careful not to set the place alight."

"It is so damp I do not think that it will easily burn."

"Then you'll be smoked like a herring instead."

"I do not need the lantern. You must take it. You must not walk through the streets alone in the dark."

"I can manage. It's not that late. It just feels like it because it's been such a long day. And you do need the lantern. There are rats in this warehouse."

"In that case I accept most willingly." He grinned at her. "I can fight people but of rats I am afraid."

She laughed with him, admiring the courage that could joke in such adversity, but the next moment his face grew serious. "What's wrong?" she asked.

"Molly, you think that poor, dead lady was my mother, do you not?"

She hesitated, choosing her words with care. "I think she may have been."

"I too think that it is possible and yet it seems an idea very strange." Molly waited patiently for him to put his thoughts into words. "It is true my sponsor spoke much of my father but rarely of my mother. I thought nothing of that. He was my father's friend. He told me what a great fighter he was, and how brave. But perhaps he did not speak of my mother because he knew that she was alive in England. That she had abandoned me and had denied her past."

"Does that make you angry?" She spoke softly, afraid to release the emotions he was labouring to control.

"It makes me sad. I have thought about this much in the past few days. I do not blame her for concealing her shame. For a woman to have a child without marriage is a terrible thing and I do not know the... the... things that were happening around her."

"The circumstances," suggested Molly.

"Yes. And I do not know what forces were put upon her to give me up. But I could have known her. Even now I am a man grown it would not have been too late. We could have talked together. She could have told me what she liked to do with her days. She could have told me about my father, not the soldier but the man. And I could have told her about my life and what my country is like now."

Molly searched for the right thing to say. "She liked to draw. There are sketchbooks full of her pictures. I think, when this is over, Lady Dewsbury would show them to you."

"I would like to see them." He spoke quietly but Molly could tell how much the offer meant to him.

*

Chapter 38

"Adelaide, where have you been? I have been most concerned about you."

Adelaide's hopes of slipping unnoticed into the house disappeared as her aunt bustled down the stairs to greet her. "I'm sorry. I didn't mean to worry you." She noted, with dismay, that her aunt was already dressed for dinner. It must be later than she'd realised.

"But where have you been?"

"I've just come from St Mark's Church, ma'am."

"Are you telling me you've been there the whole afternoon? You're not taking to religion are you? Your parents wouldn't like it if you became a nun."

Adelaide bit her lip, trying not to smile. "I have no thoughts of entering a convent."

"You may well be forced to if you parade yourself around the streets alone at night," snapped her aunt.

"I was not alone. The vicar was kind enough to escort me home."

"The vicar?" Aunt Susan's gaze sharpened. "I see. It wouldn't be a great match but you could do worse. I wonder I did not think of him before. Of course he is not a proper vicar, because St Mark's isn't a parish church, just a Chapel of Ease, but he's young and it's his first living and I understand from Mrs Boyle that he's got expectations. I suspect she's got her eye on him for her eldest girl. It doesn't do to be hasty. I'll consult with your parents and, if they approve, I'll invite him to dinner next week."

"Please do not do so on my account." She did not want any more suitors. Her aunt's promotion of Henry Russell's pretensions was enough to bear.

"Nonsense Adelaide. We must consider your future. Some churchmen can rise to eminence as great as any secular gentleman. Think of dear Reverend Wilberforce."

Adelaide did not point out that she'd never met the previous vicar of St Mary's, the Reverend Samuel Wilberforce, who had left the parish five years ago and was now the Bishop of Winchester. His admirers spoke of him as a great patron of education and an exceptional orator, his critics referred to him as 'Soapy Sam.'

"Now hurry and change out of that dreary black, Adelaide. I wish you to look your best tonight. Dr and Mrs Russell and Mr Henry Russell are dining with us."

"I had forgotten we were expecting guests." With her new found knowledge, Adelaide felt she could not bear to sit at table with Henry Russell tonight. She thought this was an appropriate time to develop a headache and dine in her room.

"Mr Corfield called to see you," said her aunt. "He wished to speak with you."

"Indeed? Did he tell you what he wished to say?" For a moment Adelaide felt sick with dread, then reason cut in. If Mr Corfield had spoken of her latest visit to the Naval Hospital, her aunt would have already taken her to task.

"No. He would not confide in me. I always find his manners rather evasive. However I invited him to dine with us."

"But you don't like him!" Astonishment caused Adelaide to forget discretion.

Aunt Susan looked affronted. "And what has that to do with anything, pray? When one moves in Society there are few of one's acquaintances one actually likes. Mr Corfield is a personable young man. His presence here may serve to encourage Mr Russell to pursue his suit. There is nothing like the hint of a rival to do that."

Adelaide stared at her in horror. There was no escape. She would have to dine downstairs. Mr Corfield knew far too much about her misdeeds in the past few days. She shuddered at the thought of the dreadful evening ahead of her.

"Make haste to change. Where is that impertinent maid of yours? Surely she was with you while you were out?"

"I sent her to the servants' entrance." Adelaide was shocked by how easily the lie fell from her lips.

"Well I'll need her to serve at table. Bradbury has just told me that my footman has contracted a chill and one of the maids as well. I told Bradbury to send them to bed, I won't have them coughing and spluttering over my guests."

Adelaide didn't argue. It would be good to have Molly in the dining room. If Mr Corfield's questions became too pressing, she could always drop a serving dish. Although knowing Molly she was more likely to upend it over him.

"I will inform her, ma'am, but first I need her to help me change." She hurried upstairs, praying that Molly would be waiting in her room.

Molly was not there, so Adelaide selected a gown in a soft shade of lavender that fastened with small pearl buttons at the front of the bodice. Then she put on the lightest touch of paint and powder, to add colour to her pale cheeks and lips. Such enhancements to one's appearance had to be discreet. Respectable women did not use such things, but this evening she'd need all the weapons in her armoury.

By now she was rehearsing excuses to her aunt to account for Molly's failure to wait at table. If she claimed Molly had also caught cold, she'd be found out in her lie as soon as Aunt Susan spoke with her housekeeper.

Now for her hair. She'd put that off, knowing she'd find it difficult to dress. She gazed in the mirror, hoping the daytime style would do. Perhaps if she placed a wreath of flowers cleverly enough no-one would notice the stray hairs that had escaped from confinement. She made several ineffectual attempts to position it and stared at her reflection in despair.

"Let me, m'lady." Molly entered and took in the situation at a glance. She dropped her wicker basket and cast off her cloak. As she unpinned Adelaide's hair her hands brushed against Adelaide's neck, their coldness made her shiver. "I'm sorry, m'lady. It's a bitter chill out there tonight."

"I'm glad you're back. My aunt informs me that the footman and a maid are both indisposed with colds and she wishes you to wait at table."

"That stands to reason. She wouldn't want them sneezing in the soup," said Molly briskly. "Don't worry, m'lady. I know how to wait at table. Grandmama has shown me what to do. I'll ask Mrs Bradbury to give me a suitable dress."

"I hadn't thought of that." Again Adelaide gave thanks for Molly's down-to-earth good sense. A lady's maid was allowed to look fashionable, especially one who accompanied her mistress around town, but a housemaid must wear a proper uniform. She took in Molly's drab clothes, donned to escort Kemal to his hiding place, and discovered a vein of practicality in herself. "I will tell Bradbury to send suitable garments to your room. If she saw you dressed like that she'd think it strange. Now can you tell me what you've been doing while you dress my hair? Have you got Kemal safely in hiding?"

"Yes m'lady." As she worked Molly described the measures she'd taken for Kemal's comfort and safety. "Grandmama had not come home when I was there so I don't know if they've noticed Kemal has escaped."

"I fear they have. Mr Corfield has been here wishing to speak to me but at that time I had not returned home."

"It's a good thing you avoided him, m'lady. He's too clever that one."

"Too clever to let me avoid him. He persuaded my aunt to invite him to dinner."

"Oh Lord!"

"And the entire Russell family is dining here as well," added Adelaide tragically.

"Well that's good isn't it? No disrespect, m'lady, but when Mrs Tate and Mrs Russell start talking there won't be room for a gentleman to get a word in however clever he is. Especially when Mr Henry Russell's there trying to gain your attention and the doctor's prosing on the way he does."

"That's true." The picture Molly painted made Adelaide smile.

"After I left Kemal, I went back to my father's yard and sneaked a word with Tom. He said he'd go and see Kemal later tonight and he'd nip back here to tell me how he fares. And he'll bring news of Grandmama. I want to know that she is safely home."

"How is Tom going to speak to you once the house has been locked up?"

"I thought if I kept watch from an upstairs window, I could creep down when I saw him and out the kitchen door. I know where Mrs Bradbury keeps her keys."

"Do you indeed? And what if she hears you?"

"I'll have to make sure she doesn't."

"But can you see the street from your attic room?"

"Not very well, m'lady. I was wondering... I'd sit ever so quiet."

Adelaide wondered how much deeper Molly intended to embroil her in this mess. "Very well, you can keep watch from here. But Molly I've got something to tell you. I returned to St Mark's and the vicar told me that Miss Berry often went to the church to pray. She'd spoken to him of encountering someone from her past."

"We know that, m'lady."

"But listen, Molly! The vicar told me Miss Berry first spoke of this on the last day of October. He remembers because he was preparing for the Feast of All Saints. That was before the Turkish ships docked. When she saw her ghost, Kemal had not arrived. And if he was not her ghost, surely he cannot be her child."

*

Chapter 39

Molly was happy to wait at table. She knew her grandmother had trained her well but she soon realised that the between maid and upstairs maid had little idea of how to present a meal and both girls were trembling with fear. Molly became the perfect servant, working hard to make the dinner party a success and winning approval from Cook and even a word of praise from Mrs Bradbury.

When the guests were assembled, Mrs Tate requested Dr Russell to escort her into the dining room, asking Mr Corfield to take in Mrs Russell and Mr Henry Russell to escort her niece. As they walked through, Molly saw Henry Russell pat her mistress' hand and noted Lady Adelaide's ill-concealed distaste.

Mrs Russell was wearing one of her better quality gowns but Molly thought that iron grey was an unfortunate choice for a woman of her age and complexion. In contrast Lady Adelaide looked beautiful in her soft lavender and Mrs Tate was elegant in dark blue silk. Dr Russell was dressed with his usual restraint but, to Molly's mind, his son looked ludicrous, wearing a brightly coloured waistcoat and one of the new style cravats that stuck out like a bow. It made him look as though a giant butterfly was trying to lift his head from his shoulders. Molly saw Mr Corfield regarding him and caught a glint of amusement although it was swiftly veiled. Mr Corfield himself had honoured the occasion with formal evening wear and was resplendent in a dark, long-tailed coat and trousers, high collared white shirt and white cravat and an elegant but restrained waistcoat of cream silk intricately embroidered with thread of a slightly darker shade.

At first the talk held little of interest. Over the oysters in a garlic and herb sauce Mrs Tate expressed relief that her cook had not yet succumbed to the illness that was laying low so many of her servants. During the cream of celery soup, she and Mrs Russell bemoaned how servants these days had ideas above their station in life. This topic continued to dominate during the consumption of the fillets of sole that formed the third course. The male Russells, father and son, looked bored, but Mr Corfield seemed interested. He enquired whether male servants were easier to come by now Britain was no longer at war and so many soldiers were seeking new employment. Mrs Russell declared that she employed no footmen, such servants were only for foolish people who wished to waste their money on vain show. Molly had to admire the skill with which Mr Corfield placated Mrs Tate, who was quite reasonably offended by this attack, while encouraging Mrs Russell to elaborate on the theme.

The main course was roast turkey, carrots in dill sauce, Potatoes Marie and Brussels sprouts in mustard sauce. Molly hoped the rumbling of her stomach could not be heard. There would be plenty of leftovers for the servants to eat in the kitchen but not for a long time yet.

Henry Russell took over the conversation to boast of a hunt he had attended in West Sussex. He was insistent that Lady Adelaide should turn out on the hunting field this year. He'd heard she was a capital horsewoman. If finding a mount were a problem, he had plenty of good friends who'd be delighted to oblige him by providing her with a suitable horse. His friends were eager to meet her. He'd been singing her praises and they longed to make the acquaintance of such a paragon.

Molly realised Mr Russell had arrived for his dinner engagement slightly drunk and was getting more foxed with every glass he took.

"Thank you sir, but I do not care for the exercise." Adelaide emphasised the snub by turning to Dr Russell to enquire after a young lady of her acquaintanceship who had been injured when a spark from the fire had set alight her skirts. Mrs Tate took up the theme, stating that all wise ladies kept green baize cloths on their pianofortes or tables in order to smother the flames if a dress caught fire.

As the meal progressed, Molly began to hope they would get through without incident. Then Mr Corfield turned to Lady Adelaide and said, "I was at Haslar Naval Hospital today."

Molly saw Lady Adelaide's hands clench convulsively on her cutlery, then deliberately relax. "Indeed sir. Did you have some interest there?"

He smiled and Molly wondered if he was baiting Lady Adelaide. "It was a matter involving that young Turkish seaman, the one you took an interest in."

"Interest?" Lady Adelaide's voice was wonderfully indifferent. "Only the interest any Christian woman would take in an unfortunate who is a stranger, injured and friendless in our land."

"A stranger maybe, injured certainly, but I think he has found good friends."

"Indeed you seem to take great interest in this unfortunate young man, Mr Corfield. Pray tell me what is your concern with him?"

"Why that of a Christian man concerned for a stranger who has met misfortune in our land." That would teach Lady Adelaide to spar with him, thought Molly ruefully.

"It's a fine hospital," said Dr Russell. "Saved hundreds of sailors and soldiers over the years."

"Yes," agreed Mr Corfield. "Although today was not their most shining hour. There were some unfortunate deaths from poisoning."

"Food poisoning eh?" said Dr Russell. "I trust they're sure it is that and not some contagion." He turned towards his wife. "We've had cholera sweep through this town before, haven't we my dear?"

"It was a most trying time," she agreed. "And even worse in London. I was constantly afraid that Henry would be struck down."

"I understand Bowman's grandmother nursed her neighbours throughout the contagion," said Mr Corfield, "and she still tends those less fortunate today. She seems a fine woman."

"Yes, a very fine woman." Dr Russell met his wife's glare and said hastily, "not the equal of my wife of course."

"Do you also go out to nurse the poor, Mrs Russell?" Lady Adelaide's voice was sweetly enquiring.

"I prefer to expend my energies doing God's work," snapped Mrs Russell.

"What work is that, ma'am?" Mr Corfield took up the probing.

"She spends many hours at the poorer parts of the town, teaching those who are on the path of sin and depravity to change their ways," said Dr Russell.

"A worthy task. Although one that is rarely successful," said Mr Corfield.

"No one has ever said the Lord's work was easy or without cost," declared Dr Russell. "But my good wife's work has prospered. She has taken children whose parents have died and brought them up, trained them as servants and taught them Godly values."

"My mother always likes to have a pet or two about the house," remarked Henry Russell, "like that idiot, Geoffrey, who's always underfoot."

"That, sir, is a most offensive remark. Apologise to your mother immediately," thundered Dr Russell. "Geoffrey is devoted to your mother. He's a loyal servant, despite his... limitations."

"Sorry mother." Henry raised his glass. "Drop too much wine you know."

Mr Corfield spoke into the simmering silence. "Bowman's grandmother was at the hospital today. I sent her safely home in my carriage." He didn't look at Molly but she felt sure his words were meant for her and felt a rush of relief and gratitude.

"That was kind of you," said Adelaide approvingly.

"Not at all. She's a remarkable woman. She was very active in saving the life of one of the victims of poisoning... a young Turkish sailor."

"She always was an interfering woman," said Mrs Russell. "Anyone of sense would have let him die and saved the hangman a job."

Chapter 40

"The hangman?" Mr Corfield raised an enquiring eyebrow. "You are labouring under a misapprehension, ma'am. The young man who nearly died from an excess of opium was not Kemal."

"Opium?" repeated Dr Russell. "How did that happen? Someone's been damned careless."

"So that young murderer is still alive?" exclaimed Mrs Russell.

"If you mean Kemal, he is to my best knowledge very much alive," said Mr Corfield, "but he's not at this moment proved a murderer. We still have the quaint custom of trial before we hang a man." He allowed a moment for these words to sink in. "Of course, his own government may wish to charge him with desertion."

"Desertion? You mean he's run off?" exclaimed Henry Russell.

"Possibly. I understand they are still searching for him on the hospital premises although I suspect he has managed to get away in some disguise."

"How resourceful of him," said Lady Adelaide.

"I don't know why you're talking about that Turk as if he's a hero," snarled Henry Russell. "He's a murdering savage who cut that woman's throat."

Molly's hands tightened on the serving dish and she contemplated the temptation of hurling it at his head.

Fortunately, before she could succumb, Mr Corfield spoke, his voice mocking, "Indeed? Do you have new information on this matter that the authorities would wish to share? Maybe you were in Gosport at that time? Perhaps visiting a friend?"

Henry Russell stared at him and turned red. He gulped and ran a finger around his collar, as if his fancy cravat has become too tight. "Me? In Gosport? Of course I wasn't. I don't know what you're getting at."

"And I wonder why you're so heated against this unfortunate young man," Mr Corfield remained languid, "when there is no evidence of his guilt."

Henry Russell glared at him, red-faced and belligerent. "What do you mean no evidence? What was he doing in the garden? That's the question. Everyone knows he was discovered where he had no business to be and his dagg…"

"Henry!" Mrs Russell broke in, her voice shrill and protesting.

"I don't know what you're complaining about, Mother. I'm not saying anything you haven't said yourself."

Molly's brain was reeling. Had Henry Russell really intended to say what she thought? She racked her brains for other words that began with dagg but found none. Surely she must be mistaken? How could Henry Russell know that Kemal's dagger had not remained in its sheath? Only she, Kemal and the killer knew that.

*

Adelaide thought this dinner party had turned into a different nightmare than the one she had expected.

Aunt Susan looked appalled at such behaviour at her civilised gathering but she spoke with quiet dignity, "I do not care for such subjects to be discussed at my table."

"My apologies, madam. The conversation seems to have grown a little heated." Mr Corfield smiled at his hostess and, to Adelaide's amazement, she smiled back.

Mrs Russell spoke in a quavering voice, "I'm sorry Susan, but I feel unwell. I regret breaking up your party but I must go home." She turned to her husband, "I would like to leave now."

"Of course, my dear." Dr Russell was already on his feet.

"Henry, I want you to come as well," pleaded Mrs Russell.

Her son looked as if he was about to protest but Mrs Tate said firmly, "Good evening, Mr Russell."

"Good evening." He spoke sulkily and walked towards the door. The care with which he moved emphasised how drunk he was.

At a signal from Mrs Tate, Molly sped into the hall to hold the guests' coats and hats. Mrs Tate and Adelaide followed their guests to bid them farewell.

As the front door closed behind them, Mrs Tate turned to Adelaide, "I apologise, my dear. You were right, that is a most unsuitable young man. I feel for his poor parents." She led the way back to the dining room. "Mr Corfield I apologise. I do hope you'll stay for the dessert courses, my cook prides herself on her fancy cakes."

He bowed to her. "Thank you, I would like to. I am very fond of sweet things." He looked at Adelaide with such mischief in his face that she blushed and found herself smiling back at him. At the same time she felt nervous. Now the sheltering presence of the Russell family had gone she was sure he'd tell Aunt Susan of her activities today.

Instead they talked of the plays that were currently popular in London and what interests in literature they shared. The conversation moved on to music and he spoke with knowledge and good taste.

"Do you play any instruments?" she asked.

"The pianoforte, a little," he admitted and moved swiftly on to describe the Great Exhibition that the Prince Consort had helped to guide into existence. It was to be held early the next year and he hoped Lady Adelaide would be able to attend. Adelaide discovered that she hoped so too, with an eagerness that surprised her.

He begged not to be left alone with his port and accompanied them into the drawing room. Adelaide's worries returned. Surely now he'd betray her to her aunt? She crossed to the pianoforte. "Would you play for us?" she asked.

His smile told her he'd seen through her request but he sat down and performed a set of sparkling waltzes. Then he turned to Adelaide. "Please, would you sing? I'd be honoured to accompany you."

Adelaide hesitated. She felt shy and her first instinct was to refuse but there was a small glimmer of excitement deep inside her.

"My dear, please sing *The Last Rose of Summer*," said Aunt Susan, "it was always a particular favourite of mine."

So Adelaide sang the old ballads she had learned in the schoolroom, and as she sang she felt like a young girl again. At her insistence Mr Corfield joined in and they sang duets. To Adelaide's amazement, Aunt Susan joined in with the choruses.

Adelaide thought how strange it was that, with all the trouble assailing them, she could spend the most delightful evening she had enjoyed for many years.

It was close to midnight when he rose to leave. "Mrs Tate, thank you for a delightful evening. I have long outstayed my welcome and I apologise."

"Not at all. It has been a pleasure." She rang the bell. After a minute she rang again, then frowned and ushered her guest into the hall. "Oh dear! I will fetch a servant to see you out. You must forgive the informality. My domestic staff is somewhat depleted." Clearly flustered, she hurried towards the kitchen, ignoring his protests that there was no need to summon a servant.

Adelaide had followed them out of the drawing room. He smiled at her. "I'm quite capable of putting on my own coat." He took it from the coat stand and demonstrated this ability.

Adelaide handed him his hat, gloves and stick.

"Thank you." He stood looking down at her, his face so grave that she felt quite alarmed. "Dear Adelaide, please believe that you can trust me."

Chapter 41

Adelaide felt an overwhelming desire to take him at his word. It would be good to have someone to advise her. But only a fool would trust a man simply because he asked her to. "That's easy to say, but you never trust me. You ask so many questions and never say what you are thinking."

He surveyed her thoughtfully. "What is it you wish to know?"

Her mind went blank. The only thing she could think to ask was an absurd irrelevance. "Why are you so interested in footmen?"

He looked surprised but after a moment he answered, "The day Miss Berry was discovered in the garden, I stayed out there after the doctor and Molly and Kemal had gone inside. Whilst I was waiting for the police officers to arrive I looked around the area near Miss Berry very carefully. It was growing lighter by that time and I found something, caught on a tree branch, as if someone had brushed against it in haste."

"What was it?"

"I found a few white hairs, curled and powdered as if pulled from a wig."

Adelaide stared at him, her mind in turmoil.

He smiled at her and continued. "Of course, yours is not the only bewigged and powdered footman in The Crescent, although his background is harder than most others to track down."

"Frederick has only been with us since October but I'm sure my aunt would have required good references." She spoke with more assurance than she felt. Aunt Susan did not always run her household wisely. For the first time since her husband's death,

Adelaide recognised inside herself a desire to manage her own household again.

"I trust so but I would prefer not to ask her directly about her footman. From me such an enquiry would appear odd but, if you would be so kind, you could discover his antecedents for me without occasioning comment."

Adelaide thought this explained Mr Corfield's sudden willingness to confide in her. She might have known he wished to use her in some way. "What have you discovered about his background?" She didn't see why all the information should go one way.

"Remarkably little. I know his name is Frederick Pearson and he is not by birth or upbringing a Hampshire man. That in itself is not suspicious, many householders prefer their servants to come from a distance, it can complicate things when they have local ties."

She wondered if he was teasing her about Molly and the turmoil she had caused, but she didn't rise to the bait. She was too horrified by the thought that Miss Berry's killer could be part of their household. She shivered.

"However, there could be a dozen innocent explanations for those strands of wig in the garden." Mr Corfield must have seen her fear. "And there's no reason to suppose it was your footman."

In a flash it came to her that, quite recently, she'd noted that Frederick's wig had been in disarray. Surely that was on the day Miss Berry's body was discovered?

He took her hand. "What is it Adelaide?"

She was about to tell him when the kitchen door opened and he hastily released her and stepped back. Aunt Susan bustled along the hall, followed by Molly, who was tying her apron. As she drew nearer,

Adelaide saw the red dampness of her hands and realised she must have been helping with the washing up.

"Mr Corfield, I apologise," said Aunt Susan. "I fear my household is in disarray. Even more of my servants are unwell. I must contact the Agency and get them to send through applicants for the post of butler and parlour maid immediately."

"It must be a difficult task to choose the right applicant," said Mr Corfield.

"It is indeed. Especially for a position of great trust."

Adelaide saw her chance and spoke swiftly, "Mr Corfield was complimenting you on your footman, ma'am. He said he had rarely seen a better turn out. Where was he last employed? I am sure it must have been in some great house?"

Her aunt looked gratified. "He was with Lady Haskell over in Dorset."

"Indeed? I am acquainted with Lady Haskell," said Adelaide. "I did not realise she was a friend of yours?"

"I have not met Lady Haskell, but she supplied excellent references for Frederick. He came to me through the local agency. I always employ, an excellent firm that…" She recalled herself. "But I do not know why we are discussing my servants. Such subject matter can be of no interest to Mr Corfield."

"On the contrary, ma'am. But I must take my leave now. Thank you for a most enjoyable and informative evening." His bow was nicely graded to take in both of them, but Adelaide was sure the words were meant for her.

*

Molly was so weary she could hardly stand. After the terror and exhaustion of the past days it had been hard work to wait at table and to clear up afterwards. To be fair, Mrs Tate had been horrified when she realised Molly was engaged in the menial task of washing dishes. Her status was equal to the housekeeper and the cook and they'd taken themselves off to their rooms before the clearing up began. But Molly had lived for many years in a household with just one young, all-purpose maid and she was used to turning her hand to whatever needed to be done.

At least the mundane tasks had given her time to think about what Henry Russell had said this evening. Or almost said. The word had been so swiftly cut off that she thought nobody else had picked up on it. Although she couldn't be sure about Mr Corfield, there was little he missed. Jeremy had said Henry was often in Gosport without his parents' knowledge but surely it couldn't be common gossip around the dock area that Kemal's dagger had been found beside the body? Perhaps she was mistaken about what Henry had intended to say.

The worst of it was that she couldn't tell Lady Adelaide she'd kept such an important part of the story from her. Fortunately, as she assisted her to undress, her mistress seemed preoccupied with discussing what Mr Corfield had told her about footmen to notice anything amiss. Molly had always considered Frederick a harmless, rather dull young man, and knew that the erstwhile butler had regarded him as adequate but not exceptional at his job. However, when she thought about it, he had seemed more nervous than usual in the past few days.

She reassured Lady Adelaide that the footman had been safely in his sickbed when she'd sent the hall boy to him to offer a hot drink. To her relief, Lady

Adelaide didn't ask her not to go out and meet Tom that night, although she did beg her to take care.

As she sat by Lady Adelaide's window Molly found herself drifting into sleep. She jerked awake. By the light of the single candle she'd set in the window she saw her mistress seated beside her, a warm woollen shawl wrapped over her nightdress. "Don't worry, Molly. I'll keep watch with you."

"Thank you, m'lady." Molly knew she should refuse this offer. It wasn't proper and Lady Adelaide had endured a gruelling day as well, but common sense told her that she could not keep awake and someone had to keep a sharp lookout. It was important to know all was well with Kemal and if Tom hung around outside these gentry houses for too long it was likely he'd be taken as a thief.

"Molly." Lady Adelaide's light touch on her arm summoned Molly from sleep. "I'm sure there's someone out there. I saw them in the shadows."

Molly leaned forward, watching and listening. "Tom would whistle. It's our signal."

"I can't hear anything."

"Nor can I. I don't think it can be him. Are you sure you saw someone, m'lady? Perhaps it was a trick of the darkness. Shadows are funny things."

"You may be right."

They sat in silence, staring into the darkness for some time, then a soft whistle echoed eerily through the still night.

"That's Tom." Molly started to her feet and signalled with the candle, to show she had heard. "I'll go down to meet him."

Lady Adelaide laid a restraining hand on her arm. "Give Tom this note and ask him to deliver it to Hasan."

"Hasan?" Surprise was followed by anger. How could Lady Adelaide think about her flirtation with Hasan when Kemal's life hung in the balance?

"I wish him to meet me tomorrow morning. He is the only person we can trust and he must wish, as we do, to help Kemal."

"Very well, m'lady. I must go down to Tom. It's not safe for him to be lingering outside the house."

"Do you really intend to steal Mrs Bradbury's keys?"

"I've already done so, m'lady. She went to her room quite early and I sneaked in and took them just after we'd finished washing the dishes. That way I could make some excuse if she woke up."

Molly didn't tell her mistress that even the most heavy-handed thief was unlikely to rouse the housekeeper. It was common knowledge amongst the servants that Mrs Bradbury was partial to a few glasses of wine when she retired to her room, but if it was brought to Lady Adelaide's attention she'd have to inform Mrs Tate. Molly didn't like Mrs Bradbury but she felt sorry for her. Being in domestic service for close on forty years must take its toll and to finish up the leftover wine after dinner was always considered part of the butler and housekeeper's rights.

"Don't worry, m'lady. The keys hang on a peg just inside her room and I'll slip them back easily enough when I've spoken with Tom."

She stole silently down the stairs and towards the kitchen but paused to listen outside the door of Frederick's room. He and the hall boy slept down here near to the kitchen, as did the butler, when the mistress had one. It was their duty to guard the silver plate and other household valuables, but the hall boy was a lazy lump and, once curled up in his cubbyhole, he was unlikely to rouse.

There was no sound from Frederick's room. She crept on until she reached the scullery door and bent to draw back the bolts. But it wasn't bolted. That startled her. Surely Mrs Bradbury could not have forgotten to secure the house? She turned the key, eased the door open and slipped quietly through.

"I'm here, Mistress." Tom appeared beside her, making her jump.

"Is all well, Tom?"

"Aye, nothin' to fret about. Your Grandmother is home and your sailor friend is lyin' snug and safe."

"Is he really all right? It's a cold, damp hole to house a sick man."

"He says he's slept in worse. He's a fightin' man. He's a fine fellow, isn't he? For all he's a foreigner."

Molly smiled. "Yes Tom. He's a very fine man. I've this note for you to deliver to Hasan, Kemal's officer friend on the Mirat-y Zafer. Take it first thing tomorrow and mind you don't get into trouble. Go home now. But when you next see Kemal tell him I will come to visit him soon."

"I will, Mistress."

"Thank you, Tom."

Back in the house she closed the door. For all her care, it creaked. She paused, listening intently, worried that Frederick might have heard and rise from his bed of sickness to investigate. Reassured by the silence of the house, she locked the door but did not bolt it. Better to leave it as she'd found it.

She slipped into the housekeeper's room and replaced the keys. They chinked together as she slid them onto the hook. It made her heart lurch but Mrs Bradbury didn't stir.

Back in the corridor she realised she hadn't removed her cloak. It would cause comment tomorrow morning if any of the servants noticed it wasn't on its hook in the passage outside the kitchen. Cursing her own stupidity she hurried to hang it up. As she reached up to do so she heard a telltale creak. It was the sound the kitchen door made when closing. It clicked shut. Paralysed by fear, she heard the key turn in the lock, then the bolts were dragged across. Before she could gather her startled wits and move, she heard footsteps drawing closer. She pushed back into the concealment of the servants' hanging cloaks and watched as a tall figure moved in her direction. Huddled in her flimsy hiding place she prayed that he'd go past.

*

Chapter 42

"But why would Frederick be sneaking back into the house at such an hour when he was believed to be sick in bed?" demanded Adelaide. Even in the privacy of The Crescent garden, deserted on such a cold morning, she kept her voice lowered.

"I don't know, m'lady. All I know is what happened. It was dark in the passage but he passed as close to me as you are now. If he hadn't been dazed with fever he'd have seen me." Molly shuddered.

Adelaide stared out across the bay. The terrace overlooked the coast and in summer it was a delightful walk. This morning the sky was sullen grey, the sea dark and tumultuous. They'd left the gate to the garden unlocked because Adelaide hoped Hasan would contrive to meet them there as she had asked.

"What would you have done if Frederick had seen you?" she asked.

"Screamed."

"You'd have roused the household?" Adelaide was appalled at the fuss that would have caused. It would probably have resulted in the dismissal of everyone concerned.

"It would have been worse for him than me. My cloak was hanging up in its right place, scarcely damp. And Mrs Bradbury's keys were back on their peg. No-one could prove I'd left the house. But his greatcoat was soaked and he still had the key to the kitchen door clutched in his hand."

"You considered that while you were hiding in the darkness? I'd have been too terrified to think."

"No, I thought of that afterwards. At the time I'd have screamed because I was afraid."

"But how did Frederick gain possession of a key to the kitchen door? At this time, Mrs Bradbury is the only servant with a key and you had hers. Surely he would not have dared go to my aunt's private parlour and steal it from her desk?"

"No, I think he's got his own. It's no great trick to nick a key and get another cut. That way he could get in and out of the house at night whenever he wished to." Adelaide was horrified to hear a wistful note in Molly's voice.

The more Adelaide considered the situation the more afraid she felt. Frederick, whom she'd always considered a quiet, inoffensive young man, could be the killer. There was no bolting the door against him. He was within their citadel. For the first time she fully realised that the rich and mighty had no real power; they were vulnerable to their servants.

"I wonder what Frederick does when he creeps out of the house at night?" said Molly.

"I presume he goes out to meet someone."

They stared at each other, the same thought in both their minds.

"You think he went to meet Miss Berry?" said Molly. "But that makes no sense. If he used to go out to meet Miss Berry, why venture out now she's dead?"

"I don't know," said Adelaide. "Do you think he could be Miss Berry's son?"

"He's about the right age," said Molly. "And he's swarthy enough. He could easily be foreign but the same could be said for a lot of men."

"He came to live here in mid-October, that's about the right sort of time. But, if so, surely he must have been in communication with her for several weeks? Why should he suddenly do such great harm to her?"

Molly shook her head. "How can we tell? Perhaps she rejected him again. Or she found out something bad about him and threatened to expose him."

"You told me she was not killed in the Garden. Where could a man in Frederick's position have committed such a violent deed and remain undetected?" She hoped Molly was not going to tell her that such a crime would be possible in her aunt's house.

"I don't know," said Molly helplessly.

Adelaide felt like screaming with frustration, but ladies must not make unseemly exhibitions of themselves. "We have no proof that Miss Berry's death has any connection with Miss Berry's child. Indeed it's only speculation that she had a child. Lady Dewsbury didn't really know. There could be a different reason for her death."

"But if that's so, we don't know what it is. We can't clear Kemal's name if we have no idea where to start."

Adelaide knew the time had come that she'd been dreading. She had to go to Lady Dewsbury and confess the theft and loss of Miss Berry's letters. "Lady Dewsbury asked me to call upon her today. Let us return to the house now." It was past the time she'd asked Hasan to meet her and it seemed probable that he could not come.

As they retraced their steps a scruffy figure approached them stealthily.

"Tom!" exclaimed Molly. "What are you doing here? Is something amiss?"

"Nothing's wrong, Mistress. I brought this letter for her ladyship. It's from the Turkish sailor. Not Kemal. The one that looks at you like you're a smell that's got up his nose."

Even Adelaide had no difficulty in relating this description to Hasan. Somewhat affronted, she held out her hand and accepted the note.

My Pearl,
I regret I cannot comply with your request and come to your aid. For you I would attempt any endeavour, but I will not aid the man of whom you speak. He has betrayed his country and his comrades. His desertion is a disgrace. If I discover his whereabouts I will do my duty and inform my Captain, so that he may be taken and brought to justice.
I remain eternally your devoted servant,
H.

Adelaide read the note and reread it. She felt numb. She became aware of Molly's anxious gaze and handed her the note then realised she could not read French. She translated it, aware that her voice sounded cold and remote.

"Playing it careful, isn't he?" said Molly scornfully. "Not even mentioned any names."

"Yes." It confirmed what Adelaide had feared deep in her heart. For all his protestations of devotion, Hasan would always look out for his own interests.

As they left the Garden a post chaise drew up outside the Anglesey Hotel and Mr Corfield climbed down. He looked stiff and weary.

"Good morning, Lady Adelaide. It's a cold day for a walk."

"And a cold day for travelling," she replied. "Have you journeyed some distance?"

"I fear that's obvious from my appearance, ma'am." His smile acknowledged her riposte. "I have journeyed into Dorset to visit a mutual acquaintance."

She could guess which mutual acquaintance he meant but she was surprised that he'd undertaken such a gruelling journey to check on her aunt's footman. "You have travelled through the night? In this cruel weather?"

He smiled. "I was fortunate to hire a particularly hardy set of postboys."

"You must be very tired."

"A trifle, but it seemed necessary. I had reason to think my errand was urgent. Kemal could be retaken at any time."

She wished to ask why he took such an interest in Kemal. What importance could a young Turkish sailor without wealth or connections have for him? But she was sure he would not answer and the question of Frederick's integrity was vital to the welfare of her aunt's household. "Did Lady Haskell tell you anything about Frederick?"

"Lady Haskell was away from home, which was perhaps a fortunate circumstance. A kind lady but inclined to gossip. Her butler answered my questions without enquiring why I was asking them."

"Yes?" she prompted him.

"He told me that Frederick Pearson had been an excellent footman and a young man of impeccable background and character." He paused, and Adelaide realised he was delaying for effect. It was the first time she had ever known Edwin Corfield to show off. "He died last March. I went to the churchyard and visited his grave."

*

Chapter 43

Molly stood at the end of the passage that led to Frederick's room. Her mouth felt dry, her heart was beating fast. Standing beside her, Lady Adelaide looked equally anxious. She spoke quietly but with great urgency, "This is not wise, Molly. I should have told Mr Corfield about Frederick. I don't know why I didn't speak out but it's not too late. I can send for him and tell him what we know."

"No, m'lady. Please, don't tell Mr Corfield... not yet. We still don't know what his game is. There's a chance that Frederick had no connection with Miss Berry and I've got more hope of getting him to open his budget than Mr Corfield has."

Lady Adelaide looked doubtful. "How can he be innocent when he came here under a false identity? Don't argue, Molly. As soon as my aunt returns, I must tell her what Mr Corfield has discovered. It's my duty to do so and if I do not I am sure Mr Corfield will."

Molly thought, if she'd been Lady Adelaide, she'd have kept quiet and let Mr Corfield bear the brunt of the mistress' wrath. It stood to reason she'd be angry. She'd devoted her morning to arranging for the employment of a new butler and parlour maid and would be outraged, on her return, to learn that her footman was a fraud.

"I'll go and speak to him now," she said, determined to act before she lost the chance. Kind mistress though she was, Lady Adelaide could never comprehend the depth of the gulf between the Drawing Room and the Servants' Hall. Once accused of wrongdoing by the nobs, Molly was certain Frederick would close up like a clam.

"Cook has prepared some broth for the invalids, m'lady." The thought of healing broth made her recall Ahmet and Kemal. "I've just remembered something. The poisoned broth that nearly killed Ahmet, there was no way Frederick could have taken that to the hospital, he was here all day."

"I thought of that," said Lady Adelaide. "Mr Corfield didn't tell me much but I gather he thinks Frederick may be part of a much larger conspiracy."

"Suspicious cove, isn't he?" commented Molly. Showing disrespect to her betters helped to boost her courage. "I'd better go and see how Frederick's faring. The hall boy said he's in a poor way this morning."

"That's hardly surprising, considering he was out in the cold last night," retorted Lady Adelaide. "I will stay nearby. If you need me you must scream."

"No, please m'lady. You lingering in the basement would cause the servants to talk, those that are still on their feet. I'll keep my distance and he won't harm me in the house."

Molly spoke with more courage than she felt. As she entered Frederick's room she could not shake off the fear she'd felt last night.

"I've brought you some broth," she said. "And some hot ale with healing herbs. It's what my Grandmama gives people when they're laid low like you."

"Thank you." His voice was hoarse and croaky and the hand he held out to take the tankard was shaking.

"Here I'd better help you." She forgot her promise to keep her distance and approached the bed to steady the tankard. "If you spill this on the bedclothes, I'll be in trouble with the laundry maid as well as with Cook. She's rare put about because I used one of her pans to heat the ale."

Her deliberate informality had the desired effect. He smiled at her, although it was a feeble effort. "Thank you. You're very kind."

She felt a fleeting pang of guilt. She was not being kind, she was manipulative and sly, lulling her prey into a sense of false security. But if Frederick wasn't a killer, it would be better for him if she found out the truth. Of course, his name wasn't really Frederick Pearson. She wondered what he was truly called.

"I saw you last night. What were you up to?"

He stared at her, his face stricken. "I don't know what you mean."

"I saw you," she repeated. "It's no good lying. Your coat's still crumpled in the corner, dripping wet, and so is the lantern you used. And if the mistress orders a search through your possessions they'll find the key you stole to sneak out at night."

"You've told her?"

"Not yet."

"You mustn't! I won't let you!" He struggled upright and grasped her arm. His grip was cruel and she knew she had no hope of breaking free.

"Let go of me." Molly managed to sound calm although she was desperately afraid. "I've left a note for my mistress. If you try to silence me she'll know who to blame."

"Silence you?" He released her arm. "I wouldn't. I didn't mean to hurt you. I'm sorry. Please, don't tell. I mustn't lose my place."

He sounded young and bewildered. Molly found it hard to believe he was the killer they were seeking. She thought he might lash out in fear and panic but, if he had harmed Miss Berry, he seemed incapable of the devious, ruthless planning necessary to implicate Kemal.

"What do you do when you sneak out?" she asked.

He didn't answer and he wouldn't meet her eyes.

Cautiously she drew nearer to the bed. "You're in serious trouble. People have been looking into your past. They know you're not Frederick Pearson, he's dead and buried these past ten months. So who are you and what's your game?"

To her dismay, he put his hands over his face and sobbed.

"Stop that!" she commanded. "It won't do you any good and if the other servants hear it'll be all up with you. Where do you keep your handkerchiefs?"

"Top drawer," he mumbled.

She went to his cupboard and found a large, coarse handkerchief, poor quality for an Upper Servant like Frederick. "Here you are. Dry your eyes and blow your nose."

The brisk nursery tone was effective. He obeyed and, after a few moments, lay back on his pillows, gazing up at her, still sniffing and shaking but more or less in control.

"Who are you?" she asked.

"Frederick Pearson."

"Don't give me that slum, Frederick Pearson's dead."

"Frederick John Pearson's dead. I'm his cousin, Frederick Robert Pearson. We were both named for our grandfather, but in the family we always called him John."

"And it was your cousin who was footman to Lady Haskell?"

He nodded miserably. "We always thought John would be the one who made his way in the world. He got good places with wealthy families. Even when Lady Haskell let him go because she was travelling abroad she asked him to come back to her when she returned."

"Is that why she gave John a reference? So he'd get work while she was abroad? I wondered about that." Molly thought it was like putting together a segmented map, every piece made sense when it was put in the right place. "I thought you must have forged them."

He shook his head. "No. John kept them even when he went back to Lady Haskell. He was proud of all the good things they said about him."

"What about you? You trained as a footman too, that's plain to see." He'd not have been able to bluff for two days, much less two months, if he hadn't known the basics of his job.

"Not as big houses. Not as good families. Never as good as my big cousin." He sounded sad rather than bitter.

"Is that why you decided to take his place?"

"No!" He looked shocked at the idea. "I did it because I had to. I got into trouble and I lost my place and had no chance of getting another one."

"What did you do?"

"I got a girl into trouble."

"Oh I see."

He must have seen disapproval in her face. "It wasn't like you think. Kitty was the only girl I've ever looked at in that way."

"What happened to her?"

"She was the between maid for the family where I worked. They dismissed us both when they discovered Kitty's state. I married Kitty but both our families said we'd shamed them. Kitty's got a great aunt who lives in Gosport who said she could stay with her, as long as she worked hard to earn her keep. So we moved here, where nobody knew what we'd done, but without a good reference I couldn't get a place. And all the time John's were burning a hole in my valise."

"Why did you keep them?" Molly suspected their continued possession made him less innocent than he was pretending to be.

"John was so mortal proud of them. I couldn't throw them away like they was rubbish. I didn't think I'd get away with it. I'm only twenty, six years younger than John. He was always my hero. I don't know what he'd think of me making use of his references like I did."

"I'm sure he'd understand." Molly felt sorry for him.

"I hope so. He was a good man, was John but always a stickler for doing the proper thing. His father was a butler, mine was just under-gardener."

"Is that where you go at night? You creep out to visit Kitty?"

"I have to. She's so lonely and her spirits get so low. She's only sixteen and the baby is frail. Kitty frets we won't rear her but I tell her God wouldn't be so cruel as to take her from us."

"What's the baby's name?" Molly warmed to him. There was no doubt he loved his child and his young wife.

"Rosie."

"If you tell me where they live I could ask my Grandmama to call on them. She's good at healing and helping babes to thrive."

He stared at her. "You'd do that for me?"

"Of course I would."

"Thank you. I'd be grateful and so would Kitty."

Molly resolved, if she could, she'd rescue Frederick and his family from the trouble that Fate and their own folly had landed them in.

"I don't know what will become of us if I get turned off... or worse."

Molly thought if she could call the tune she'd keep his secret, but she wasn't paying the fiddler. Lady Adelaide and Mr Corfield knew about Frederick's deception and gentry often didn't look at things like sensible folk who had to work to live.

"Frederick, a few nights ago, around the time poor Miss Berry died, you were in the garden weren't you?"

That took him by surprise. He stared up at her, eyes dilated, face grey, and gasped, "I didn't do it! It was nothing to do with me!"

Chapter 44

Frederick cowered back against the bed. Molly felt sorry for him but pity wasn't going to prevent her from discovering what he knew. "But you saw something, didn't you? A scrap of your wig was found in the garden. What were you doing there? Surely you didn't meet Kitty there, in the cold and dark?"

"You won't tell?"

"Not unless I have to in order to save an innocent man's life," promised Molly.

His expression made it clear that he did not think this was a sufficient guarantee but she looked at him steadily until he admitted, "Sometimes Kitty comes here to visit me in my room."

"Really?" Molly felt astonished admiration. When it came to breaking rules Frederick was far more adventurous than she was.

"She doesn't do it often but there's not much risk since Mr Aiken left. Kitty's great-aunt looks after Rosie for her."

"And Kitty had been here with you that night?"

He nodded. "I was taking her home and we'd just left the house when I heard someone coming. The garden gate was open, so I took her in there to hide."

"What time was that?"

"Just after two in the morning."

"What happened next?" Molly leaned forward eagerly. "Tell me what you saw."

Frederick shook his head. "I didn't see anything. I kept my head down and told Kitty to do the same."

"You know something." Molly spoke firmly. "It would be better to tell me."

He looked at her fearfully. "Someone came through the gate and along the path. I'd been hiding with Kitty in the shelter of a tree but then I took her away behind the Bath House and lifted her over the railings and climbed out of the garden after her."

"What did this person who came through the gate look like?"

He shook his head. "I couldn't see."

Molly wondered if Frederick was telling the truth. A man in his position might find it wiser to look the other way.

"I heard something."

Molly's heart leapt. Had he heard a voice? Or even better a name?

"It's nothing much." Frederick spoke apologetically. "It was the sound of wheels, a barrow or something dragging along the path."

"Oh I see." Molly struggled to conceal her disappointment. She stood up. "I'll do my best for you, Frederick, but, before I leave, you'd better give me that key."

As she left him she was aware of disappointment and felt ashamed. She'd hoped Frederick was the killer because the nobs would accept his guilt. It would be far harder to prove anything against Mr Henry Russell. The more she thought about it, the more convinced she was that he'd been about to refer to Kemal's dagger being left beside Miss Berry's corpse. She tried to think of a way of trapping him that would not endanger herself or Kemal. Without confessing to Lady Adelaide and begging for her help it seemed a hopeless task.

*

When they arrived at Lady Dewsbury's house, Adelaide instructed Molly to wait in the entrance hall. She'd rather go through the ordeal of confession alone.

Her heart sank when she found Admiral Daley sitting with her hostess. She had great regard for the admiral but if she did not tell the truth now she feared she never would. Years of rigorous training came to her aid and she listened with well-feigned interest to the old sailor's anecdotes. Within minutes the Admiral rose to leave. "I promised to drop in on Russell."

"Is Dr Russell a particular friend of yours?" said Adelaide, gently fishing.

"I wouldn't say he's a particular friend but he's an old one. I first met him over twenty years ago. At that time he was fond of travelling. Used to be a dashing fellow, though you'd never know it now. Poor devil, he lives under the cat's foot sure enough."

Lady Dewsbury cackled with laughter, "Dreadful woman."

Adelaide said nothing, she felt like a governess in charge of two outspoken children, but she could not deny the truth of what they'd said.

As soon as the Admiral departed she took the plunge. "Please Lady Dewsbury, I've got something very important to tell you."

"Dear me, that does sound serious. Tell me what's wrong."

After a halting start the story was easier to tell than Adelaide had expected. Despite her embarrassment, she took pains to make it clear she'd condoned Molly's behaviour and the responsibility was hers.

When she came to a halt Lady Dewsbury was looking grave but her first words were reassuring, "You poor child, you must have found that story very hard to tell."

Adelaide bowed her head, unable to meet her eyes.

"I am sorry Ellen's letters have been lost and pray they do not resurface in a manner that causes harm to my poor friend's reputation, but the blame is as much mine as it is yours or Molly Bowman's."

"How can that be?" Astonishment made Adelaide to look up.

"I knew that Molly was the sort of girl who'd rummage until she reached the truth. I sent her up to Ellen's room in the full knowledge that she would search for any enlightenment she could find. I wished her to discover the truth, but your involvement surprised me."

Adelaide blushed. "I know such behaviour is unladylike."

"Fiddle faddle! Every gentlewoman should uphold the search for Justice. You are a woman of character, my dear."

"Thank you. I don't much feel like a woman of character. It's so hard when one does not know whom to trust."

"Trust yourself," came the prompt reply, "and you can trust young Molly and her grandmother. And I will give you any support I can."

"Mr Corfield asked me to trust him."

Lady Dewsbury looked doubtful. "He's a clever man, too deep for me to see through. If his heart's as good as his head he'd make a fine ally, but I cannot be sure."

That settled it. Adelaide decided not to tell Mr Corfield about Frederick's explanation until she felt sure it was wise.

Lady Dewsbury said gravely, "Adelaide, I have a commission for you."

"Of course, ma'am, anything I can do."

"I wish you to take Ellen's sketch books and look through them. I am haunted by the conviction that they hold the truth of poor Ellen's past."

"Willingly, if you trust me to do so, ma'am."

"Of course I trust you, you foolish child. The only person I would trust for such a task. I will instruct my footman to carry them to your residence."

"I will accompany him, ma'am." She would not allow the books to leave her sight.

Ten minutes later, as she and Molly walked ahead of the laden footman along the street, Adelaide saw a familiar figure. Hasan had abandoned subterfuge and came to meet her, arrogantly certain of his welcome. "My Pearl."

"I have nothing to say to you, sir." French could sound romantic but it was also a good language for anger and contempt.

"You are enraged?" He sounded surprised. "But you must understand, I spoke out of duty."

"Surely you have a duty to aid your comrade, sir?"

He made a dismissive gesture. "I meant my duty to you. I wished to save your reputation. You are not always wise."

Anger blazed through her. "You have no duty to protect me, sir. What is more, you have no right. Excuse me, I have no time or desire to speak with you." She walked into the house, her head held high, leaving him gaping after her.

"Well done, m'lady," said Molly.

Adelaide stared at her. "But you cannot speak French."

"I don't need to." Molly giggled. "His face said everything."

Chapter 45

It was past midnight when Molly presented herself in Adelaide's room. "I'm ready, m'lady, I'll be off now."

Adelaide felt concerned. She and Molly had both rested that afternoon, but Molly still looked pale and subdued. Adelaide hoped it was just the effect of the plain, dark dress she was wearing, which she had brought from her home the other night. She felt sure Molly had something on her mind, something that she was unwilling to confide.

Molly moved swiftly across the room, her stride much longer than it usually was. "It's strange. I never thought I'd get used to frills and stiff petticoats but now it feels odd without them."

"I wish you didn't have to go tonight, Molly." Adelaide's bedchamber was warm, with a cheery fire burning in the grate, a bitter contrast to the tumultuous, blackness of the outside world. "Stay here and tomorrow we'll find a way to visit Kemal by daylight."

"I'm sorry, m'lady, but I must go. I've got to see Kemal. Tom slipped by to tell me he's getting restless. It stands to reason. He's bound to fret lying there alone in the dark. If he tries to leave before he's fully fit he's going to get caught."

"If Tom's not careful, your father will find out what he's up to and turn him off."

"Tom is careful and Grandmama wouldn't let Pa turn him off, not when he's serving me. Anyway Pa's away for the night. He's over to Southampton on business."

"But aren't you afraid to go out alone, Molly?"

"Not as much as I used to be, I'm getting quite used to being out after dark. At least I don't have to creep into Mrs Bradbury's room and steal her key. I made Frederick turn his over to me."

"Was that wise?" protested Adelaide.

Molly smiled. "I didn't let on I was planning to use it. I told him I was taking it to stop him falling into temptation to sneak out again. I said it was for his own good."

Adelaide drew back from discussing Frederick. She had not yet told her aunt about the footman's deception. Molly had urged her to forgive and forget and pretend she'd never known but Adelaide had been the mistress of her own household and this felt wrong. "Do you plan to take with you the clothes you altered for Kemal?"

"Not tonight, m'lady. It might encourage him to try and leave."

"Put them out of sight in a drawer then." Better to conceal them in her room than in Molly's, in case any of Molly's fellow servants tried to pry.

Molly obeyed her, then moved towards the door. "Goodnight, m'lady."

"There's no need to bid me goodnight. When you return, I want you to come and tell me you're safely home. I will not be asleep. I too have an investigation to pursue."

After Molly left, Adelaide lit the working candles Molly used to sew by. She sat at the table and opened the first of Miss Berry's sketchbooks. She turned the pages, scanning the images, but part of her mind kept worrying at her numerous concerns. There were so many complications in her life: Edwin Corfield, Hasan, Henry Russell... at least Aunt Susan no longer wished to promote his interests. Then there was Frederick; despite Molly's cajoling she had a duty to her aunt. Above all there was Molly, risking so much to save

Kemal. And Kemal himself, courageous and civilised, a stranger in a strange land.

What was she searching for in these sketchbooks? Poor Lady Dewsbury was clutching at straws. Nevertheless she kept on looking.

She was on the fourth book and felt no sense of foreknowledge when she focused on a sharp, exquisitely drawn image and stared in disbelief.

*

What Molly had said to her mistress wasn't true. She had grown more accustomed to being out alone after dark but it still scared her. All the way from The Crescent she felt as if someone was following her. Twice she stopped, listening intently. She thought she heard stealthy footsteps that halted a few moments after her own, but she could not be sure. She called herself a nervous ninny and sped on.

As she approached the derelict warehouse her fear deepened. The dark building looked so grim. She caught a glimpse of a lurking figure. Relief washed through her. She whistled softly and Tom sidled out of the shadows and approached. Irritation mingled with her relief. He must have waited in The Crescent and followed to watch over her, but did he have to terrify her whilst protecting her?

"What are you doing here, Tom?" She spoke in a whisper, although her tone was sharp. They were too near Kemal's hiding place for her to risk raising her voice.

He looked surprised. "Nothing bad, Mistress. I was having a yarn with Kemal. I brought him a meat pie and some ale like your Grandmother told me to. Then I stayed to talk. There's no harm in it. Your Grandmother said I could. It helps to pass the time for him and I like to hear his tales."

"Then you didn't follow me from The Crescent?"

"No mistress." He looked anxious. "Should I have done so?"

"No. I thought I heard something." She disliked the knowledge her nerves had played her false.

"You're bound to get frightened, out here alone in the dark. It's not fittin' for a young lady. Don't worry, while you're talking with Kemal, I'll slip back and tell the Mistress all is well and then I'll come back and wait and see you safely home."

The way he spoke made her feel like he was a man and she was a mere child. Annoyance tempted her to reject his escort, but that would be folly. "Thank you, Tom. Give my Grandmama my love."

The door to the warehouse was unlocked, but that made little difference; the structure was so flimsy it would not keep out any marauder. Gingerly she pushed the door open, entered the building and made her way up the stairs. They creaked and shuddered. If Pa didn't demolish this building soon it would fall down by itself.

As she entered his hideaway it was clear that Kemal had heard her coming. Raised on his elbow he was staring anxiously at the door. "Molly? What are you doing here so late? It is not safe for you. Is something wrong?"

"I wanted to see you." She moved to kneel beside him and rested her hand on his forehead. "You're feverish."

"It is nothing, by tomorrow I will be well. But you must not stay here."

"I'll go quite soon but please let me stay and talk for a while. Lady Adelaide sent you a bottle of wine." She took the bottle and two glasses out of her basket and poured. She wasn't sure she really took to this foreign wine. It hadn't got the sweetness or warmth of her grandmother's blackberry cordial but she needed something to give her courage to talk to Kemal.

She sat down beside him on the narrow pallet and huddled close to him for warmth. She told him about what Lady Adelaide had discovered from the vicar of St Mark's, which made it improbable that Miss Berry had been his mother.

When she finished he was silent for a long while.

"Kemal?"

"It is strange. I had told myself she was my mother. I know now it was never true, but all the same I feel... bereaved."

"I'm sorry."

"It does not matter. Nothing has really changed." He forced a smile. "I wish that it would prove my innocence but your police will not care about such things. Tell me, what else has been happening?"

Glad to change the subject, she told him of her suspicions regarding Henry Russell and how hard they'd be to prove.

Kemal looked solemn. "Promise me you will not challenge this man alone?"

"I promise." That would be foolish rather than brave.

"There's something else." She told him about Frederick's deception and what he'd heard on the night of Miss Berry's death.

"A barrow," he said thoughtfully "that is strange."

"Why?" asked Molly.

He stared past her into the middle-distance as he struggled to think back. "It was in the street, after I was struck down. I was dizzy but as I raised myself I saw some tracks. They had cut through the ice that coated the ground. But it was too narrow, I think, even for a hand-cart. They were like this." He reached out and drew lines in the dust beside the bed.

Molly frowned as she looked at them, her own memory stirring. "I've seen prints like that, quite recently. But it wasn't outside the garden, it was at Miss Berry's funeral. It was..."

"You always were a meddling girl."

They had not heard the newcomer's approach and both turned to stare at the figure in the doorway, holding a pistol and levelling it straight at them.

*

Chapter 46

Adelaide sat staring at the sketch. After all their speculation, the answer was so simple, almost too simple. The man in the picture was heavy featured, with hooded eyes and a wide, sensual mouth. He was the image of Henry Russell but she knew she was looking at a picture of Miss Berry's lover; the man she called Habib. No wonder, when she first encountered Henry, Miss Berry thought she had seen a ghost.

A sharp rustling noise made Adelaide jump. It came again and she realised it was caused by small pebbles being thrown against her window. She abandoned the final sketchbook, stood up and looked into the darkness. She could see a slight figure but she did not know who it was. He bent to gather another handful of stones. The movement brought him under the street light and she recognised Tom. She opened her window and hissed, "Go round to the back of the house. I'll come down."

She took the door key from her aunt's desk and met him at the back step, gesturing him to move with her some distance from the house so that they could speak without rousing any of the sleeping household.

"What's wrong?"

"It's Mistress Molly. She's in trouble."

"Tell me."

"She went into the old warehouse... the place we stowed Kemal... and I was just goin' to leg it to tell the Mistress what was goin' on when I looked back and saw some other cove wanderin' round outside the warehouses. And he was carryin' a barker and was all covered up in a black cloak so I couldn't see who he was. I think he was lookin' for the warehouse where Kemal's hid. I should have tackled him. He weren't that big a cove. But I was worried if he let loose with that barker folk 'ud come runnin' and then they'd find Kemal. I didn't know who to tell. Master's away for the night and the other lads won't turn out for the likes of me. And the Mistress is an old lady for all she's full of rumgumption. I know the yard where the bone-setter leaves his nag so I prigged it and came to you."

Adelaide stared at him in dismay. "But what can we do? By the time we've summoned help it will be too late."

Tom looked stubborn. "We gotta try."

"Of course we have." Adelaide thought rapidly. "Wait here a moment Tom." She fled upstairs to her bedroom and rummaged in her bureau drawer taking out all the ready money she possessed. She ran down again and handed it to Tom. "Find me a vehicle. Be as fast as you can."

"The nag's outside, tied to the garden railings."

"I can only ride side-saddle, Tom. Get anything, any cart will do. Meet me in the street. I won't be long."

He ran to do her bidding. She returned to her bedchamber. Molly was right, petticoats were too hampering and she had no riding dress with her. She remembered the bundle of clothes Molly had intended for Kemal. She put them on although she wore her own ankle boots. Even on the tightest notch the belt was too loose for her, so she secured the trousers with a silk scarf knotted through the loops. She bundled her hair under a cloth cap and gave one startled look at the stranger reflected in the mirror. These clothes felt very odd but she could understand why men had so much more adventure in their lives.

She went to the sketchbook that contained the picture she'd recognised and tore it out. She ran down the stairs and stepped into the darkness.

Fortune was with them. Despite the late hour, Tom had hailed a hansom cab that had just delivered some visitors to the Anglesey Hotel.

"He'll take us right back into the town, Madam," he said proudly. "He says the guards on the gates know him and they'll let him through."

"That's excellent, Tom. Now give the driver directions to the warehouse."

"But I'm comin' with you. I can tell him the way."

"No, Tom. I need you to run an errand for me. You must run back to the hotel. Here's my visiting card. You are to speak to Mr Edwin Corfield in person. Tell him what has happened and give him this picture." There was no time left to wonder whom to trust but her instincts told her this was right. "I don't care how you do it but you must see him."

"I'll do it if I have to mill the ken," he promised and set off, a small, disreputable figure about to storm the most exclusive hotel in the town.

Harried by fear, Adelaide found the journey interminable, even though the hansom cab rattled along at a good pace. It was only after Tom had left that she wondered what he'd do if Mr Corfield were not at the hotel.

*

"Mrs Russell!" Molly found it hard to drag her eyes from the weapon that was levelled straight at her. "Don't be so foolish! You know you wouldn't dare to use that gun. There'd be someone near who'd hear and run for help."

Mrs Russell smiled grimly. "If you think I wouldn't shoot you, you're a bigger fool than I took you for."

Molly spoke even louder, "I left a note for my mistress. I've told her everything." She could only pray that Tom had returned. The walls of the warehouse were flimsy and Tom's ears were sharp.

"Indeed?" The steel blue eyes assessed her. "I wonder, are you telling me the truth?"

"Of course I am."

"How much did you tell her?"

"Enough," bluffed Molly.

"In that case I will have to deal with her as well."

"You won't get away with that."

"I assure you I will not fail." The cold look flickered briefly to Kemal. "And do not think that if I shoot the girl, you will overpower me. This weapon fires more than one bullet without reloading and I can easily kill you both. My husband purchased this weapon for protection when he has to go about his business in the night and he taught me how to handle it. I am an extremely good shot."

Molly forced a note of scorn into her voice. "I'm not a stranger like Kemal. I'm a girl with family. They would never rest until they discovered who'd harmed me."

"Nonsense. A local girl of loose character and her Turkish paramour elope to avoid Justice. Far from creating a fuss, your father and grandmother will never hold up their heads again. It is not hard to make people disappear. The teaching hospital is always glad to receive paupers' bodies for their students to dissect."

Everything inside Molly shrivelled with fear. As a Christian she knew it should not matter what happened to her body once the soul had departed but the image of the dissecting table was hideous. She took a deep breath and said, "Lady Adelaide is an Earl's daughter. You wouldn't dare harm her."

Again she was treated to that mirthless smile. "You have no idea what I dare." Silence engulfed them.

Molly tried desperately to think of something to say that would distract this madwoman. The longer she kept her talking, the more chance that help might come.

"I really thought you would have worked it out." Mrs Russell sounded contemptuous, as if pitying the poverty of Molly's understanding.

"No," Molly struggled to keep her voice steady, "I thought it was Henry."

"My son? He wouldn't have the courage." Despite the contemptuous words her voice softened when she spoke of him. "What made you suspect him?"

"Last night, at Mrs Tate's dinner, he started to say something about evidence against Kemal and you hushed him. He knows that Kemal's dagger had been left beside Miss Berry's body, doesn't he?"

She nodded. "He overheard me talking. I was telling his father I'd heard a rumour, during my work converting the sinners on the docks, that you and the Turk had concealed vital evidence. I needed my husband to convince the authorities to take action. It was careless of me, but even the greatest Generals can miscalculate. I did not know Henry had come home. I would not trust him to keep a still tongue, he talks too much, especially when he has been drinking. Of course he did not know the significance of what he said last night. In fact he had forgotten where he heard the rumour. By tomorrow I will have convinced him he heard it from one of those loose women he consorts with."

"You know about that?" gasped Molly.

"I know everything about my son."

Molly couldn't hold back. There was little to lose, Mrs Russell intended to kill them anyway. "But you aren't his mother, are you? And Doctor Russell isn't his father. He's Miss Berry's son."

Chapter 47

"How did you know?" demanded Mrs Russell.

Molly took a deep breath and began to speak, slowly and quietly, determined to spin out her tale for all she was worth. "Miss Berry was upset because she'd seen someone who made her think she'd seen a ghost. When we heard about Miss Berry's past everyone assumed Kemal was her love child but today we discovered that Kemal had not landed when she first saw her ghost. It was about that time your son, Henry, met Miss Berry when he came to her aid after Lady Dewsbury's wheeled carriage broke. He told Lady Adelaide that he feared Miss Berry had hurt herself because she turned so pale."

Mrs Russell tossed her head. "She had the impertinence to claim that Henry was the image of his father. Such nonsense. Henry is English to the core."

Molly thought it couldn't be nonsense if Miss Berry had recognised him at first sight but she said, "Did she not know who he was? She must have seen him before. You've lived in Angleseyville for many years and so had she."

"We do not move in the same circles and Henry is not at home a great deal. I had met her in company with Lady Dewsbury, and my husband had encountered her when he attended the household in his professional capacity, but she had never seen my beloved son before. She was never informed about who adopted her bastard and we did not know her identity. Her brothers insisted that she changed her name. They did not wish to share her shame."

Molly noted that, in the same sentence, Henry could be both Mrs Russell's beloved son and Miss

Berry's bastard. "All those years and you didn't realise who Miss Berry was?"

"No, nor did I wish to know. Henry is mine. It was a great grief to me when I could not bear a child. So many false hopes, so many miscarriages and then Henry, my own baby. My husband was travelling in Turkey at the time. He was part of an expedition that searched out medicinal plants. That woman's brothers were leading a similar expedition. Knowing my husband was a doctor they brought the child to him and requested he found the child a home. They apologised for asking such a favour of him. They could not know that they were offering him the thing we had prayed for. That is what Henry is to me, the answer to my prayers and the sign of God's blessing on my work. And that woman had the impertinence to come into my house and claim my son. She was going to tell him. I couldn't bear that. And what if she decided to tell the world? It would have ruined his career, his chances of a great marriage. It would have ruined everything."

"And so you killed her?" Molly's throat felt dry. Her voice was a cracked whisper.

"Of course I killed her. What else could I do? It was quite simple. I invited her to my house when I knew James was going to be with a patient for much of the night."

"What about your servants? Weren't you afraid they'd notice something amiss?"

"I told the maids to take their day out and gave them permission to spend the night at their parents' home. The three of them are sisters and like to go out together. I do not usually allow it but, for once, I did." She gave a thin smile. "They were grateful for my generosity. I do not care for footmen and have no male servants apart from the butler and the boy who runs my errands. The only other domestic I employ is Cook. She is married to my butler and they never venture from their quarters after I have given them leave to retire for the night."

"You planned it all out?" whispered Molly.

"Of course. A good staff officer always gets the details right. My father was a military man you know. I told her to come late at night when everybody was asleep. I told her that she could talk to Henry but she had to keep our meeting a secret. She came and I showed her into my private sitting room and killed her. It wasn't difficult. I've often assisted James with operations in the past. All it required was resolution and the foresight to put down an old rug to cover the carpet."

'She really is mad,' thought Molly. She felt sick.

"I disposed of the body after the rest of my household was asleep."

"You didn't use a barrow to take Miss Berry to the Garden, you used Lady Dewsbury's wheeled chair. The one Henry had offered to have mended," said Molly. "How could you return it for Lady Dewsbury to use at the funeral?"

"It seemed appropriate." Mrs Russell smiled. "If I hadn't thought of the wheeled chair I would have ordered Geoffrey to carry her to the Garden."

It took Molly a moment to recall who Geoffrey was, then she remembered Henry Russell's contemptuous words at dinner last night. "Geoffrey's the idiot you rescued from destitution and took into your service?"

"Yes. I really believe he'd do anything I commanded. I didn't want anyone to ever track the woman's death back to me or my family and I'd already planned how that Turkish sailor would be blamed. Geoffrey had taken the message to lure him there and we lay in wait for him. My husband has a stick with a weighted handle. He carries it for protection. That night I had made sure he could not find it when he left. It was very effective in rendering the Turk unconscious." She cast a contemptuous look at Kemal, who was listening quietly, with no reaction showing on his face. "I had kept Geoffrey with me to carry him into the Garden so that he would be discovered lying next to that woman's corpse, but you came along and interrupted us." She gave Molly an evil look.

"I hope you don't expect me to apologise," said Molly. Now the first shock was past she was sure that Mrs Russell did not wish to shoot them. Even the most inexperienced medical student might be expected to notice a bullet wound in a corpse.

"You have been a nuisance, but I knew, if I set Geoffrey to watch, you would lead me to your paramour. You didn't keep me waiting long."

Molly felt angry at her own carelessness. "Did you kill Jeremy Bray as well?"

"That insolent police officer? Yes. He made me very angry. I struck him with my husband's stick, then I had Geoffrey transport him to the harbour. I told Geoffrey to roll him into the water but he was afraid, so I did it myself."

"But why? What did Jeremy do to deserve that?"

"He discovered me in his house. I had just found the letters he had taken from the Turk. Of course I had to kill him, he would have ruined everything."

"How did you know the letters existed?"

"That Berry woman had spoken of them. I told her to bring them with her when she came to visit me but she didn't do so. And you stole them before I could visit poor, dear, blind, helpless Lady Dewsbury."

*

The driver put Adelaide down a short distance from the building as she'd requested and pointed it out to her. She paid him and he drove off. Left alone in the dark, narrow lane, she was shivering with a mixture of cold and fear.

The warehouse loomed black and menacing, darker than the cloudless night sky, but in one corner of the upper storey she could see the glimmer of a light. The door was open and she slipped inside.

*

"How did you know I'd taken the letters?" It frightened Molly how much Mrs Russell did know.

"After you and your meddling mistress left Lady Dewsbury I asked to go to that woman's room to retrieve a book of sermons I said I had lent to her. There was a letter lying on the floor. I knew there were others and you must have taken them."

"But why did Jeremy take them from Kemal?" asked Molly.

"The fool believed they were love letters from this Turk to you. I destroyed them. I had to. Sooner or later they would be translated and heaven knows what they say."

"They said nothing." Kemal spoke for the first time. "Nothing to harm you."

"How irritating." She glared at him. "It would have been so much simpler if you'd died. Those nurses' deaths are all your fault you know. What's that? I heard a noise." She stood up, as if to investigate.

"A rat," said Kemal. "This place is full of them."

"How unpleasant. Still I will not be here for long. I must go now. I've enjoyed our conversation. I did not wish you to die without knowing how pitiful and foolish all your efforts have been, but it's time to end it. I must be in my room before James awakes and comes to minister to his poor invalid wife."

"Dr Russell really knows nothing of what you've done?" asked Molly, incredulous.

"Of course not. And nor does Henry. My husband is, and always has been, determinedly blind to that which he does not wish to see. He did not even question when he came home on that morning and I sent him to discover what was happening in The Crescent. All I had to do was tell him that I had looked out of the window and seen that Turk moving stealthily in that direction. Not that it was as successful as I'd hoped. I thought I could depend on him to raise the alarm and have the Turk imprisoned, or better still, shoot him when he tried to escape, but he allowed that Corfield man to over-rule him. Weak as water. I should have known I could not rely on him. I have always been the driving force in my family. Now it is time to call an end." Keeping a careful distance she drew a small medicine bottle out of her shabby reticule, withdrew the bung that sealed it and poured the contents into the two glasses of red wine. She did all this one-handed. The pistol in her other hand did not waver. "Now drink."

Molly searched her mind desperately for some further delay. She was sure the noise outside hadn't been a rat. Just a few more minutes and there was a chance that help would come. No strategy came to her. She tensed herself, ready to tackle Mrs Russell. She would not die without a fight.

"Drink," repeated Mrs Russell.

"Wait," said Kemal. "I wish first to say my prayers."

*

Chapter 48

The timbers creaked and Adelaide froze. Then she heard Kemal say the sound had come from a rat. She'd worked herself onto a small landing just outside the room where they were imprisoned, and was in a position to hear everything and, by peeping, see a bit. She thought Kemal knew she was there, but she wasn't sure. There was a piece of loose timber lying by her feet, cautiously she bent down and picked it up. Its solid weight felt reassuring in her hand but she was still desperately afraid. The woman was insane. She'd heard enough to be sure of that. If she didn't act soon Molly and Kemal would die.

A hand clamped over her mouth. Her assailant drew her back to lean against him. Her heart thumped and her senses swam. A voice hissed in her ear, "No sound." She knew who it was and felt reassured. He released her and moved to stand beside her. Edwin Corfield, as immaculate as ever, save that he too was carrying a pistol. He handled it with the air of quiet competence that characterised everything he did. "Stay here." The words were a soundless whisper but she understood.

He eased open the door and slipped inside the room. For a moment Mrs Russell didn't notice him, she seemed engrossed in Kemal, on his knees and uttering a loud, fervent, foreign prayer. Adelaide saw him level his pistol then hesitate. She felt heartsick. Edwin could not bring himself to shoot anyone, certainly not a woman, in the back. He was wagering his life on reaching Mrs Russell before she turned.

Mrs Russell sensed his presence and spun round. The dual reports of two pistols rocked the building, sending down showers of wood dust. Edwin staggered and fell. Mrs Russell swung swiftly back and fired at Kemal who was scrambling forward. He stumbled, clutching his left leg.

"Keep back!" The deadly weapon was moving between Molly and Kemal. Edwin lay motionless, the vivid red stain spreading across his chest.

There was no time to think of danger. With a scream of fury, Adelaide leapt into the room and struck Mrs Russell with the wood she held until the older woman fell to her knees. Molly was there, helping to hold her down, and Kemal wrestled the pistol from her. It was then two police officers came pounding up the stairs.

Adelaide dropped her makeshift club and ran to Edwin. Desperately she looked around her for some cloth to staunch the blood. In that moment she bitterly regretted the loss of her petticoats.

"Here, m'lady." Molly pushed past her and tore off Edwin's neck-cloth, then she pulled open his coat and shirt. "Wad my shawl and press down here. We've got to stop him bleeding." She turned to deal with Kemal's injury and to berate the bemused police officers that they should be arresting the respectable doctor's wife not the Turkish sailor. Her language was not that of a well-brought up young girl.

Adelaide pressed down on the ugly wound. Edwin's blood was warm as it trickled through her fingers. The flow slowed, but didn't stop. All around her there was movement and the buzz of voices but she was on an island, held prisoner in a fog of blood and silence. Pressing ever harder on the wound, although her arms trembled from the force.

"Please God, don't let him die." And then, in answer to her whispered prayer, Molly's grandmother walked into the room.

*

Molly felt as if the world, already shaky, had turned upside down. Whatever was Grandmama doing here?

Her Grandmother paused briefly on the threshold, taking in the scene with one incisive look..

"Let that young man go." Her quiet authority cut across Molly's protests and Mrs Russell's shrill demands that they took the wretch to prison where he belonged. The two policemen released Kemal.

"Sorry, ma'am, but we've got our orders," said the older policeman.

"Then keep Kemal in one corner and this lady secure in the other," said Grandmama. "I understand a more senior officer is on his way."

"Yes, ma'am." Despite Mrs Russell's objections they obeyed.

Grandmama turned from the police officers and knelt beside Lady Adelaide, taking over the care of Mr Corfield.

There was a scuffling sound on the stairs and Tom appeared, hauling a lanky youth, taller than him but skinny and plainly dressed. The boy was snivelling pitifully. He broke free of Tom and ran to Mrs Russell, falling on his knees before her and sobbing, "Oh Mistress, what are we going to do?"

"Be quiet, Geoffrey," she snapped. "Say nothing or they'll take you and hang you."

"That is the boy who delivered the message and your bookmark," said Kemal.

"Tom, where did you find him?" demanded Molly.

"Found him outside lurkin'," said Tom. "Thought I'd bring him in and find out his lay."

"But what are you doing here?" repeated Molly.

"The guv'nor there got busy." A jerk of the head indicated Mr Corfield "Soon as I told him he sent his manservant off with a message for some police nob and told me to fetch your grandmother."

"Tom, run for Dr Harvey," commanded Grandmama. "Bring him here as swiftly as you can."

"Yes Mistress. As soon as this cove's got out the way." There was loud huffing and wheezing as the senior police officer hauled himself up the stairs. He was a portly gentleman and the room was small. Molly hoped the floor would not give way.

It was hard to tell what shocked the senior policeman most: Mr Corfield's parlous state, Lady Adelaide's unmaidenly clothes or being forced to arrest a respectable lady who was a pillar of the Church. To give him his due he grasped the situation and swiftly dispatched Geoffrey to the lock up, Kemal back to the Naval hospital under a watchful but not aggressive guard, and Mrs Russell to his own house to be kept under the watchful eyes of two police officers and his housekeeper until a doctor with suitable experience in dealing with maladies of the mind could be summoned to assess her condition. Molly thought bitterly that there was no being hauled off to the lock up for the respectable and wealthy Mrs Russell.

The young local doctor arrived and he and Grandmama consulted quietly together. "We'll take him to my son's house," decreed Grandmama. This startled Molly. She wondered what Pa would say when he got home tomorrow. There'd be no way of hiding what they'd done.

"That will be best." The doctor nodded. "I cannot remove the bullet while he lies in this filthy hovel. I think he should survive being transported that short distance." Despite his agreement he sounded far from confident.

"I'm going with him," said Lady Adelaide.

"So you shall, my dear, but we must allow the policemen to carry him down." The softness of Grandmama's tone warned Molly how very badly hurt Mr Corfield must be.

They lifted him carefully and eased him through the door and down the stairs. To Molly it seemed terrible and strange to see the consummate puppet master lying so limp and pale. The strings had fallen from his hands and his marionettes were dancing on their own.

Chapter 49

Molly sat with Grandmama in her small sitting room, the basket of household mending on the floor between them. Molly's fingers were active but her mind was wandering. It was seven days since the nightmare in the warehouse. This small room, with all its keepsakes from Grandmama's past, had always been her favourite sanctuary but now she wanted to be downstairs, in the parlour, where important business was being discussed. She sighed.

"Cheer up, Molly." Her grandmother looked up and smiled.

"I can't cheer up. I'm worried." And very cross that she'd been banished. This had been her adventure, hers and Kemal's, and now they were excluded from its conclusion.

"What if they still try and put the blame on Kemal?" Henry Russell was part of the august gathering and he'd do anything to prevent the truth about his mother coming out. The important visitors had given plausible reasons for holding their meeting in her father's house but she suspected its insignificance was the greatest advantage.

"Surely if they hadn't accepted his innocence they wouldn't have let him return to his ship?" Despite her reasonable words Grandmama sounded troubled. "It was fortunate Mr Corfield had written such a detailed report outlining his suspicions."

"Yes." Molly felt deeply grateful for that. Along with the picture from Miss Berry's sketchbook that Lady Adelaide had discovered, Mr Corfield's report had ensured Kemal's release. "I never thought we'd escape without scandal."

"That was thanks to you," said Grandmama.

"Maybe." It certainly wasn't thanks to Lady Adelaide. Even when they'd got Mr Corfield safely here, she had refused to go home. Steadfastly she'd insisted on staying while they dug the bullet out of his shoulder. The operation over, she'd spurned any suggestion she should leave. She'd sat at his bedside, holding his hand, as if her grasp could keep him anchored to this world.

In the end, Molly had taken it upon herself to insist that Lady Adelaide wrote a brief note to her aunt, explaining that she'd been called away to visit a sick relative of her late husband and that she had taken her maid with her. It was a feeble story but Molly hoped it might prevent the mistress from raising an outcry in search of her truant niece. Before dawn, with Tom as escort, she'd gone back to The Crescent and slipped into the house. A few minutes later she'd left as quietly as she'd entered, taking with her suitable apparel for herself and her mistress and leaving the note for Mrs Tate.

On the way back she'd commanded Tom to retrieve his stolen horse and return it to its owner's yard. With any luck it would not have been missed.

And it seemed that her ploy to save her mistress' good name had worked. In the last week gossip had scurried throughout the town, but all the talk was about how Dr Russell had been struck down by an apoplectic fit and Mrs Russell had been taken to a private nursing home, and, rumour following rumour, soon after came the suggestion that she'd been confined in an establishment that tended the insane.

Thinking of this, Molly asked, "Grandmama, what will become of Mrs Russell? Will they hang her?"

Her grandmother laid down her sewing. "I think they will decide she is too unwell to be brought to justice. Although there is much talk throughout the town, I have heard no hint that she has committed any crime." She sighed. "When Henry was still in leading strings, his mother adored him and spent every minute in the nursery. It was later, when he went off to school and grew away from her that she became the bitter, unhappy woman that you knew."

She glanced at the china clock on the mantel. "I hope they will be finished soon. I do not wish to leave before it is all settled but I promised to visit Frederick's wife this afternoon."

"Do you think their little girl will get well?"

"I think so, although I will continue to visit throughout the winter months. Frederick's wife is young and inexperienced and very lonely, poor girl. The aunt she lives with doesn't mean to be unkind but she's not a woman with any sympathy for nervous fancies."

"At least Frederick still has his employment." The events of the last two weeks had driven his misdemeanours from Lady Adelaide's mind and Molly was sure that, between them, she and Grandmama could convince her not to tell Mrs Tate how she'd been deceived.

The door opened, and a quiet voice enquired, "May I enter?"

"Kemal!" She sprang to her feet, scattering thread, needle case and scissors, then checked her impetuous desire to run to him. It was the first time she had seen him since that night in the warehouse. "Are you all right? What are you doing here?"

Her father spoke from behind Kemal. "The gentlemen using my parlour sent for him but, while he's waiting, he has my permission to speak with you alone." Pa looked troubled and Molly was sorry for it, in the past week he'd been very kind.

Grandmama put down her mending, rose and made for the door. She paused and smiled at Kemal. "My dear boy, I am glad to see you restored to your health and rightful position."

"Thank you, Madam. Without your help and that of Mistress Molly I would certainly have been hanged."

"As I said on our first meeting, that would have been a most grievous waste." She left the room and Molly's father shut the door, leaving Molly and Kemal alone.

She stared at him in silence, feeling suddenly shy. He was looking well, although still limping slightly from the minor leg wound he'd received last week. She wondered why he had returned to speaking of her as Mistress Molly. It put a distance between them that she didn't know how to bridge.

He took her hand and kissed it. "Dear Molly, are you well?" he asked.

"Yes. Are you?"

"Yes. Thank you for all that you have done to aid me. Did you or her ladyship get into trouble because of what occurred?"

"No. It was all right." When Lady Adelaide finally agreed to return to her aunt's house, Mrs Tate was so full of the story of Dr and Mrs Russell's indispositions that she had accepted without question that her niece had been summoned to the death bed of her late husband's great aunt. Although she had commented, as an afterthought, she'd thought the old lady had died some years ago.

"What about you? Did you get into trouble for going absent without permission?"

"No. Hasan spoke for me and they will not punish me."

Molly thought one day she'd tell Lady Adelaide that Hasan had done one unselfish deed but she did not think her mistress would really care.

"Your good father has given his permission for me to speak with you."

"Yes?" She was surprised Pa had left them alone together. She found it impossible to believe that he had given his blessing if Kemal had asked him for her hand. But, if Kemal had gained permission to address her, she didn't know how to answer him. She wasn't sure that she wished to be married yet, even to Kemal. Then she looked at his troubled face and understood. "You're going away, aren't you?"

"Not for some weeks but then I must. It is my duty to return with my ship when our mission is complete. Also I wish to. I must speak with my guardian and tell him what has occurred... and ask him questions."

"Questions?"

"I have never really asked about my parents. I think he never wished me to. But he is growing old and I have realised how easily a man's life can slip away. I want to know the truth."

"And when you have your answers?"

"Then, when my time in the navy is complete, I will make my way back to England and find employment here." His voice was steady but his eyes were anxious. "And I will pay court to you, if you are still unmarried and you permit."

Happiness overwhelmed her. It was the perfect solution. It gave her time to do some of the things she'd dreamed of before she had to settle down to housekeeping and childbearing, but, at the same time, she'd know that Kemal would return to her.

"I would like that." She spoke stiffly, behaving with a propriety that would have astonished her mistress. Since Kemal was safe from both murderer and hangman, she was no longer living in a reckless romance. Sensible Molly, the hard-headed tradesman's daughter, was ruling her again and warning her that it was only two weeks since she had first met Kemal

"Will it be very long before you return?" The question slipped out. Perhaps good sense was not as dominant as she wished.

"Not long, I promise you. A year at most. And I will write to you. Will you reply?"

"Yes." And yet she felt troubled. "Our lives are so different, Kemal."

He smiled at her. "In your language the name of my ship is the Mirror of Victory."

She understood immediately what he meant, "And when I was a child, Grandmama told me about one of our greatest Admirals who won a famous battle in a ship called the Victory."

"We are not so very different. If we..."

The door opened and Pa entered. His face was grim and Molly wondered if he'd had his ear to the door, making sure they behaved themselves.

His first words dispelled her suspicions. "I wanted to warn you, there's trouble in the parlour."

"How do you know?" demanded Molly. Surely they wouldn't have told her father their precious secrets?

He shrugged. "They forget they're in a working man's small house. They're talking loud enough for anyone in the kitchen to hear."

"What are they saying?" Molly felt fear claw through her once again.

"They're talking about the lad here. They're saying how the easiest course would be to blame him for everything and have him hanged. You'd best head off, lad, and keep clear of them."

Kemal shook his head. "Thank you, sir, but no, I have run enough. If a man keeps on running, soon he will not know how to stop."

Molly discovered it was possible to feel overwhelmingly proud of someone and wish to shake them both at the same time.

"As you think best, lad." She could hear the admiration in her father's voice. In other circumstances it would make her heart rejoice but at this moment she was too afraid.

*

Chapter 50

There were only four people in the parlour but to Adelaide it seemed very full, even though, for a working man's abode, the room was of reasonable size. She wondered if that was because of the Important Gentleman from London. Lord Harmer was powerful in Government circles and an acquaintance of her father. It was as if his eminence had expanded to fill the cooper's modest house. Or maybe it was Henry Russell, loud voiced and struggling to impose his will. His anger and bewilderment were exacerbated by his obvious deep hurt. She felt sorry for him but that didn't mean she'd give way to his demands. The final person was the quietest of all. Adelaide did not look at him but, in every fibre of her being, she was aware of him.

"I see no reason this Turkish sailor shouldn't take the blame." Henry Russell repeated the argument he'd already made, as if by battering his point home he would eventually prevail. "I concede it's not reasonable to hang him, but we could send him back to where he came from and say he died of cholera. We could wait until he's underway and then give out that he was the dead woman's bastard and he'd killed her when he found out."

Adelaide noted with incredulity the way he'd swept aside the fact that he was Miss Berry's bastard, not Kemal.

"That is not possible," she said crisply. Everyone present turned to stare at her. "As I explained, I am here at Lady Dewsbury's request as her representative. She insists that Miss Berry's name remains unsullied."

She met Henry's eyes then shifted to take in Lord Harmer. "Lady Dewsbury asked me to warn you that if anyone, however powerful, attempts to drag Miss Berry's name through the mire, Lady Dewsbury will create a scandal that will reverberate throughout Society. Not merely in this quiet town but in London also." Before anyone could protest, she stated her own stance, "And if anyone tries to make Kemal the scapegoat, I will reveal the truth."

"You wouldn't dare," blustered Henry Russell. "Your reputation isn't untarnished. You wouldn't risk another scandal."

"I would dare," she retorted, "even if I have to petition the Queen."

There was a shocked silence, broken by a soft voice, weak but incisive. "My apologies, Lady Adelaide. If my arm weren't in this wretched sling I'd knock the fellow down. For all your bullying, Russell, there will be no blame cast on Kemal. I will not allow it."

"You won't allow it, Corfield? What the devil is it to do with you?"

"It is a great deal to do with me." He spoke to Lord Harmer. "My commission, as you know, came from the highest powers. It is to ensure that there is no ruffling of the smooth relationship between our country and the Ottoman Empire. At the moment the situation is delicate, and diplomatic concerns must over-ride all others."

Lord Harmer nodded his agreement. "You're right of course, Corfield. I'm afraid the truth will have to come out. Bad business, but I don't see how we can hush it up. There's going to be a lot of talk, Russell, and I don't say it won't affect your career."

"It will kill my father."

Adelaide thought that might be true. Her aunt had told her that, several days after his apoplectic attack, the doctor was still scarcely able to speak and could barely move. Adelaide had never liked Dr Russell but she pitied him. What must it feel like to know that one's wife was capable of such a crime? And she had sent out her husband, an innocent dupe, to find Miss Berry's body. Although there were times when Molly had made wry, cynical remarks that had caused Adelaide to wonder if the doctor could be as totally ignorant of his wife's crimes as she had claimed.

"Any scandal could have diplomatic repercussions," said Edwin Corfield, "but I may have a solution,"

"Indeed Corfield? Please tell us," said Lord Harmer hopefully.

"I understand there was a young man who was involved in Mrs Russell's crimes?"

"Geoffrey Briggs," said Henry Russell. "He's feeble minded. He's still in the lock up. They can't get any sense out of him, all he does is cry and beg to see my mother."

"And is it true that this young man has no family of his own?"

"Yes. Father a drunken sailor, mother a drunken whore. Both of them dead."

"Mind your language, Russell. There's a lady present," exclaimed Lord Harmer.

"I'm sorry, I'm sure." The sulky tone of the apology made it clear he regarded Adelaide as unworthy of respect.

"What is your plan, Corfield?" asked Lord Harmer.

"It's simple enough. The deaths of the nurses and that unfortunate police officer can be passed off as accidents but Miss Berry's death cannot. Therefore, for the benefit of the curious world, Geoffrey Briggs can take the blame for that. I am sure Lady Dewsbury will recall some incident that roused his rancour.

Perhaps Miss Berry reprimanded him for impertinence or dishonesty and threatened to report him to Doctor Russell."

"An excellent solution," said Henry Russell. "Thank you Corfield."

"It may well do." Lord Harmer was more cautious. "Hanging's no more than the boy deserves. He was privy to the crimes."

Everything in Adelaide rose up in outrage at this callousness. She stared at Edwin and shivered. She couldn't bear to think he'd hang a foolish, wretched boy to serve his political masters. "He is not a killer!" she protested.

Edwin smiled at her. "I thought transportation rather than the gallows, but a boy like that might not survive a penal colony and so I'd suggest one of the free colonies. I know a man who's taking his family over there. He'd be pleased to take a hard-working, obedient lad who needed a fresh start. Especially when his fare was paid and he had a suitable sum to ease his way."

He looked meaningfully at Henry Russell who nodded his surly agreement. Adelaide thought Henry would have preferred Geoffrey to be hanged and gone for good.

"The man I have in mind will have to be told that the boy's ended up in trouble through being misled by other stronger characters," continued Edwin. "He's a decent fellow and won't mistreat the lad."

Adelaide remembered someone else who had lost everything through Mrs Russell's crimes. "There's also the mother of the young policeman who was killed. She has been left destitute and facing the workhouse."

"I will ensure that Mr Russell makes her a suitable allowance," promised Edwin, "not that anything can console her for such a loss. And there will be restitution for the families of the dead nurses too." He smiled. "You will be regarded as a public benefactor, Russell."

Henry Russell scowled and seemed about to protest but he encountered Lord Harmer's stern gaze and muttered a sulky, "Very well."

"A satisfactory solution." Lord Harmer rose to his feet. "I'll inform the necessary authorities if you'll make the arrangements, Corfield."

"Certainly, sir."

"Tomorrow," said Adelaide, "Mr Corfield must rest now."

"Of course. Glad you're recovering, Corfield, you've done an excellent job."

"I'll see you out, sir," said Adelaide "and you, Mr Russell."

"Thank you Lady Adelaide." Lord Harmer beamed at her. "Good day, Mr Russell. I hope your father recovers his good health."

Mrs Russell was not mentioned. She had already passed beyond the pale.

Chapter 51

As Adelaide closed the door behind the visitors she thought how strange it was that she felt so at home in this small house. Of course she'd spent much of the last week here. The first two days, when Edwin had been close to death, she had scarcely left his bedside. Her devotion had won the grudging acceptance of Edwin's taciturn valet.

When she returned to the parlour Edwin smiled at her. He was white and weary but there was a hint of mischief in his look.

She said the first thing that entered her mind, "Edwin, are you a spy?"

The humour deepened. "Without trumpet or drum, creeping behind enemy lines? Not the job for a gentleman, my dear."

She knew that was so. All her breeding and upbringing declared spies should be despised. Nevertheless the reply was on her lips, "It's work for a brave man. One who does not hide behind a uniform."

"But would you marry a spy?"

She stared at him, suspecting mockery, but he was regarding her with desperate earnestness. She was silent as she thought the matter through. Her first marriage had been a nightmare but she had always known that she would have to marry again. The only alternative would be to live the rest of her life as a dependant in the house of one of her relatives. And she would hate that. Her temperament and training both meant that she enjoyed the independence and responsibility of being mistress in her own house.

She chose her words carefully, "I'd marry you, if you are asking me."

"Of course I am." He struggled to rise. "But I can't get out of this chair."

"You don't need to." She sat down beside him.

"You haven't asked me about my birth or fortune. All you know of me is that I am engaged in an occupation that can be reprehensible."

"That doesn't matter to me." In all her life she had never felt so supremely confident. By teaching her to love and trust, Edwin had set her free from the shackles of guilt and fear that had been forged by her late husband's cruelty and disgrace.

"And what of your father?"

"My father married me off to a profligate gambler and he has sponsored the pretensions of the adopted son of a murderess. I do not think his judgement is infallible."

He laughed. "The adventures of the past two weeks have had an effect on you. However I trust we may not be totally cast off. My birth is respectable, if not noble. My fortune is also respectable, although I'm a younger son. Indeed my job title is respectable, They call me a diplomat, even if the truth is somewhat grubbier."

"Edwin, what do you do?"

"When diplomatic trouble is brewing they send me to smooth it down. When it erupts they send me to clear it up. Sometimes I work with the police, or army, or navy, sometimes with diplomats. Sometimes I work with the sort of people I will not be bringing home to dine with you. At the moment the Government is preoccupied with strengthening our relationship with the Ottoman Empire, despite the efforts of various other Powers."

"And you thought the sailors in the training ships could be used to cause trouble?"

"I thought it possible. There have been one or two training accidents that had a hollow ring. It's hard to tell whether the danger was in my imagination, or, by putting out certain warnings, I averted it. The irony is that the biggest danger came not from a foreign saboteur but from an obsessed madwoman." He winced and she knew his wound was paining him.

"You must go to bed now. I'll fetch your man to support you upstairs."

"In a moment. Adelaide, when will you marry me?"

"Today if you wish."

"I would indeed wish that but it would require a special licence and embarrass your family. No sense in kicking up dust if there's no need. As soon as I'm fit to travel I'll visit your father. Now fetch Kemal for me, my dearest. I must speak to him."

*

Whilst Kemal was in the parlour, Molly waited outside. She was sorely tempted to listen at the door but she refrained because Mr Corfield was sure to know.

At last Kemal came out, shutting the door behind him. He looked thoughtful.

"What did he want?" she demanded.

"He told me what had been decided and hoped that I approved."

"Lady Adelaide told me. I suppose it's for the best." Molly couldn't forgive Mrs Russell or her husband. She remembered Dr Russell's lies, evasions and the weapon concealed in his coat pocket as he urged Kemal to run. He may have been his wife's tool but she felt certain he was not her innocent dupe, despite her boastful claims..

"Also Mr Corfield said, if I returned to England, he would wish me to take up a position as his secretary," continued Kemal. "He said he needed a man with my knowledge of languages and my fighting capabilities."

Molly thought the latter sounded like a strange quality for a secretary but she didn't say so. She had a pretty good idea of what Mr Corfield's lay was.

"What did you answer?"

"That I must ask you what you would wish."

That was easy. It required no thought at all. She smiled at him and pushed him back towards the parlour. "Say yes," she commanded.

Historical Notes

The characters and events in Strangers and Angels are fictional, apart from a few famous historical characters. Gosport and the historical sites described are factual.

Gosport is a naval town on the south coast of England. It shares a harbour with Portsmouth. The historical buildings referred to all existed, including The Royal Clarence Yard; Haslar Hospital; the Floating Bridge; Gosport Railway Station; the Anglesey Hotel; St Mark's Church; The Crescent and its garden.

In 2017 the Railway has gone; the magnificent Floating Bridge has been replaced by ferries that serve foot passengers; the Royal Clarence Yard has been adapted into housing and leisure premises and a similar fate has befallen Haslar Hospital and its grounds; St Mark's Church has been demolished and so has the Reading Room and Bath Houses, and housing has been built which blocks the garden view across Stokes Bay.

The Crescent is still standing, as is the Anglesey Hotel. The Friends of The Crescent Garden have restored all they can of its past elegance, placing a fountain where the Reading Room once stood. The restoration has been so well done that the garden has achieved Green Flag and Green Heritage Awards. A similar transformation has been carried out by the Friends of St Mark's Churchyard, who have restored graves and monuments, and cleared the neglected churchyard.

Last but not least, the place that was the initial inspiration for the novel, The Turkish Burial Ground. Initially the Turkish sailors who died from accidents or disease were buried in the grounds of Haslar Hospital, the place where many of them died. A few years later these bodies were exhumed, along with many other dead sailors, and transferred to the newly established Clayhall Cemetery. Full Military honours were accorded to the dead as they were transported along the aptly named Dead Man's Lane. All of Clayhall Cemetery is beautifully and reverently maintained, including The Turkish Burial Ground.

Contemporary crime books by Carol Westron

Crime Series set on the South Coast

The South Coast Crime books form an overlapping series of police procedurals where characters and events from one series interact and impact on the other, mirroring real life, where police personnel often work over a large area within their county.

Books in the South Coast Crime series:

The Terminal Velocity of Cats
(Mia Trent Scene of Crimes) published 2013
About the Children
(Serious Crimes Team) published 2014
The Fragility of Poppies
(Rick & Annie Evans) published 2016
Karma and the Singing Frogs
(Mia Trent Scene of Crimes) published 2017.

The books are separate and all stand by themselves

Printed in Great Britain
by Amazon